OF FATE AND PHANTOMS

MINISTRY OF CURIOSITIES, BOOK #7

C.J. ARCHER

C.J. ARCHER

To Joe, Samantha and Declan. All my love.

CHAPTER 1

LONDON, NEW YEAR'S EVE, 1889

"*Y*ou look beautiful," Lincoln whispered, enclosing my hands in his.

We stood in the corridor between our rooms on a freezing New Year's Eve. Lincoln's warmth, however, chased away the chill. A tendril of his hair skimmed his brow. He didn't plan on tying it back for the ball. Apparently pirates cared nothing for grooming.

"Thank you," I murmured, a blush rising up my throat and infusing my cheeks. "You look rather dashing yourself."

"Pirates aren't supposed to look dashing." He eased back, taking my hopes of a kiss with him, and rubbed his bristly jaw. "Perhaps I should have started the beard a day earlier."

"Not too dashing," I quickly reassured him.

Who knew that such a self-confident man cared so much about looking the part of a pirate for a masquerade ball? He'd gone so far as to purchase a new shirt, complete with ruffled sleeves at the wrist, a wide leather belt, and a tricorn hat that he'd thrown in the dirt as soon as he got it home. Apparently pirates couldn't be seen in brand new hats. At least not the roguish pirate that Lincoln wanted to portray.

1

"You will look frightening once you put on the eye patch," I said. "We maidens will tremble in our shoes."

He leaned in again, as far as the broad skirts of my Georgian costume would allow. "I hope to scare away all but the bravest of maids."

I tried to think of a quip in response, but my mind went blank when his lips caressed the corner of my mouth and he palmed my waist. I felt the light pressure even through the corset boning.

"I'll save a dance for you," I said.

"Save them all for me. I won't be dancing with anyone else."

"You should. People will talk if you only dance with me."

"Let them."

"You want them to gossip?" I asked.

His lips curved into one of his rare smiles, but this one held a touch of mischief, an even rarer commodity. "I want them to know you're mine."

In the week since Christmas, Lincoln and I had settled into a pattern that fell somewhere between friendship and betrothed. We were neither, and yet sometimes, like now, it felt like we were both. I had not plucked my engagement ring from its velvet bed in the ring box, but that didn't stop us from touching hands as we passed in the corridor or sat next to one another at dinner. Only once had we kissed passionately, in the privacy of the parlor the day after he emerged from his sickbed.

That kiss had not been repeated, not even on the single occasion when we'd found ourselves alone in the house one Sunday morning. He'd retreated to his study and I'd gone to find him. I wasn't sure what I hoped would happen, but I was certainly not expecting him to order me to leave. He'd sought me out later to apologize, blaming his abruptness on concern for my virtue and his lack of willpower. I'd laughed but he had not.

Lincoln's hands dropped to his sides, and his gaze shuttered. "We shouldn't be doing this. Not here. Not now."

Not now.

It was a reference to our status as a couple, or lack of it. I knew he wanted to be engaged again, and that his offer awaited my response in the form of putting the ring on my finger. Yet I wasn't ready to give up my newfound freedom. I had a small house of my own now. I had a roof over my head here at Lichfield Towers, and I could make my own decisions regarding my life, my person, and my future. I didn't want to jeopardize that, and certainly not with a man who'd proven to be unpredictable. And yet, I loved him. That could not be denied.

"You're right," I said on a sigh as I moved away. "It wouldn't do for Lady Vickers to see." A few months ago, I hadn't cared a whit for propriety, but things had changed since then. Not the least of it, the arrival of both Seth's mother and my friend Alice. Where before I was still something of a street urchin in my thoughts and behavior, I was now more aware of the necessity to act my age of nineteen. It was time to fit back into a society that had been alien to me for so long and be the sort of person they could both be proud to associate with. My newfound maturity could be attributed to facing down the twin evils of the Queen of Hearts' army and the headmistress of the School for Wayward Girls. Escaping that place alive would bend even the most stubborn will.

I went in search of Alice, and together we put on the wigs and masks we'd purchased during the week. The gowns had been discovered in a trunk in the attic, having been left there by the previous owner of Lichfield. They'd required minor repairs and airing out, but they were otherwise perfect.

We met Lady Vickers, Seth and Lincoln at the appointed hour. I bit back my giggle at Seth's foppish Georgian attire, complete with powdered wig and beauty spot. He'd insisted on matching our costumes, and wanted Lincoln to do the same to identify us as a group to the other guests. Lincoln had refused to dress as a dandy and decided on the pirate outfit instead. His argument that he matched the same era of our costumes had been unassailable, much to Seth's frustration.

Seth slapped on his hat, blew its long black feather off his face, and held his arm out to Alice. "You do look smart," he told her.

Smart? That was the best he could do? For such a charming man, he wasn't always at his most charming with her. Indeed, he even seemed a little overwhelmed by her. She was uncommonly pretty and possessed an air of aloofness.

He must have realized his response lacked enthusiasm because he added, "And beautiful. Lovely. A vision."

"And historically accurate," Alice said. "More or less."

Lady Vickers followed them out, her scowl directed at Alice's back. The severity of it became lost, however, with all the tinkling of the beads and tokens attached to the hem of her gypsy dress, visible beneath her fur coat. I'd tried to tell her that the beading and colorful dress were a cliché, and that gypsies didn't wear such ostentatious outfits, but then I'd have to tell her how I knew. Lady Vickers, for all her strength of character, might not like knowing that the woman she'd taken under her wing had visited a gypsy camp with a man who was half-gypsy himself.

I glanced at that man now and accepted his arm with a smile. "Are you sure you'll be warm enough?" I asked, eyeing his jerkin and doublet. He wore no coat.

"Charlie," he chided. "You promised."

"I promised not to ask if you were all right, not if you were warm enough. Besides, I said *at* the ball. We haven't arrived yet."

"Next time I'll be more specific."

"You have been ill, Lincoln, not to mention injured." And the evening air already felt icy. Frost would settle on the lawn overnight and into the bones of the homeless who could not find adequate shelter, as I knew all too well.

"I'm neither ill nor injured anymore."

"You may have recovered from your ordeal, but I have not." I left him contemplating that as Doyle, the butler, held the carriage door open for me. "Do you have enough blankets for warmth, Gus?" I called up to our coachman and friend. We really did need to find a proper coachman to take over his duties, as well as a housekeeper and maids. Lichfield was ready for them, and so was I.

"Thank you, Charlie." Gus patted his coat pocket where he kept his flask. "All set."

Seth leaned out of the carriage and spoke loudly enough for Gus to hear. "Don't worry about him. His skin's so thick nothing penetrates it."

"Unlike yours," Gus said. "It's so delicate you have to wear furs and feathers."

"It's a *costume*."

Gus snorted. "You told me you cobbled it together from pieces found in your own wardrobe. Costume, my ar—"

"Let's go!" I said, pushing Seth's shoulder. He retreated back inside the cabin.

The carriage was too crowded for five people, two of whom wore voluminous skirts. I didn't realize until Lincoln shut the door without joining us. The coach rocked as he climbed onto the seat next to Gus. I tried not to think of him sitting out in the cold, but memories of him lying unconscious in his bed after the kitchen explosion assaulted me anyway. That nightmare had occurred too recently for my liking. Not even he could be fully recovered yet.

As if she sensed my concern, Alice kept the conversation lively all the way to the Curzon Street residence of Lady Vickers' friend, Lady Hothfield. A footman opened the carriage door and we lowered our masks and shed the blankets keeping our knees warm.

"This is rather grand," Alice whispered as we stepped inside the house onto crimson carpet.

The spacious entrance hall was indeed grand, with the central staircase diverting into two at the landing and wrapping around the walls leading up to the next level. Lamps and a central chandelier blazed with light, catching the gilt in the frames, furniture legs and the tip of the spear clasped in a semi-naked statue's hand. The white marble Grecian's modesty was maintained by a flimsy red cloth that looked as if the flick of a finger could dislodge it.

I curled my hands into fists. "A little grander than the school," I agreed. "But don't tell the ghost of Sir Walter that I said so."

She grinned, I was relieved to see. When she'd first arrived at Lichfield, any mention of the castle prison we'd both been sent to in Yorkshire made her shiver with awful memories of her time there. It was good to see her putting that experience behind her.

Another footman—there were an awful lot of them—escorted us up the stairs toward the music. Lady Vickers introduced us to our host and hostess in the ballroom, but I had no illusions about our importance to them. We were merely there thanks to Lady Vickers herself, not because we held any interest for Lord and Lady Hothfield. Their greetings were polite enough, but it was Seth who earned most of their attention.

"It's been so long since we saw you, dear boy," Lord Hothfield exclaimed, slapping Seth on the shoulder. "You look as fit and strong as ever. What have you been up to?"

He didn't get a chance to explain, or lie, before Lady Hothfield spoke. "You haven't changed." She tapped Seth's chest with her fan. "Always such a handsome boy." She swapped the fan to her left hand, opened it then giggled behind it. "How we have missed you, dear Seth. How long has it been? Too long, I say."

Seth's face reddened. I bit my lip to stop my smile. He'd told me the day before that he wasn't looking forward to seeing Lady Hothfield again. Their last meeting had been in her bedchamber, over a year ago, before Lincoln had employed him. I'd been utterly flabbergasted by his admission, because she wasn't at all the type of woman he admired or desired. Indeed, she was much older than Lady Harcourt, one of his most recent lovers. It had taken a few probing questions before I realized that Seth had most likely slept with her for money. In fact, he'd only answered my questions after I promised to help him avoid Lady Hothfield.

I was about to do my duty and ask him to join me when his mother ushered him away. Lady Hothfield's gaze lingered on Seth until he disappeared into the crowd.

Lincoln, Alice and I followed, only to divert as Lady Vickers introduced her son to a small gathering of ladies. He cast a hapless glance at us over his shoulder, but I thought it best to leave him alone for the time being. He needed to get these initial introductions over with at some point. It was, after all, his mother's reason for attending.

"This room is lovely," Alice said, gazing up at the six dazzling chandeliers above. "And don't all the costumes look marvelous? Did you see Queen Elizabeth?"

"I couldn't miss her with that hair." I pointed my chin at a Roman senator and his wife, dressed in the outfit of an ancient Roman noblewoman. "I like what she's wearing. Next time, I'll try that."

"Do you recognize anyone you know?" Being taller than me, Alice could see over some of the heads and further into the ballroom.

"It's hard to tell with their masks in place," I said.

"There's Lord Gillingham," Lincoln said, nodding at one of several Georgian fops in the room.

"So it is. I can tell from the walking stick."

"And his wife is over there."

My gaze followed his to a group of women, their ages indeterminate thanks to their masks. "Which one?"

"The medieval princess in green."

"Are you sure? Her hair is darker."

"She's wearing a wig."

"Then how can you tell it's her?" Alice asked.

Lincoln hesitated before saying, "She's the right height and weight."

"There must be dozens of women here the same size as her," I said, indicating the hundred or more guests. "Come now, Lincoln, tell us. How do you know?"

Again, he paused. Was he reluctant to give up this knowledge? "It's no single thing. Some of her face is visible. Her mouth and chin, her throat and ears."

"Her ears?" Alice laughed, only to stop abruptly upon Lincoln's glare. He managed to instill as much steel with one eye covered by the patch as two perfectly good ones.

"She also has a broad set to her shoulders, and tilts her head to the left when she's listening. Her hands are quite large and she tucks them behind her back most of the time, perhaps because she feels self-conscious."

I looked down at my hands. They were average sized, but I could well believe they were smaller than the shape-shifting Lady Gillingham's. According to Lincoln, who'd seen her in her beast form, she resembled a wolf, and not at all human. I was wildly curious to see her change, but didn't dare ask. If she was self-conscious about her hands, imagine how she'd feel about a hairy, beastly body?

Alice blinked slowly at him through the holes in her mask. "You're entirely serious, aren't you? Are you so observant with everyone?"

"He is," I told her. "It's a skill."

If I didn't know Lincoln so well I would have been jealous that he observed so much about another woman, but I knew he probably had a dozen little ways of telling me apart from others my size. Lady Gillingham was not special.

"Oh, look, here comes another pirate," I said as a gentleman of impressive stature approached. "His costume is not nearly as unique as yours, though, Lincoln."

"It's Marchbank," he said.

I squinted as the man joined us. I could see the scars on his face now that he was closer. The broad brimmed hat, long black wig and large eye patch had hidden much, but not those.

"Good evening, Charlie, Fitzroy," he said. "Excellent costumes."

I introduced him to Alice then we fell into a discussion about the costumes. No one mentioned the recent events at Lichfield. The night General Eastbrooke had almost killed Lincoln, tried to kill me, and had blown up our kitchen was rarely discussed, even by those of us enduring the rebuilding of the kitchen. I, for one, had difficulty digesting the horror, and part of me didn't want to. It wasn't so much the horror of the injuries and destruction but of the general's betrayal. He'd been the closest thing to a father that Lincoln had, and yet he'd gone to great lengths to attempt to control and undermine him.

"I wonder what the prince and his cronies will wear," Marchbank said, watching Lincoln closely.

Lincoln went very still. "Prince?"

"I see you haven't heard."

Lady Vickers took that moment to burst through the crowd, her grin as broad as her handsome face. "You will never believe who is set to come tonight."

"The prince," I said.

Her smile wilted but only for a moment. "Isn't it exciting! I wonder who he'll bring with him. He always attends parties with a group of lively, charming royals. Such a charming man himself. I do hope his sons come, although I don't think they move in the same circles, more's the pity. You simply *must* meet him, Charlie, and you too, Alice. And Fitzroy, if you wish. I'll introduce you."

"You know him?" Alice asked.

Lady Vickers waved her hand airily. "We've met." It was hardly the same thing, but she seemed so excited that I didn't want to say anything to deflate her.

"Which prince?" I asked, glancing at Lincoln. He stood stoically, his hands at his back, and his face bland, although I could tell from the stiff set of his shoulders and firmness of his jaw that this news affected him. His father was the Prince of Wales, first in line to inherit the throne.

Lord Marchbank and the other committee members knew. No one else did, perhaps not even the prince himself.

"*The* prince," Lady Vickers said, as if I was a dimwit for asking. "The Prince of Wales."

"I thought you already knew," Marchbank said heavily.

Lincoln didn't respond. "We didn't," I said. "This is a surprise."

Lincoln had never looked shocked at anything, yet his unblinking immobility was the closest to it I'd ever seen. He'd been caught unprepared for this meeting, something he loathed.

"I'm not sure I want to be introduced," Alice said. "Perhaps I'll wait here by the wall, out of the way. But Charlie should go."

"I insist." Lady Vickers' voice rose with her excitement. "Particularly if he brings some young gentlemen with him, if not the young princes themselves. They're the perfect age for you, Alice."

"Me!" Alice blurted out. "I'm just an ordinary girl."

"You're a beautiful, charming girl, just the sort to catch the eye of any gentleman. Charlie is too, of course, but we all know she's not available."

I studiously avoided glancing at Lincoln. Alice thanked Lady Vickers for the compliments but expressed a wish to avoid meeting the prince and his party. I agreed with her point of view. From what Lincoln had told me about the one encounter he'd had with his father, at another ball some months prior, the prince thought of women as playthings, there for his enjoyment. I didn't want my friend embroiled with a rich, titled scoundrel. I didn't want her going the way of Lincoln's mother—abandoned and with child. Alice had no family who cared for her, and we were her only friends. I would protect her from men like that. Fortunately, I didn't think I'd have any difficulty on that score. She was one of the most sensible girls I'd met.

Lady Vickers, however, seemed determined. She alternately begged and reasoned with Alice, until she finally gave up and ordered Alice to meet the prince when he arrived.

"There you are," Seth said, joining us, all smiles. Smiles which he directed mostly at Alice. His mother's lips tightened. It was then that I realized why she'd pressed Alice so hard to meet the prince. She hoped someone else would capture her eye—someone other than her son.

Perhaps she ought to be introducing Seth to eligible ladies, and not Alice to gentlemen. The infatuation seemed entirely on his side, not hers. From the small hint she'd given me, I gathered that Alice saw Seth as an amusing person, but she had no interest in him. He, however, couldn't take his gaze off her.

He thrust out his hand. "Will you dance with me, Alice?"

She paused. Her gaze flicked to his mother. Lady Vickers' nostrils flared. "I can't think of a single reason not to," Alice said, accepting his hand.

Lady Vickers watched them go then stormed off. Lord Marchbank had also disappeared, although I hadn't noticed him go.

I clasped Lincoln's elbow. "You don't have to go anywhere near him if you don't want to."

We stood side by side, watching couples assemble on the dance floor, neither of us speaking. A troubling thought struck me.

"You won't do anything foolish, will you? In the prince's presence, I mean."

His gaze slid to mine. "When have I ever done anything foolish?" At my arched brow, he added, "Disregarding the time I sent you away."

"And the time you kidnapped me. And when you—" I cut myself off before I mentioned the darker things he'd done. "Never mind." He was in no mood to be reminded of them or treat them lightly.

"I won't do anything foolish tonight," he said. "I won't speak to him at all."

"Then neither will I." I took his hands in mine. "You promised me a dance."

We moved to the edge of the dance area and waited for the music to end and another tune to begin. It was a waltz, and it necessitated us to be close to one another, much to my delight. As with everything he did, Lincoln was a very good dancer and made me feel like I was better than adequate, which was quite a feat given my lack of lessons.

We moved aside when the dance ended and made our way to the refreshment room. Lincoln retrieved a cup of tea for me but nothing for himself, then we fell into quiet conversation.

A few minutes later a woman dressed all in white with a white mask rimmed with seed pearls entered. Dark hair trailed down her back, stark black against the white, a tiara sparkling in the light from the chandelier. Voices rippled around her, following her path to the footman holding the tray of ices. I thought the chatter was because the cut of her bodice was too low, but then I realized it was most likely because the woman behind the mask was Lady Harcourt. Ever since her secret past as a dancer became public, society madams had snubbed her. Apparently Lady Hothfield had decided to make an exception.

I was in two minds as to whether we ought to acknowledge her when she spotted us. She didn't approach, however, but simply bowed her head in greeting, set down her ice without touching it, and glided out again.

"She'll probably ask you to dance later," I said to Lincoln.

"I doubt it. I'd wager she's given up."

"On you? Unlikely. Losing is not in her nature."

He turned to me. "You don't need to fight her, or anyone. I'm yours."

A lump rose in my throat. I swallowed. "If I did have to fight, I would win. My right hook is rather good."

He chuckled quietly. "That it is, Charlie."

We'd restarted our training sessions after Christmas. Lincoln had been teaching me how to fight off an attack, with and without weapons. Even though the supernatural imp in my necklace could save my life, it needed to be out of its amber orb to do so, and I may not always be able to summon it. Knowing that I was capable of throwing a punch as skillfully as any pugilist made both Lincoln and I feel better. It also allowed us to touch one another without raising eyebrows.

A man wearing ordinary evening clothes of tailcoat, black waistcoat and white tie sauntered over to us. I recognized him from his lazy, arrogant walk, and the fact that his black mask—the only item of clothing befitting a masquerade ball—covered very little of his face. I tried to hide my distaste of Andrew Buchanan, but I doubted I succeeded.

"Well, well, if it isn't Bluebeard and his mistress," he drawled, looking me over with a critical eye. His gaze settled on my breasts, somewhat insignificant affairs compared to those of his step-mother, Lady Harcourt. He sniffed.

Neither Lincoln nor I took his bait.

"Your disguise isn't all that good, you know." Buchanan's little finger wiggled at Lincoln's chest. "I knew it was you immediately."

"You're looking for Julia," Lincoln said.

Buchanan bristled. "What makes you say that? I'm here for the refreshments." As if to prove his point, he inspected the table laden with cakes, biscuits, bonbons and sandwiches.

"She just left," Lincoln continued.

"I told you, I'm not—"

"Go away."

Buchanan backed off, hands in the air. The footman had to step nimbly aside to avoid a collision.

"He's already drunk," I said, watching Buchanan retreat to the ballroom.

"And he'll be even drunker soon."

"Do you think he'll embarrass himself? Or her?"

"It's likely."

A commotion by the door drew our attention. Surely Buchanan hadn't made a fool of himself already. Whispers of "He's here" rippled across the room to us.

"The prince," I announced.

"Shall we dance again?" Lincoln asked.

"Is that wise? Perhaps we should stay in here."

"I'm not going to attack him, Charlie, or confront him. I simply want to dance with you."

"Oh," I said and bit my lip.

"Besides, have you ever seen a member of the royal family?"

"No."

"Then now's your opportunity." He held out his hand.

I placed mine in it. "You're going out there, near him, just so I can catch a glimpse of a prince?"

"Is that such a bad thing?"

"Not at all." Yet I didn't quite believe that he was doing it for me. There must be a small part of him that wanted to observe his father, too, even from a distance.

We exited the refreshment room, but couldn't catch sight of His Royal Highness through the throng. Everyone seemed to want an introduction. It took a good hour before the crowd thinned and we could see the man himself. He was a strong looking fellow, and handsome for his age, although his florid complexion and paunch told the story of his excesses. According to Lady Vickers, the Prince of Wales enjoyed the company of women, although not that of his wife, and drank champagne as if it were water. Sometimes, he even bathed in it, but only when he frequented Paris's exclusive brothels.

"There you are." Lady Vickers caught my hand as soon as Lincoln and I ended our dance. "Come with me, Charlie, and meet the prince before he gets too drunk and makes a play for you."

My eyes widened.

She waved her hand. "You've heard what he's like."

I turned to Lincoln, but the crowd had already moved into the space between us. Apparently he had no intention of following.

We scooped up Alice as we passed, tearing her away from the conversation she shared with Seth and four others, and advanced toward the prince and his friends like an army marching on its enemy, our steps sure and steady, our gazes focused dead ahead. We were out maneuvered, however, by Lady Harcourt. She was already there, her tinkling laughter floating on the drafts. The prince laughed too, his gaze not lifting higher than her heaving bosom.

"That woman," Lady Vickers ground out between her teeth. "No one breathes that deeply. She's doing it to show off her breasts. As if we haven't already noticed them."

"We can still meet him," Alice said.

Lady Vickers' brows drew together with determination. She scanned the room. "I wonder who his friends are. Where is our hostess when she's needed? I want to be introduced to them."

"We don't need to meet his friends," I said. "They're rather too old for, er..." I glanced at Alice again.

"For me," she said flatly. "They're too old for me. Thank you for your efforts in finding me a suitable husband, madam, but I think I can manage on my own."

Lady Vickers let go of Alice's hand as if she'd been stung. "No! You can't!" She glanced behind us to where Seth stood, his focus on Alice.

"I don't particularly care to meet the prince or his friends," I said before the conversation steered too far out of control. "But thanks for thinking of me, Lady V."

She jerked my hand hard against her side. I prepared to be dragged over to meet the prince.

But we never got the chance.

A heavily accented woman's voice pitched over the music. "I must speak! I must speak to prince!"

Everyone turned toward the voice. Dancers stopped mid-step, and the band quieted.

"Who is it?" the prince demanded, trying to peer over heads.

A tall, slender woman with waist-length gray hair and tanned skin broke through the crowd. No one tried to stop her. Everyone seemed too curious to see what would happen next.

The strangest reaction came from Lady Harcourt, however. She gasped then covered her mouth with her hand. She glanced past me. I turned to see Lincoln standing there, his gaze fixed on the woman. He'd gone pale.

The woman stopped short of the prince, whose friends now tried to block the woman's path. The prince shoved one of them aside. He faced up to the woman, keeping an arm's length between them. She tipped her chin, fierce defiance flashing in the depths of eyes as black as pitch. She was a strikingly handsome woman of about fifty years, with a strong jaw and cheekbones, and a slender figure. Her clothing, however, was modest, the practical boots well worn. Not a single guest would have chosen such a drab coat and humble skirt for their costume.

"Who is she?" he asked Lord Hothfield, standing beside him.

Lord Hothfield made a noise in the back of his throat, opened his mouth and shut it again without answering. He looked like a fish, gasping on the dock.

"You know me," the woman said. "I am Leisl. Your woman, long ago."

The entire ballroom fell silent. Not a shoe scuffled, or a nose sniffled.

The prince burst out laughing, but there was an uncertain hesitance to it. "You jest, woman. I wouldn't waste my time with you. Get her out of here."

"Thompson!" Lord Hothfield bellowed. "Thompson! Escort this dirty creature from the house."

A footman grabbed the woman's arm but she shook him off with a violent motion. "I came to warn you. I see you, Prince. I see your future. You are in danger."

The prince's laughter spluttered until it died altogether. His cheeks above his beard went white. "What kind of danger?"

His question was almost lost amid the hoots and howls from his friends. "Get the mad old bat out of here," one of them shouted.

The woman pointed her finger at the prince. "I warn you. Be careful of your father."

More howls of laughter followed. "His father's dead," someone said. "God, woman, where have you been?"

The footman grabbed her again, this time with the help of another.

"I have seen him!" the woman screeched, her unwavering gaze still on the prince, even as the two men ushered her away. "He will bring you much trouble! Heed my warning! You know I speak only true to you. You *know* this!"

The men pushed her forward and she stumbled. They stopped her from falling, and roughly dragged her away. The crowd parted, the women wrinkling their noses in disgust. One man spat at her.

"Disgusting gypsy," muttered a woman near me. "They ought to be barred from entering the country."

Gypsy.

I spun round to Lincoln, but he didn't notice me. He

forged his way toward the footmen and the gypsy, who shouted at them to leave her alone, that she would walk unassisted. They did not let her go.

Not until Lincoln gripped their shoulders and tore them away from her. Away from his mother.

CHAPTER 2

"What are you doing, man?" bellowed one of the prince's friends. His voice rang clear across the room now that the band and guests had gone silent. "Let them escort her out. She's making fools of us all."

Lincoln placed his hand on the woman's lower back and said something to her that no one else could hear. She glanced sharply at him. I tried to determine from her face if she somehow knew he was her son, but her features quickly schooled and she allowed him to steer her out of the ballroom. Lincoln had never met his mother, but he knew her name and where she lived from the file in the ministry's archives.

I picked up my skirts to follow.

"Who is he?" The prince's voice sounded remarkably close. I glanced over my shoulder to see him, Lady Harcourt and our host on our trail. "Hothfield?"

"I am not sure, your highness," Hothfield said. "My wife will know."

"He's Lincoln Fitzroy," Lady Harcourt said. "Of Lichfield Towers in Highgate."

"Never heard of him," the prince said. "Does he know Leisl, do you think?" His use of her first name wasn't lost on me. He remembered her. He must.

"I rather think he does," she said.

I caught up to Lincoln and Leisl in the entrance hall, standing in the shadows beneath the staircase. He nodded at something she said and her lips parted. Her knees buckled but he caught her and guided her to the chaise.

"That's velvet!" Lady Hothfield cried. She stood between her husband and Lady Harcourt, her fan fluttering violently at her chest. "Get up! Get up! You're ruining my furniture with your dirty clothes." She barreled past the prince, but I blocked her with my arm.

"Her clothes aren't dirty," I said in as mild a voice as I could manage considering the way my blood boiled. "She's not doing you any harm sitting there."

"Don't be ridiculous," Lady Hothfield snapped, shoving my arm away. "She tried to assassinate His Royal Highness the Prince of Wales! In my home!"

"Steady on, m'dear, " Lord Hothfield said. "There was no assassination attempt."

"Don't be a fool. She's a gypsy!"

Lincoln stood between Leisl and Lady Hothfield. "She'll leave," he said. "She needs a moment to compose herself first."

"Why does *she* need a moment? I am the injured party! And His Royal Highness, of course." Lady Hothfield assessed Lincoln anew and made no attempt to get past him.

Lincoln crossed his arms over his chest and set his feet apart.

Lady Hothfield took a step back beneath the force of his glare. "Thompson! Thompson, remove these people at once!"

"Leave us, Hothfield," the prince ordered.

"You wish to speak to her?" Lord Hothfield blinked at the prince. "Is that wise considering what she is?"

"Indeed," Lady Hothfield said. "What if she puts a spell on you?"

"Go." The way the prince barked reminded me very much of Lincoln. Both men were accustomed to giving orders and having them obeyed, without question.

With a bow, Lord Hothfield retreated, gesturing for his wife to follow. She shot a glare at Lincoln then retreated with her husband. They passed Seth at the base of the stairs and headed back up to the ballroom. Lady Harcourt left too, her pace slower, her brow rumpled in thought.

"See that we're not disturbed," Lincoln said to Seth.

Seth nodded and headed up the stairs, taking two at a time.

The prince approached Lincoln as one would approach a dog of uncertain temperament. In Lincoln's current mood, it was perhaps wise to be cautious. He looked thunderous.

"You too," the prince said.

"No," Lincoln shot back.

I stilled. He dared disobey the Prince of Wales? "We know she's a seer," I said quickly. "We know a lot of things that may help in this situation."

The prince regarded me levelly for a moment. I thought he would order me to go too, but then he said, "Very well. Stay. Leisl, you shouldn't have come here. It's far too public."

"I cannot go to your palaces," she said. "There are too many guards. Where do you expect me to go?"

"That is not the point."

"No," Lincoln said, low. "The point is that she risked much to come here and warn you."

"Warn me?" The prince snorted. "Of what? That my dead father has it in for me? That's absurd." He squared his shoulders and stretched his neck. "Even if I believe that she has visions, it's still an outrageous claim."

"You believe," Leisl said before Lincoln could reply. "I know you. I read you...*sire*."

Had she been about to call him a different name, perhaps a more personal one that she used to use?

The prince stiffened. "This man." He jerked his head at Lincoln. "How do you know him?"

Leisl pushed to her feet. The fierce set of her jaw, so like Lincoln's, spoke of her cool determination, yet the slight quiver of her lower lip softened the effect. "I have just learned that he...he is my son."

So Lincoln had told her that much in their brief encounter tonight. *My son*, she'd said, not *our*.

"Fitzroy," the prince murmured, mulling over the name that meant son of a king. He looked at Lincoln anew. "How old are you?"

"My age is not the issue here." In centuries past, Lincoln's impertinent answer would be considered an offence worthy of a beating. Nowadays, the prince simply flared his nostrils in disapproval. "The point is, you treated Leisl abominably this evening. Apologize."

"I beg your pardon?" the prince spluttered.

"Apologize to her."

My breath hitched. Leisl sucked in her top lip and half shook her head.

"I will not!" the prince bellowed. "She charged in here, uninvited, frightened the other guests, then proceeded to spout off about my late father. Why in God's name should I apologize to her? It is she who ought to apologize to me." His gaze flicked to the woman he'd known intimately on at least one occasion.

"We have both wronged the other," Leisl said. "So long ago."

Lincoln opened his mouth, most likely to protest. As the only one there who had his best interests at heart—and I included Lincoln himself in that assessment—I decided to step in before he spoke. This little family reunion wasn't going at all well and he had the potential to make it so much worse.

"Water under the bridge," I said in a light, breezy voice. "Perhaps we ought to discuss Leisl's warning. I think we'd all like to hear more about it."

The prince narrowed his gaze at me as I moved to stand alongside Lincoln. "Who *are* you?"

I bobbed a curtsy then lowered myself a little more. How low should I go? I almost lost my balance as I stood again, but Lincoln grasped my arm and steadied me. "My name is Miss Charlotte Holloway," I said. "I'm a friend of Mr. Fitzroy's."

"Miss Holloway, you claimed you know things that may help in this situation, but I think it's best if you leave this to me and Fitzroy.

"She stays," Lincoln said before I could respond. At the prince's arched brow, he added, "The supernatural doesn't frighten her."

I wouldn't have put it like that. Some of the supernatural frightened me terribly.

Leisl rose and stepped in front of me so that I couldn't see the prince's reaction. She touched my cheek, her gaze connecting with mine. She sucked a sharp breath through her teeth and her fingers curled on my cheek. The nails scraped my skin but did not break it.

"Yes, you can help," she said. "You see the dead. I cannot."

I could do more than see the dead. I could raise them and control them. I thought it best not to mention that in front of the future king of England, however. Although I doubted he had the power to reinstate a law to burn witches at the stake, I didn't want to take that chance.

Leisl turned to the prince who looked somewhat stunned

after her pronouncement. At least he didn't call anyone mad, or demand my arrest. "I came to warn you, sire. You are in danger from your dead father."

"How can a spirit harm me? Are they not made of air?"

"I do not know. It is not clear."

He snorted. "Seeing the future is an imprecise science, is it?"

"The unclear can be changed. The clear cannot. Good fortune is with you tonight, sire. My son and his bride will help if you allow it."

"Oh! I'm not his bride," I said with a silly laugh that I wished I could take back as soon as it escaped my lips.

"I...I..." The prince smoothed his hand over his evening jacket then tugged on the cuffs. "I ought to return upstairs. You must leave now."

"But you are in danger!"

Lincoln placed a hand on her shoulder. "You've done all you can."

The prince held Lincoln's gaze for a very long time before breaking it to once again take in every inch of him...of his son. Did he see the similarities? Did he know or suspect? It wasn't clear from his expression, now closed and unreadable. It was so very like the mask Lincoln sometimes wore to hide his emotions that my breath hitched.

The prince turned sharply and strode up the stairs. Leisl gathered the lapels of her coat at her chest, her dark eyes focused not on the man she'd lain with in her youth, but the man who was the product of that union.

"You were such a little thing." She touched Lincoln's arm and, when he didn't move away, squeezed. "Now you are strong. Fierce."

"Tell me what you know about the danger," he said. "What have you seen?"

Leisl's fingers sprang apart and she let him go and

stepped away. I wanted to chastise Lincoln for his coolness toward her when she must be feeling quite emotional to meet her long lost son. But I couldn't do so here, in front of her and others. Seth, Alice and Lady V approached cautiously down the stairs.

"It was his father," Leisl said emphatically. "He may wish to harm his son."

"How, when a spirit has no form?" Lincoln asked.

"I do not know."

"You said you saw it, in your vision. If you didn't see how it harmed him, then what, precisely, did you see?"

"No, no, not see a vision. Not..." She clicked her tongue in frustration. "Not like I see you now. I see it as feeling, in here." She touched her chest. At Lincoln's continued frown, she added, "You do not see my breath, yet you know I breathe. Yes?"

"I understand," I said. "It's an instinct that's nagging you, not an actual vision."

"An instinct," Lincoln said flatly.

"As *you* instinctively know when I'm near or in danger. You don't see the pictures in your mind's eye, but you do know." I touched his chest over his heart. "In here."

He closed his hand over mine and drew it to his side. "You're supposed to be a strong seer," he said to his mother. "I thought you could see pictures, visions."

"I do, with some. With the prince, it is in the heart only. Is instinct," she said with a smile at me. "As your bride say."

Lord and Lady Hothfield arrived along with the butler and footmen. It would seem we weren't welcome to see in the New Year. Lord Hothfield asked one of the footmen to have our carriage brought around, and another fetched our coats. Lady Vickers praised the ball and the esteemed guest list, but Lady Hothfield ignored her completely. Lady Vickers thrust out her considerable chest, threw back her head, and backed away. She bumped into the Greek statue. A moment later, she stepped away, a small smile on her face. The crimson cloth covering the statue's nether region disappeared into the folds of her skirt.

I bit my lip, but couldn't stop my grin. Seth and Alice both followed my gaze to the white marble statue, now entirely naked. Seth pinched the bridge of his nose while Alice giggled into her hand.

Lord and Lady Hothfield hadn't yet seen. They continued to sport scowls as the footmen produced our coats. I put mine on and caught Leisl observing me. Could she see into a person's past as well as their future? What did she see in mine?

"You are not medium," she said quietly. "You are more."

I glanced at Lincoln. Neither of us answered.

"Do not fear me," she said. "I do not harm the woman my…my son loves." She reached for his hand, but he moved away. Her face fell.

I took her hand instead. "Forgive him," I said. "He needs time."

She nodded and held my hand briefly in both of hers before letting go.

"If you need anything, we can be found at Lichfield Towers in Highgate. Take care, Leisl."

Alice hooked her arm through mine. "We'd better go," she whispered. "Lady Hothfield is looking at us so fiercely, I can feel her glare stabbing me."

"You!" Leisl took a step backward, her huge eyes fixed on Alice. "You are door."

"Door?" Alice tried to laugh but it fell flat. "Charlie, what does she mean? Why is she looking at me like I'm the devil?"

"The door to other worlds," Leisl muttered, taking another step back. She pulled out a necklace from beneath her bodice and held it up. The flat oval pendant attached to the leather strip sported a roughly hewn etching of a blue eye. It was identical to one I'd found in Lincoln's possession some time ago. He'd told me his mother had given it to him when he was a baby. It was all he had of hers.

"What is she doing? Is she cursing me?" Alice's voice rose in panic and she sidled closer to me.

"Nothing like that," I quickly assured her. "It's for her own protection."

"She knows what I am? What my dreams do? How? How can she know?"

"I'll explain later." I took her hand and steered her toward the door.

"Alice?" Seth fell into step beside us. "You look pale. Allow me to escort you."

"Oh!" cried Lady Vickers. "Oh my! Oh dear, how *wicked*."

I spun round to see Lady Vickers pointing at the statue, her other hand shielding her eyes.

"I cannot bear to see such…such filth!" she screeched.

Several faces peered over the balustrade to see what all the fuss was about. More than one gentlemen snickered, and a few ladies too, while an older woman covered her young companion's eyes.

"I want to *see*, Mama," the girl whined, clawing at her mother's hand.

Lady Hothfield's cheeks turned the color of the carpet. "Cover it up at once! You there, your jacket!" She dragged the hapless footman's jacket from his shoulders then flung it back at him. "Cover up the offensive area! Quickly!"

More guests peered down, and several giggled while others shook their heads in disgust. This level of society wasn't used to seeing nakedness in their entrance halls, not even on statues. Indeed, for some, nakedness in any room was abhorrent.

Gus arrived with our carriage. Lincoln climbed up beside

him while we four piled inside and pulled the blankets over our laps. Lady Vickers produced the statue's loin cloth and waved it in front of Seth's face.

He shoved it away. "You're drunk."

She flicked the cloth at him. "How else am I to get through evenings like those?"

"I thought you wanted to go."

"And be whispered about behind my back? Be snubbed at every turn? That is not my idea of a pleasant evening, Seth."

"Then why accept the invitation at all? Indeed, why go to so much trouble to secure an invitation in the first place?"

"To force them to smile politely at me when I greet them. I want them to know that their malice did not bury me." She patted his cheek. "And to ensure you will be accepted into society once again."

"Why do you care so much about that? I don't want it."

"You may not want it, but you need it. You don't want to get to my age and regret that you made a poor match because you didn't have access to the best ladies in your youth."

He stared at her. "I am lost for words."

"That's quite all right, dearest. You may thank me when your wits return, but please do so before I die. Or Charlie can summon me and you can tell me then."

Seth shook his head. "This conversation is one of the strangest I've ever had."

"Speaking of strange, thank goodness that gypsy woman arrived when she did," Lady Vickers said. "She certainly livened up a rather dull event. Not to mention the gossips have someone else to whisper about now."

"She was quite a crackpot," Seth agreed.

"Don't call her that in front of Lincoln," I warned them.

"Why not?"

I didn't want to tell them that Leisl was his mother, but I

needed to explain why they must temper their comments in his presence. "She's a seer and so is he."

"He is?" both Lady Vickers and Alice said.

I saw no reason not to tell them. They were both aware of the supernatural and had kept the household secrets to themselves so far. Neither would want to jeopardize their situation at Lichfield by gossiping about us. "He is," I said. "His skill is minimal, however. He doesn't so much as have visions, as feelings about certain things, and an awareness about, well, about me, mostly." I didn't mention the vision he had that day we kissed. It was a private matter, a vision of both of us, together and happy.

I told them about Leisl's vision regarding the prince, and how he'd scoffed at her pronouncement.

"I wonder how his life will be in danger from a ghost," Seth said. "I can understand his reticence to believe her, particularly if he doesn't believe in the occult."

"He believes," I said. "The look on his face when she told him suggests he does."

"I wonder if that's how they met," Alice said. "She seemed to know him, although he denied it. Perhaps she told him his fortune at the fair once."

"He wouldn't attend the fair." Lady Vickers held up the statue's loin cloth and studied it back and front. "It's more likely she's one of his conquests."

"Mother," Seth growled. "Not in front of the young ladies."

"Tosh. They're not silly girls, and I'm not imparting anything they haven't already heard." She tucked the loin-cloth into her bodice. "This will make a lovely handkerchief. I'll take it with me to all the dinner parties and luncheons this week. I think it will be quite the sensation."

Seth groaned. "I blame America."

"For what?"

"For turning you into this shameless hoyden."

She laughed. "America is not to blame for that. It was my darling George's influence." She winked at Alice and me. She spoke often of George, the man who'd risen from footman to be her second husband. He'd been the love of her life. Alice and I enjoyed hearing stories about their time in America, and how wonderful George had been to her before his sudden death. Seth, however, usually walked out of the room.

He sighed and squeezed the bridge of his nose. "Are we nearly home?"

* * *

"I GOT LEFTOVER PLUM TARTS," Cook said from the depths of the pantry. "Butter biscuits and two slices of orange cake."

"No bacon or eggs?" Gus asked, taking a seat at the kitchen table. He and Doyle had seen to the horses and coach upon our return, while Lady Vickers had retired immediately, with the assistance of her maid, Bella. The rest of us gathered in the kitchen where the range was still warm.

"It ain't breakfast," Cook said, setting a tray laden with food on the table.

Gus pounced on it, but Seth slapped his hand away. "Ladies first." He slid the tray toward Alice.

She took a biscuit and thanked him. Seth smiled then slid the tray closer to himself, away from Gus. It didn't stop Gus from reaching over and grabbing a tart.

Lincoln, standing at the stove, poured hot chocolate directly into cups that I handed out to everyone. Doyle didn't want one, and nor did he eat. He looked tired.

"Perhaps you should retire," I said quietly to him.

"Not while Mr. Fitzroy needs me," he said.

"I don't need you," Lincoln said, sitting beside me. "Charlie's right. You should retire."

Doyle looked as if he would protest but then seemed to

think better of it. There really could be no arguing with Lincoln on this score. He'd never required the services of a valet before, and there was nothing else for Doyle to do. "Very good, sir. I'll see that all the doors are locked before I go up. Goodnight everyone, and a very happy new year."

At some point on the journey home, the clock had ticked past midnight and into 1890. A new year and a new beginning.

"How be the evening?" Cook asked once Doyle was gone. We kept no secrets from Doyle, but sometimes the men didn't feel as if he was one of us since he'd only joined the Lichfield Towers staff recently.

"Interesting," Seth told him. "My mother caused a commotion that means we'll probably never get invited back to the Hothfields."

Gus chuckled. "The more I know of your mother, the more I like her."

Seth wrinkled his nose. "If you marry her, I will *not* call you Papa."

That got everyone laughing, even Seth.

"She wasn't the only one causing commotions," Lincoln said.

I touched his knee under the table, wanting him to know that I supported his decision to discuss Leisl and her vision with the others. He rested his hand over mine.

"My mother showed up."

The kitchen filled with gasps, including my own. I hadn't expected him to tell them *that*.

"That gypsy is your mother?" Seth asked.

"Romany," I corrected. "They don't like being called gypsy."

"Could you not see the resemblance?" Lincoln asked.

"A little, now that you mention it," Seth said with a shrug. "But...if she's your mother, who's your father?"

Lincoln's fingers flexed around mine. "That information is not important."

Seth pressed his lips together and concentrated on his cup.

Lincoln briefly told Gus and Cook about Leisl's vision.

"The question is, what do we do now?" I asked. "The prince ought to be protected."

"How?" Cook asked. "He doesn't believe in her visions."

"He believes," Lincoln said. "He doesn't want to admit it."

"He'll be quaking in his jeweled slippers tonight then," Gus said with a snort.

"We should visit him tomorrow," I said.

Alice laughed softly. "Charlie, one doesn't simply pay calls on the royal family."

"There must be a way of getting word to him."

"Why not approach it a different way?" Seth asked. "You could summon the spirit of the dead prince consort and ask him if he's going to do something nasty to his son."

"That's a foolish plan," Gus scoffed. "He ain't going to admit it, for one. And what's he going to do in spirit form?"

"Haunt him to death," Cook said. "That's what I'd do."

"Haunt your own son!"

"Maybe the Prince O' Wales is a right turd and deserves it."

Seth nodded slowly. "He doesn't treat his mistresses all that well once he tires of them."

"They tell you that?" Gus asked, his mouth cocked in a sly grin.

Seth's gaze flicked to Alice. "Of course not. Why would I be in communication with the mistresses of His Royal Highness?"

"Got enough of your own to worry about, eh?" Cook's belly shook with his deep laugh.

"Half-wits," Seth muttered. "The point is, Cook may be

right, and the prince consort might want his son to toe the royal line and straighten up now that he's middle aged. It won't be long before he'll take over the throne, but the way he acts, he won't be taken seriously by the public or government. It's not just the numerous mistresses; it's the parties, holidays and exorbitant expense. His lifestyle does not come cheaply or discreetly."

"That's a good theory," Alice said, "but his carefree lifestyle is not new and the prince consort has been dead a long time. Why threaten him now?"

"Perhaps the queen's ill and the ghost of her late husband knows it. Perhaps he sees the urgency now."

"I think the theory has merit," I said, "but if the spirit simply wants to scare the Prince of Wales, why is Leisl so concerned?"

"Perhaps she's overreacting," Seth said.

Alice bristled. "Because we females tend to?"

Seth held up his hands, warding her off. "Not at all," he said at the same moment Gus mumbled, "Aye."

Seth rolled his eyes. "And you wonder why no one wants to marry you."

"You ain't married neither," Gus shot back.

"That doesn't mean I haven't had proposals." Seth stood. "I'm going to bed. Alice, Charlie, can I escort you to your rooms?"

He escorted us along with Lincoln. My bedroom was a little down the corridor from Lincoln's. After Alice and Seth retreated to theirs, he steered me into the recessed doorway and rested his hand on the doorknob, barring my entry.

"Goodnight," he murmured.

"Goodnight," I whispered back.

He took my hand and placed it to his lips. He skimmed my knuckles with a kiss that was not quite a kiss, yet made my skin tighten and my blood thrum. He stepped away, much too soon, and strode toward his door.

"Oh. Wait," I said. He stopped and I caught up to him. "Lincoln, are you all right? Tonight must have been very trying for you."

He nodded. "I'm fine."

He did seem fine, but perhaps he was hiding his true feelings. "Are you sure?"

"Yes."

"Very well. Goodnight." I turned away but stopped abruptly. I turned back only to see that he'd not moved.

He arched a brow.

"The thing is…" I toyed with the leather ties on his jerkin. "You can't possibly be all right. You saw both your mother and father, not to mention your mother now knows your name and where to find you. Don't you wish to seek her out and talk to her more? Aren't there questions you wish to ask her?"

"No."

I searched his face and peered into his eyes to see if he spoke the truth. I saw nothing in them that would indicate he was covering a deep hurt. "I don't understand," I said, more to myself than him. "How could the meeting not have affected you? It affected me and they're not my parents."

"I dislike my father," he said. "That hasn't changed since the last time I saw him. And I don't know my mother. She's a stranger to me."

"Yes, but she at least seemed nice. And she is your mother, Lincoln. That must mean something."

He clasped my hands in his and looked down at them. "Perhaps I lack the sentimental part in my heart that others have."

"You were sentimental about me. You fetched me from the school."

"Because I missed you." He kissed my nose and circled his arms around me. "I knew you, Charlie, and I was lonely without you. I needed you and wanted you. I've never known my mother so how could I miss her?"

I rested my cheek against his chest and listened to his steady heartbeat. "That makes sense. And yet it doesn't explain why I'm so curious about her."

"You have a curious nature. You wonder about everything whereas I simply accept."

"Sometimes."

His arms tightened. "Sometimes."

I closed my eyes and let him hold me in a blanket of warmth until he eventually set me aside. "Go to bed or we'll stand here all night."

"Goodnight."

"Try not to lie awake and plot ways of forcing me to speak to Leisl again."

I sighed. "You know me too well."

* * *

LINCOLN and I resumed training in the empty ballroom late the following morning. Dressed in my loose fitting attire, complete with men's trousers, we punched, kicked and wrestled ourselves into a sweat. Or rather, I sweated. Lincoln didn't even breathe heavily, something which Alice commented on when we finished and he left the room. She, Seth and Gus had watched us train, sometimes assisting. Alice stood near the window, fascinated that I could throw quite a solid punch.

"Does anything exert him?" she asked.

I laughed. "Sometimes. This, however, is nothing for him. Maddening, isn't it?"

"If I hadn't seen him weak from the explosion when I arrived here, I would have wondered if he was human at all."

"You're not the only one who wonders that," Gus said, returning the baton to the sideboard cupboard.

"That's why we're so surprised to hear that Leisl is his mother," Seth said. "I'm still reeling over the news, in fact. I thought he was made, not born."

I rolled my eyes. "Don't let him hear you say that."

"Why not? It's not like he has feelings that could be hurt with a little teasing."

I was about to protest but he was right. While Lincoln had proven to me that he did have feelings that could be bruised and battered just like mine, a few humorous barbs from a friend wouldn't so much as leave a mark.

Lady Vickers strode into the room. "Here you all are. Good lord, Charlie, what are you wearing? Are those *trousers*?"

I plucked at the lightweight cotton. "Training attire. I rather like wearing them. It allows me to do this." I performed a side kick which would have revealed far too much if I'd been in skirts.

Lady Vickers pulled a face. "You are a unique girl."

"Thank you. I think."

"Go and change then meet me in the parlor. I want to discuss advertising for a housekeeper and maids."

I sighed. "I suppose it's time. We can't go on as we have. Poor Doyle is run off his feet all day, and Bella, too."

"A good attitude," Lady Vickers said, nodding. "You might as well join us, Alice."

"Me?" Alice blinked. "Oh, I don't think so. It's not my place."

"Do you have anything better to do?"

"I…I haven't made plans."

"She was going to take a walk with me," Seth said.

"It's raining," his mother said.

"A walk inside the house. Along the corridors, around the ballroom..." He crooked his arm for Alice to take.

She hesitated then took it with a cautious glance at Lady Vickers. Lady Vickers scowled and marched out of the ballroom. I had a feeling Seth would be getting another lecture from her later. Ever since Alice had arrived and Seth had shown an interest in her, mother and son had been at loggerheads. She did not approve of a poor girl from the merchant classes for her one and only child.

I changed quickly then headed down to the parlor at the front of the house. Lady Vickers sat reading correspondence by the rain-slicked window. I looked out at the low gray sky and sighed. There would be no quiet walks in the wintry garden with Lincoln today.

A dark object moved on the drive. I squinted through the window and tried to make out the shape. "I think we have a visitor," I said as the shape became a coach pulled by a matching pair of grays.

"In this weather?" Lady Vickers lowered her correspondence to her lap. "Well, well, someone must have made quite an impression last night. Where's Seth?"

I rubbed the window pane to clear the fog. "The poor coachman and footman. They have umbrellas but they're not offering much shelter in this weather."

"Can you see who it is?"

"No. They aren't getting out."

"Can't blame them for that, but how are we supposed to entertain them if they won't come in? Perhaps they are in need of another umbrella. Can you see the escutcheon on the door?"

"The rain is too heavy. The coachman and footman are wearing red and gold livery. It's very striking. Do you know anyone—"

"Red and gold!" She shot to her feet and nudged me aside. "Good lord. I don't believe it."

I frowned at her then at the footman now approaching up the front steps. "Who is it?"

She turned to me, one hand pressed to her stomach, the other at her throat. "Don't panic, Charlie."

"I'm not. Who is it?"

She clasped my shoulders and sucked in a breath that swelled her chest. "Oh Charlie, this is a monumentally important day in your life. Mark it in your diary. This is the day royalty came to Lichfield Towers."

CHAPTER 3

$\mathcal{I}$ hurried to the entrance hall where Doyle received the drenched footman.

"I'll await Mr. Fitzroy's reply," the footman said, handing Doyle a note.

Doyle went to take it upstairs when Lincoln appeared on the landing. He must have seen the coach arrive too. He accepted the note and read it.

"Doyle, an umbrella, please." There was no hint on his face as to the contents of the note.

Doyle handed him an umbrella and Lincoln headed outside, the footman at his heels. We shut the door to keep out the driving rain.

"Do you think it's the Prince of Wales?" Lady Vickers asked. "Or the queen herself?"

I paced the entrance hall until Lady Vickers ordered me to be still. How could I be still when Lincoln might have to confront his father again?

Seth and Gus approached from the direction of the service area at the rear of the house. "Why are you all gathered near the door?" Seth asked.

His mother clasped his arms, her face alight with excitement. "Someone from the royal household is here!"

"Blimey," Gus muttered. "Who?"

The door suddenly opened and Lincoln entered. He handed the thoroughly wet umbrella to Doyle who raced away with it, dripping water onto the tiles.

"Well?" Lady Vickers asked. "Who was it?"

"The Prince of Wales," Lincoln said, his gaze connecting with mine.

"I knew it!" Lady Vickers clapped her hands. "What did he want?"

"To summon Charlie and me to the palace. He didn't say why, but it must be about Leisl's vision."

"Me?" I blurted out. "Go to Buckingham Palace? Don't be ridiculous. I can't go there. I'm a nobody."

"Did you not once say that you're Her Majesty's necromancer?"

I gave him a withering glare. "That was a joke, Lincoln, and you know it."

"The fact is, you *are* her necromancer. Although they've never been aware of our existence, we work for the crown. We've been summoned and we have to go."

"Can't you go alone?"

"No. This is a ghostly matter, and you see ghosts."

I needed to practice my curtsy.

"When word gets out about this, you'll be the envy of everyone." Lady Vickers lifted my arms and inspected my simple woolen dress. "You must change."

"Word about our visit is not to leave this house," Lincoln told her. "If we're recognized upon our arrival, then so be it, but gossip about the visit will not be traced to here. Is that clear?"

Lady Vickers bowed her head, all demure acquiescence. "Of course. Now, Charlie, your dress."

"I'll wear the blue," I said.

"Why at the palace?" Seth asked. "Why not here? He did come all this way to speak to you, after all."

"He came in person because he didn't think an invitation in the hands of footmen would be safe enough," Lincoln said. "He doesn't want the world to know that he's taking Leisl's warning seriously. The meeting is to be at the palace because his mother wishes to attend."

"The queen!" My stomach churned. "I am to meet the queen?"

"After lunch."

"I can't possibly eat! Lady V, can you show me how to do a proper curtsy so that I don't lose my balance?"

Her eyes brightened. "It will be my pleasure. I've always wanted a daughter to teach the art of curtseying." She strode off to the parlor. "Come, Charlie, we'll begin immediately."

Seth frowned at me as I passed. "I feel as though I'm being replaced."

* * *

BOTH SETH and Gus insisted on driving us to Buckingham Palace, so in the end, Lincoln allowed them to sit together on the coachman's seat, but Gus held the reins. They drove us through to the palace courtyard and deposited us at the steps. Two footmen in the distinctive red and gold livery led us inside.

I tried very hard to act as if I walked the halls of palaces every day, but my wonder must have been clear on my face because Lincoln looked amused. How could he not gawp at such opulence? We were led through room after room filled with golden candelabras, vases and frames, ornately carved furniture, doors, and ceilings, and finely detailed frescoes. The lengths of thick drapes puddled on the floor and soft carpet woven with crowns deadened our footsteps. The blue and pink walls took me by surprise and didn't appeal to my tastes, but they did suit the palace's splendor.

It would take a lifetime to fill a house this size with so many things. The queen may be old, but not old enough to decorate every inch. This place had evolved over many years, and she was merely its current occupant. Each resident had stamped their presence here in some measure and left behind tangible memories. I had always been somewhat resentful that the royal family lived in such luxury when people starved on the streets, but now I understood why they couldn't simply sell a painting and feed the homeless. In a way, they were not theirs to sell.

"So much to take in," I said quietly, staring at the painting of a man wearing a tricorn hat. "Look at all the gold."

"Seen any spirits?" Lincoln asked, his voice low.

"Not yet."

The footmen led us through to a series of more sedate rooms, not so richly decorated. A small woman of middle age wearing an elegant charcoal colored gown waited in front of a closed door. "Good afternoon, Miss Holloway, Mr. Fitzroy. I am the Honorable Mrs. Charles Grey, lady in waiting to Her Majesty. I apologize for the double escort, but we had a break-in recently and security has increased."

"A break-in?" Lincoln asked.

"A minor nuisance. Nothing was taken." The Honorable Mrs. Charles Grey didn't meet either his gaze or mine. "Now, before you meet Her Majesty, there are some things of which you ought to be aware. When you first greet her, you must address her as Her Majesty, and thereafter as ma'am. A small curtsy is required of you, Miss Holloway, and a bow is sufficient from a gentleman. Do not present your back to her, offer to shake her hand, or touch her in any way. If she stands, you must both stand too. Ready?"

She opened the door before either of us could respond and announced us. Compared to the public rooms we'd just traversed through, this room was positively cozy in size and decoration. The fireplace was modest, flanked by two vases taller than me, and in the room's center stood a round table that looked too solid to move. A figure swamped in black silk and lace sat on the sofa, her heavy features lifting a little in curiosity before settling into regal aloofness.

I sank into a curtsy and rose without losing my balance. Lady Vickers would be pleased. Lincoln's bow was more of a nod and I wasn't sure it would pass protocol.

"Good afternoon, Miss Holloway, Mr. Fitzroy." The queen's voice was as robust as her person. "Take a seat. My son will be here shortly."

We sat on the chairs at the table. Who else had sat here? The prime minister? Princesses? Best not to think about it. It wouldn't do to giggle nervously in the presence of the queen while discussing the matter of her dead husband.

The silence stretched as we waited. I felt compelled to fill it, and couldn't rely on Lincoln. "You have a lovely home, ma'am." *Ugh*. Perhaps I should have stayed quiet.

"Thank you," the queen said. "You live with Mr. Fitzroy at Lichfield Towers, I believe."

"I do."

"As his ward?"

"Yes." Not really, but our living arrangements would only expose us to speculation and innuendo and I couldn't abide that from a woman whose moral streak was wider than her person, according to Lady V.

"And what is it you do, Mr. Fitzroy? Or are you a man of leisure?"

"I am not," he said.

"He's the least leisurely person I've ever met," I said.

She pinned me with her deep-set eyes, as shrewd as they were grim. No, not grim, sad. This woman still mourned her husband, so the newspapers claimed. How that must dampen the air here and infect it with her misery. No wonder her eldest son did the exact opposite of his mother and enjoyed himself.

The Prince of Wales entered at that moment. We rose, and I curtseyed while Lincoln nodded again. The prince stood by the crackling fire, his hands at his back. If he stood and the queen sat what were Lincoln and I supposed to do? The Honorable Mrs. Charles Grey hadn't given us a clue. Lincoln sat again, so I did too. As if it were a signal, the prince also sat. He had not taken his gaze off Lincoln.

He knew.

"My son imparted the events of last evening to me," the queen said. "All of them. Apparently you claim to have knowledge of spiritual matters."

Lincoln hesitated barely a moment before saying, "Some, ma'am, yes."

"And you are the son of that gypsy woman."

"Leisl. I believe so, although I cannot be certain. I'd never met her until last night."

"Who raised you? Your father?"

"A man known as General Eastbrooke, a commander in Your Majesty's army, now deceased."

"He was not your father?"

"No."

"Then who is?"

Lincoln hesitated again. "I cannot be certain." Before the queen could ask him more questions, he turned to the prince. "Are we to understand that you believe Leisl's pronouncement after all?"

The prince settled back in the chair and stretched his legs under the table in a rather relaxed manner that had his mother pursing her lips. "I've met her before, and I have reason to believe she speaks the truth."

"What reason?"

"I beg your pardon," the queen snapped.

I sank into my chair, wishing I'd taken charge of the conversation and not left it up to Lincoln. He was as subtle as a bull.

"Private reasons," the prince said. He smiled charmingly. Too charmingly. I didn't quite believe it. "Mr. Fitzroy, I admit to being intrigued by you last night, as much as Leisl's vision. I had asked you how old you are and received no answer, so this morning, I sent my secretary to the General Register Office."

Good lord! I couldn't believe he'd done such a thing. I couldn't believe he'd admit it. I may have done the same thing a few months ago, but I had good reason. I was living with Lincoln yet he'd been something of a stranger to me. I needed to know more about the person under the same roof as me.

"You learned nothing," Lincoln told him. "The record of my birth has been lost, if it ever existed."

The prince confirmed this with a nod. "I find that odd, don't you?"

"Not at all. Perhaps Leisl failed to register me. Perhaps she recorded my birth under a Romany name."

"Why didn't the general do it?" the queen asked.

"I don't know. You would have to ask him that."

"You said yourself that he's dead."

Lincoln didn't tell her that I could summon him. Either he wasn't ready to mention my necromancy or he knew I never wanted to see the general again, even in spirit form.

The prince opened his mouth to speak but the queen lifted her hand and he closed it again. "This meeting is to discuss the gypsy's vision, not Mr. Fitzroy's family."

"Very well," the prince said. "The matter of his family can wait." Wait, but not dropped altogether. "I believe Leisl genuinely saw something in her visions that worried her," he went on. "And I would like you, Mr. Fitzroy, to discover what it is and then disarm the danger. Can you do that?"

"I believe so."

"How?" The queen leaned forward, no mean feat considering her size and the deep sofa. "How can you? What qualifies you?"

"I am the head of an organization that monitors people in possession of supernatural powers."

I lifted my brows, but they didn't rise as high as either the queen's or prince's.

"Is this a joke?" the prince bellowed.

"We're an ancient organization now known as the Ministry of Curiosities, but we've had other titles in the past."

"A ministry?" The queen looked to her son. "Why haven't I been informed of it?"

"Not an official ministry," Lincoln said. "We are not under the parliamentary umbrella. Making us official would make us public, and I don't think the public are ready to hear about the supernatural."

"Oh, I don't know," the queen said idly. "Spiritual matters are all the rage now. One of my ladies claims to have attended a séance several years ago where a real medium spoke to the ghost haunting his widow. Apparently this woman was very convincing."

The prince closed his eyes and heaved a sigh. "Mediums aren't real."

"They are," Lincoln said. "As are a great many people with interesting abilities whom you would dismiss as frauds or tricksters. The ministry catalogs them and their families to ensure we know where they are and what their talent is. It's important to trace lines of ancestry, since paranormal traits are inherited. It protects them, as well as the nation."

The queen gave her son a triumphant look, then turned her attention to Lincoln. "Do you have a list of true mediums? Will you send it to me?"

He shook his head. "I won't be releasing that information to anyone. Not even to you. It's far too dangerous—"

"I am your queen! I command you."

"There's no need for a list," I said before Lincoln got himself into more trouble. "I can summon your husband for you. Indeed, I think it's an excellent idea to ask him if he has any knowledge of Leisl's vision since she named him. It seems like the next logical step."

The queen and prince both stared at me, mouths ajar in a most un-regal manner. "But you're such a little thing," the queen said. "And so young."

I simply shrugged. "Age has nothing to do with one's supernatural ability. It's something I was born with."

Beside me, Lincoln's fingers curled into a fist on the chair arm, but he didn't try to silence me.

"You can talk to the dead?" the queen asked.

"I can, and I see them too."

"What do they look like?"

"Mist shaped like their living self."

"Remarkable," she said on a breath.

"What other supernatural abilities is your so-called ministry aware of?" the prince asked.

The queen flapped a black lace handkerchief, produced from the depths of her silk skirts. "You must summon the Prince Consort, Miss Holloway. Immediately. What do you need to begin? A drum? Cymbals? Bertie, close the curtains."

The prince didn't rise. "We ought to learn more about this ministry first. I'm not prepared to accept Mr. Fitzroy's claims yet. Not without proof."

"Miss Holloway is my proof," Lincoln shot back.

"You believe Leisl," I said gently. "And Lincoln is her son. He wishes you no disrespect, nor does he want anything from you in return. We're not asking for money or a royal seal of approval. We simply want to know what Leisl meant, too. There's no harm in doing this, I promise." To the queen, I said, "I don't require darkness or any paraphernalia. I can summon him anywhere at any time."

"What if he won't come?"

"He will come for me." As a necromancer, spirits had no choice but to appear when summoned, even those that had crossed to their afterlife. For a medium, the spirit could only come if they hadn't yet crossed. The difference made my power so much more frightening. That, and the fact necromancers could force the spirit to occupy a dead body. "Are you prepared for this, ma'am?"

"Yes. Oh, yes, I have waited a long time." She seemed taller all of a sudden, younger, and a gleam lit up her eyes. "Do not disappoint me, Miss Holloway."

"We will expect proof that you speak to my father," the prince said. "If you're lying to us…"

I swallowed. "What is his full name?"

"Francis Albert Augustus Charles Emmanuel of Saxe-Coburg-Gotha," the queen rattled off.

I had to call him twice because I missed one of his names the first time. The second time, however, I breathed a sigh of relief as the mist coalesced in the corner of the room then floated toward me, slowly forming the shape of a distinguished looking man with a high forehead and impressive side whiskers. He looked around, first at me, then at the others in the room. He settled on the sofa near his widow and laid a hand over hers. She didn't respond.

"Are you Albert, the Prince Consort?" I asked.

The queen pressed her handkerchief to her chest and her gaze flicked around the room. "He's here? Where? Where?"

"Sitting next to you." I nodded at the ghost.

The queen tentatively put out a hand. It went right through him. "I can't feel him."

The Prince of Wales rose. Hands behind his back, he bent toward the spirit, a deep frown on his brow. "Proof, Miss Holloway."

Sir?" I prompted. "Are you the Prince Consort?"

"I am he." The ghost had a faint German accent but a clear voice. He waved a hand in front of his widow's face. "Who are you?"

"My name is Miss Holloway and this is Mr. Fitzroy. I'm a...I can summon spirits."

"Clearly." He nodded at his widow. "Can she hear me?"

"They can't see, hear or sense you. Only me. Sir, I must ask for some sign that you are indeed who you claim to be. For your loved ones."

"I understand." I don't know what the prince died of, but he sported no obvious wounds that I could see. He rose and swirled before settling once more on the sofa. "I used to call her my sweet petal because she was a rose in a thorny garden. Parliament," he clarified. "It was a name for her ears only."

"The spirit tells me that he called you sweet petal, ma'am," I said. "Does that—"

The queen caught a single loud sob in her handkerchief. "Dear heart." She reached for him and for a moment I thought she could see his shape because she stroked his cheek. But as the prince moved, her hand passed through him. "I miss you terribly, my love. It's unbearable without you by my side."

Both the Prince of Wales and the spirit glanced at me and then Lincoln. I understood their concern. It was awkward enough hearing the words of an unhappy widow to her dead husband, but hearing them from the monarch's lips made me feel like I'd committed treason. She looked vulnerable, sitting on the sofa in her widow's weeds, her eyes full.

"Tell her…" The prince consort looked to the corner of the ceiling where I'd first seen him. "Tell her that my soul aches for her." He nodded at me when I hesitated.

I repeated his words. The queen's sob filled the room.

"She has grown rather fat," he said. "Do not tell her that," he hastily added.

"It has been some years since your death," I told him.

"Twenty-eight years," his son said.

"Twenty-eight long years," the queen added, her voice warbling.

"That long?" Prince Albert's spirit stood and circled his son. "He looks older than me when I died. A fine looking fellow, though. Tell him that."

I repeated his words for the Prince of Wales who seemed momentarily taken aback by the praise. "Er, thank you."

"There is so much I must tell you," the queen said, pushing herself forward on the sofa. Gone was the regal bearing, the haughty tilt of her chin. She looked like any other elderly widow meeting a long lost loved one again. "Where to start? We have…" She counted on her fingers then shook her head. "I'm not entirely sure how many grandchildren. More than thirty. But our dearest Alice and Leo have both passed on. Oh! But you must know that! How are they?"

"Er…" The ghost looked to me.

"They're happy," I said for him. I didn't know if he communicated with other deceased persons, but I did know that it was important to the queen to think of them meeting their father in a better place. "Sir, we've summoned you here for a specific reason."

"Not yet," the queen said. "I'm not ready. There's more news I must impart."

Her son laid a hand on her shoulder. "Very little of it will be for Miss Holloway's and Mr. Fitzroy's ears."

Her lips pinched, as if she suddenly remembered who she was and that we were nobodies. "You're right, Bertie. Go on, Miss Holloway. Let's get to the bottom of this mystery."

"A seer known as Leisl approached the Prince of Wales last night," I began. "She claimed to have had a vision where you endangered his life."

"Me?" The spirit shimmered. "How can that be when I have no physical form?"

"We don't know," I said. "Do you have any ideas?"

"Perhaps she's a crackpot."

"She's not," I said. "She is a genuine seer."

"How do you know?"

"We know her to be truthful."

Prince Albert grunted. "Very well, I shall take your word for it, Miss Holloway, but the truth is, she must be wrong on this score. I have no reason or desire to harm any one of my family. The very notion is absurd and abhorrent. Your seer must have misinterpreted what she saw."

I repeated his words for the others.

"There." The queen shot her son a speaking glance. "I knew it. The gypsy was wrong or mischief-making."

"Wrong, perhaps," Lincoln said, "but not mischief-making. If she wanted to cause problems, she could have done so before now and in far more dramatic ways."

The Prince of Wales stiffened and his eyes narrowed as he once again searched Lincoln's face. "What do you mean?"

Lincoln calmly rose. He was taller than the prince, his shoulders broader, his frame leaner. Yet the prince didn't shy away. "Do you wish me to elaborate?" Lincoln asked. "Here?"

The prince's jaw worked and he lowered his head. "It

would seem we are no better off than when we started. The meaning behind Leisl's vision is still a mystery."

"Your lady mentioned a break-in," Lincoln said. "What happened?"

"Is that important?" the queen asked.

"It may be."

The Prince of Wales strode to the fireplace and rested his elbow on the mantel. "Not exactly a break-in. The palace is a hive of activity at all hours. Servants come and go. No one needs to break windows to get in, they simply need to act as if they ought to be here."

The spirit strode to the window and looked out to the garden. "It never would have happened in my time."

"Was anything taken?" Lincoln asked.

"A portrait of the two of us taken shortly before..." The queen's lower lip quivered. "Before you became ill, my love," she said to the empty space beside her. I didn't have the heart to tell her he was no longer there.

"I remember it," he said, coming to sit beside her again.

"I kept it on the side table in the small music room."

"Was anything else taken?" Lincoln asked.

"Not that we noticed." The Prince of Wales glanced around the rather cluttered room. There were so many things—how would they even know if one little picture went missing?

"My private letters were disturbed," the queen said.

"What?" her son bellowed. "Why didn't you tell me?"

"That is no way to address your queen," the ghost said at the same time his widow said, "Do not speak to me in such a manner, Bertie."

"Apologies," the Prince of Wales said tightly.

"I didn't think it important until now." She dabbed her handkerchief to her nose. "Nothing was taken, you see."

"You mentioned a genuine medium earlier," Lincoln said.

"Were you never tempted to commission her to contact your husband?"

"The queen is above that sort of thing," the Prince of Wales said.

"I did make inquiries, as it happens." The queen's short, blunt hands screwed up her handkerchief. "I never told you, Bertie, because I knew you wouldn't approve. In fact, I've consulted no less than five mediums. The first four were all frauds. I knew that almost immediately. The fifth, the one recommended by my friend, was different. First of all, she was reluctant to come here. When I insisted, she obliged, but refused payment. We wandered the palace and gardens for hours, but she sensed no spirits. She explained that she can only communicate with spirits who have not crossed to their afterlife. Spirits who linger here usually have something they need to do before they move on, a score to settle. Since she couldn't see my husband's spirit, she said that meant he had died a contented man and departed this realm."

Two sets of living eyes and a pair of dead ones fixed on me.

"If that's the case," the Prince of Wales said slowly, "how can *you* speak to my father, Miss Holloway?"

It would seem I had to admit it after all. I glanced at Lincoln, but he offered no guidance. He was leaving the decision to me. "I am not a medium," I told them. "I am something rarer, known as a necromancer. I can summon a spirit no matter where they are."

"Remarkable," both princes murmured.

"The name of this medium?" Lincoln asked the queen.

She tore her stunned gaze away from me. "Why do you need to know it when she wasn't able to see my husband's spirit?"

"I like to know things," he said simply.

She pressed her fingers to her temple and closed her eyes.

"I don't recall her name but she's married to the heir of the Preston viscountcy."

"I know the current viscount," the Prince of Wales said. "Beaufort is the family name."

"That's it! Mrs. Emily Beaufort."

"There was some scandal a few years back where the heir married a common girl whose coloring was, shall we say, not typically English."

"I found her to be quite charming," the queen said.

I knew her too. Or, at least, knew *of* her. She was listed in our archives. While I didn't have a memory as good as Lincoln's, her name had stuck with me because of her link to the Preston viscountcy. There were very few peers of the realm with supernatural abilities.

"Is there anything else we ought to know about the break-in?" Lincoln asked. "Or any other unusual events at the palace that may have a bearing on Leisl's vision?"

"Not that I can think of," the queen said. "Bertie?"

He shook his head, but did not meet her gaze.

"Miss Holloway and I will take our leave." Lincoln nodded at me. "Send His Highness's spirit back, Charlie."

"No!" the queen cried, attempting to push herself out of the sofa only to fail and give up. "No, you mustn't. I'm not ready. We have so much to discuss."

"He can't stay," the Prince of Wales said.

"Why not?"

"Tell her we will be together again one day," Prince Albert's ghost said to me. "Tell her I cannot stay but I'll hear her if she speaks to my spirit when she's alone. That ought to curb her grief somewhat."

I repeated his words then ordered him to return to his afterlife. His mist swirled once around the room then disappeared through the ceiling. The queen's eyes watered and her chin trembled. Her son made no move to comfort her.

"Allow me to escort you out," he said to us.

I bobbed a curtsy at the queen but she simply turned her shoulder to me and poured silent tears into her handkerchief. We left with the Prince of Wales.

A footman stood by the door, his face bland. The prince dismissed him and walked with us back through the palace.

"You held something back," Lincoln said. "What was it?"

The prince regarded him levelly. "You're used to making demands, aren't you? And having them carried out?"

Lincoln's steady gaze faltered. He hadn't expected the prince to get his measure so quickly. "My men prefer to remain in my good graces."

"And Miss Holloway? Does she do as you order?"

Lincoln's shoulders went rigid. "She has a mind that is not easily swayed when it's made up."

I huffed out a laugh then bit my tongue. I'd found myself in the middle of a battle of wills between father and son, and it might be best to be as insignificant as possible to allow them to get on with it.

"Good for you, Miss Holloway," the prince said. "A fellow should always have at least one person who can stand up to him, otherwise he becomes too arrogant."

"Yes, sir," I said, sounding utterly stupid.

"As to your question, Fitzroy." The prince lowered his voice. "You are correct. There is something else, and I didn't want to upset Her Majesty more. Only a few days ago, a man came here and demanded to see her. Her lady in waiting—can't recall which one now—thought it best that she not be troubled so summoned me in the queen's stead. It was obvious to the lady that Her Majesty would be disturbed by the visitor." The prince's pace slowed, and he once again checked behind us. He stopped altogether, and so did we. "You see," the prince said quietly, "the man claimed to be my father."

CHAPTER 4

"Good lord," I said. "Did you have him arrested?"

The prince shook his head. "I told him to go away and never return. I...I couldn't bring myself to summon the police."

"Why not?" Lincoln asked.

"He looked remarkably like my father. Exactly alike, as it happens, from his whiskers, hair style, the shape of his face. I found myself almost believing his claim. The queen would certainly have believed him, and her lady knew it. That's why she sent for me."

"What about his clothing?" Lincoln asked.

"What of it?"

"Did it look like the clothing he wore in his lifetime?"

"He died so long ago, I can't recall. He had a variety of suits, some formal, others not so much. I would say the imposter wore something unremarkable since I didn't notice his attire. To be honest, I was too busy studying his features."

"What about his voice?" I asked, recalling the spirit's German accent.

"Again, his death was almost thirty years ago. The accent

was certainly spot-on, with a hint of the Germanic." He frowned in thought. "Now that I think about it, his voice wasn't quite the same. The imposter's was deeper."

Lincoln set off again. The prince and I fell into step alongside him. "You were right to send him away," Lincoln said. "He is an imposter."

"I know," the prince said through a set jaw. "I saw my father's body. He is very much dead."

"Now we know what Leisl meant," I said. "She didn't see the *spirit* of your father, she saw the man impersonating him."

"That seems to be the case," the prince said.

"Could he have fathered another child?" Lincoln asked.

The prince's step faltered. He stopped again. "I beg your pardon?"

"That offends you?" Lincoln asked, sounding genuinely surprised.

"Yes! He was devoted to the queen."

Lincoln glanced at me. I suspected he was asking me to confirm if that was the impression I got from meeting the prince consort's ghost. "He did seem pleased to see her," I said.

"I assure you he did not stray from the marital bed," the prince hissed. "He was a good man."

Lincoln walked off. "Good men sometimes stray. Even good men of royal blood."

"And some do not."

"True," Lincoln conceded. "Some have willpower and moral fiber."

The prince slapped one hand inside the other behind his back and forged ahead. I had to quicken my step to keep up with them both. "Even men with willpower and moral fiber find themselves in need of comforts out of the marital bed," the prince said. "Although my father was not one of them."

The contest of wills had returned so fiercely that they'd

forgotten I was still there. Not that Lincoln would think such a conversation too indelicate for me. He knew I'd heard and seen things that would scandalize even His Royal Highness. I cleared my throat.

"My humblest apologies, Miss Holloway," the prince said, his face reddening. "I don't know what came over me to say such things in your presence."

"It's quite all right, sir," I said. "You are not entirely to blame."

I felt rather than saw Lincoln stiffen. "Do you know where the imposter went after he left here?" he asked.

"The East End. I had one of the footmen follow him, but he lost him in Whitechapel. My man didn't dare go further."

Considering his royal livery would have attracted undesirable attention, his reluctance was understandable. One of the footmen now opened the door leading to the courtyard. Gus and Seth straightened and urged the horses forward to collect us.

"What will you do now?" the prince asked Lincoln.

"I haven't yet decided." He nodded. "Good day, sir."

"Be sure to keep me informed at every step. Understand?"

"Perfectly."

I bobbed a curtsy. "Good day, your highness. It was a pleasure to be invited to your home and meet your mo— queen."

He took my hand and assisted me up into the carriage. "Good day, Miss Holloway. It was delightful to have your company. I hope to see you again shortly." He kissed the back of my hand and smiled as he stepped away.

Lincoln climbed in beside me and the footman closed the door and folded up the step. The coach rolled off and out of the courtyard.

"You goaded him," I said.

Lincoln arched a brow. "That's the first thing you have to say?"

"If these were medieval times, he'd have you executed."

"I doubt it. Not his own son. Thrown in the Tower to teach me a lesson, perhaps."

He said it so calmly and casually that it was easy to think that talking about the prince being his father didn't affect him. But I suspected it did. His smile did not reach his eyes. They were broody and grim.

I switched places to sit next to him, and curled into his side. He shifted his arm and placed it around my shoulders, holding me firmly. I kissed his cheek.

"I understand why you spoke to him that way," I said. "I do. But..." I sighed. "Give him a chance, Lincoln."

"To be a father to me? The time for that has long past, even if he wanted it, which I suspect he does not. I don't want or need a father." He kissed the top of my head. "You're everything I need now."

I tilted my face to peer at him. He squeezed my shoulders and set me aside. That was it, just a friendly squeeze.

I sat up straight and swallowed my sigh of disappointment. "What do you think about the imposter?"

"I think we have a problem."

"You mean the royal family have a problem—and the police. It seems to have nothing to do with us after all. Pity. I wouldn't mind returning to the palace again, or perhaps taking a turn around the garden. They're unlikely to invite us back now, unless the prince decides he'd like to get to know you better."

"He won't. Gone are the days when the illegitimate offspring of royalty enjoyed favor at court. I would be an embarrassment."

I covered his hand with mine. "You wouldn't have made a

very good nobleman anyway. You hate dinner parties and small talk."

"And fine clothes. I'd have to wear a tie all the time." He drew my hand to his lips and kissed the back. "By the way, I think you're wrong."

"About what?"

"About the matter now being one for the police and not the ministry. I think there may be something supernatural at play. The Prince of Wales mentioned how similar the man was to his father in every way. The queen's lady must have thought so too or she wouldn't have sent for him."

I shrugged. "An illegitimate son playing a cruel trick. The prince may think his father a good man, but that doesn't mean he was."

"It's a possibility, but I want to explore more."

"Explore what? How could someone make themselves look like a dead man yet not be a blood relative?"

"A body changer."

I waited for him to go on, but he did not. "Like Lady Gillingham and my two friends from the School for Wayward Girls?" I asked. "But they look like beasts in their other form, not princes."

"Something similar to them but not the same."

"Then what?"

He looked out the window. The high hedges and ornate gates of the manors on the edge of Hampstead Heath passed us by at a swift pace. "We're nearly home. I'll explain everything to you and the others there."

I clicked my tongue and withdrew my hand from his. "You're a frustrating man."

He stroked the underside of my jaw with his thumb. "There's no time for more talking."

"Why not?"

"Because I need to do this."

He pulled me closer and kissed me. It was our first proper kiss in over a week and its intensity slammed into me, sending my blood racing. I'd wanted this, ached for it, and it seemed that he'd wanted it too. He held me firmly, not allowing me to move an inch. I didn't want to. Why would I when the kiss made my body sing?

Why had he not kissed me like this in all these long days? Because he was afraid of being seen? Or afraid of not being able to stop?

It could be why he left the kiss until now, only a few minutes from Lichfield. I would think about it more when I had the chance. For now, I wanted to wallow in his kiss, his warm arms, his unconditional love, and simply enjoy what time we had left alone.

The carriage stopped far sooner than I expected. Had we passed through the Lichfield gates already?

Lincoln set me aside, putting distance between us, and drew in a ragged breath. Without so much as a glance my way, he opened the door, startling Seth. Seth eyed the fogged windows and broke into a grin.

Lincoln pushed past him. "Something you want to say?" he growled.

Seth's smile withered. "No!" He bent to lower the step for me.

Lincoln assisted me from the carriage. Behind him, Seth broke into a grin again and winked at me.

My face flushed.

"Meet us in the library as soon as you and Gus are ready," Lincoln told him. He offered me his arm and we walked in together.

Several minutes later, Seth and Gus joined Lincoln, myself, and Alice in the library. He'd decided to include her but had not explained why. Perhaps he simply thought she ought to know certain things now that she lived with us. Yet he had not asked Lady Vickers to join in.

Cook brought in tea and fruit cake and sat down. "How be the old girl, Charlie?"

"Her Majesty seemed sad," I said, pouring the tea. "I'm not sure if summoning her husband's spirit in her presence was a good idea."

"Does she look like her likeness?" Gus asked. At my frown, he pulled a penny out of his waistcoat pocket.

"A little older." I handed a cup and biscuit to Alice. "And thicker around the jaw."

"I cannot fathom meeting the queen," Alice said. "You're so fortunate. It'll be an experience you'll remember forever, and a good story to tell your children."

"It was an odd experience, overwhelming at first. Once her husband's spirit appeared, she became more...normal. I felt sorry for her."

"And the future king?"

"He's just a regular man, really, except he never called the queen Mother or Mama. I wonder if he does in private."

Lincoln and I recounted the events of the meeting. When we got to the part about the medium, Mrs. Beaufort, Seth said, "I know of Beaufort, but we've never met. They keep to themselves and their own circle. Is she listed in the archives?"

Lincoln nodded. "I see no reason to speak to her at this point in time."

"The most interesting part of our meeting occurred after we left the queen," I said. I told them about the imposter and Lincoln's theory of body changers.

"They exist?" Alice asked, her eyes huge.

"I heard rumors of one some time ago," Lincoln said. "I never found him, however, and have no proof."

"Surely it's impossible."

"Mere months ago, I thought raising the dead was impossible," I said. "And dreams coming to life."

"Aye," Gus muttered into his teacup.

Seth went to sip his tea but changed his mind and lowered the cup. "Imagine what a body shifter can do? If they can pretend to be anyone... My god. It would be chaos. Utter chaos."

"We don't know how easy it is for one to change at will into the likeness of another," Lincoln said. "Such a person must be rare or we'd have one listed in our archives."

"You said yourself that you've heard rumors," Seth said.

"Rumors are not proof."

"This imposter could be a relative of Old Prince Albert," Gus said. "Or a son born on the wrong side of the blanket."

"We considered that," I told them. "The Prince of Wales insists his father wasn't that sort of man."

Seth snorted and opened his mouth to comment, but caught sight of Alice watching him. He pressed his lips together and studied his biscuit with keen interest.

"Let's resolve this issue once and for all," I said. "I'll summon the Prince Consort again. I think everyone except Lincoln should leave the room. He may not be inclined to speak if strangers are present."

Alice rose and picked up her cup and saucer. "Of course. Come along, everyone."

Seth and Cook followed her out, but Gus hung back. "I want to meet him," he said. Upon Lincoln's glare, Gus snatched up a biscuit. "I'm going."

Once he shut the door, I looked to Lincoln. "Do you recall if it's Francis Albert Augustus Charles Emmanuel or Francis Albert Augustus Emmanuel Charles?"

"The former."

"I do hope he's not angry at us for calling him twice in one day. Or for asking such a personal question."

"It's irrelevant if he is. You're in command, Charlie, not him."

Easy for him to say. He didn't think royalty deserved special treatment. "Francis Albert Augustus Charles Emmanuel of Saxe-Coburg-Gotha, I summon your spirit here."

The mist burst through the ceiling rose like a cloud of steam from an engine and swooped toward me.

I ducked. "Bloody hell!"

"That is no way for a lady to speak," the ghost of the Prince Consort said as the mist formed his shape by the fireplace.

My spine stiffened. "And that is no way for a gentleman to enter a room, even though he may be a ghost."

His nostrils flared. "You dare to admonish me?"

"I dare. You may be a prince but I control your spirit here. Do you understand?"

He sniffed and turned his back to me. He stretched ghostly white fingers toward the burning coal in the grate even though he could feel no cold. Lincoln gave me a nod of approval.

"Why have you summoned me here?" the prince asked. "And where is here, precisely? I do not recognize this room."

"Lichfield Towers in Highgate," I said. "It belongs to Mr. Fitzroy."

The prince glanced at Lincoln, sniffed, and turned back to the fire. "Answer my first question."

I sucked air between my teeth and prepared for an irate response. "A man approached the palace claiming to be you, sir."

He clamped his hands together behind his back. "I hope they sent the crackpot away."

"He looked remarkably like you, as it happens. So like

you, in fact, that the Prince of Wales was summoned to speak to him."

"Bertie would have told the madman to take his leave."

"He did, however the incident has stayed with him because the man bore such a remarkable resemblance to you. Your son assumed it was a coincidence."

"It is."

I fanned my fingers in my lap, stretching the muscles in frustration. "Or could there be another explanation?"

The prince strode up to me. He would have been imposing in his youth, with his erect posture and the disdainful curl of his lip, but a mere mist didn't make me quake. "What are you implying?"

I glanced at Lincoln. He nodded at me to go on. "Could that man be your son by a mistress?" I asked.

The ghost shimmered and broke apart. The mist circled me, swirling and swirling until it became a blur of white. I got quite dizzy trying to follow it.

"Enough!" I shouted. "Be still and answer me."

The corner of Lincoln's mouth lifted as the ghost stilled.

"You command me." The prince's voice softened in wonder.

"I do," I said huffily. "My question is indelicate and I didn't want to ask it, but I had to. Your family may be in danger from this man. We must find him. If you can tell us anything about him, it would help our search."

"I can't tell you anything. I don't know of anyone resembling me closely enough to pass as me, nor have I ever had a mistress. There. Satisfied?"

"Thank you. That will be all. You may return to your afterlife."

The mist rose in the air. "I hope I will not be disturbed again."

"I hope that too. Very much so."

His brows shot up but then his face dissolved away and finally he disappeared altogether.

"He's gone," I said.

Lincoln rose and opened the door to let the others back in.

"We heard you shouting, Charlie," Seth said, frowning in concern. "Is everything all right?"

"He's a pompous, overbearing man." I drank the rest of my tea then refilled the cup from the pot and drank half of that.

"Need something stronger?" Cook asked.

"No, thank you. The prince insists that he's never had a mistress." I locked gazes with Lincoln. "It seems your theory is correct. So now what do we do?"

"We investigate the possibility of a person changing into the likeness of another human, as opposed to the likeness of a beast," he said. "And we see if we can trace the imposter."

Everyone began speaking at once, a dozen questions tossed out, until Lincoln lifted a finger for silence.

"Lady Gillingham may have some knowledge about shifting shape," he said.

I quickly explained to Alice that Lady Gillingham was like our two friends from school who could change form. She was not shocked or disgusted. Like me, very little perturbed her.

"Invite her to tea and see what you can learn about her," Lincoln said to me. "I will ask questions in Whitechapel where the palace footman lost the imposter. Seth and Gus will come with me."

"You think you'll get answers from East Enders?" I scoffed. "They don't like strangers asking questions."

He simply looked at me with those fathomless black eyes of his.

"Oh. Right. You've done this before."

He stood. "It's growing late. We'll go tomorrow."

* * *

LADY VICKERS HAD Doyle running ragged before Lady Gillingham's visit. Between dusting and polishing the furniture, he didn't get time to help Cook prepare. Cook had to make do with the rather inept Bella.

"She be worse than Seth," he muttered when Bella disappeared into the scullery with an armload of dirty pots. "She don't know sugar from flour."

"I'll help," Alice said, unbuttoning her sleeve. "Where shall I start?"

Cook stopped beating the dough to death and gawped at her. "Er, it be all right, Miss Everheart. Bella and me can manage."

"I like cooking and used to help out all the time back home. Please do call me Alice and not Miss Everheart."

"I...I can't," he choked out, his cheeks aflame.

"You call Charlie by her first name."

"Aye, but she weren't all proper at the start. She be like me."

"I'm not sure I'm proper now." I patted Cook's shoulder. "Let Alice help. You wouldn't want to serve Lady Gillingham something ordinary, would you?"

He pounded his fist into the dough. "I ain't never served nothing ordinary ever, Charlie."

I winked at Alice and left them to it. Doyle raced past me, his face flushed and his breathing heavy. "It won't be for long," I called after him.

He stopped to acknowledge me then hurried on his way. Poor man. But I meant it. Lady Vickers had a candidate for housekeeper lined up. It only remained for me to approve of her. Although I'd told Lady V I didn't know what qualities a housekeeper ought to possess, she insisted I have the final say since I was the mistress of Lichfield Towers. My insistence that I hadn't accepted Lincoln's proposal—his second one—fell on deaf ears.

Lady Vickers left the house mid morning to go shopping on Oxford Street, taking Alice with her. We hadn't told her why she had to leave, but merely said it was ministry business and that Lady Gillingham was less likely to talk in the presence of her peer. That appeased Lady V and she readily agreed that I wasn't a threat.

With Seth and Gus out with Lincoln, and Doyle busy, they had to catch the omnibus, much to Lady Vickers' horror. I thought she might suffer an attack of the vapors and decide to remain in her room, but she forged ahead when Alice claimed to be looking forward to spending more time alone with her.

"We really ought to get to know one another better," Alice said.

Lady Vickers narrowed her gaze. "Why?"

"No particular reason, but Seth speaks so highly of you."

Lady Vickers looked lost for words, a rare event. Whether she was surprised that Seth would speak highly of her, or worried that Alice and Seth had private conversations, I couldn't tell. I decided it was probably the latter, however, when she said, "We ought to have a new outfit made for you for the spring. Something to show off your slender figure to the young men. And then we'll promenade together in the park, just the two of us. Come along. We don't want to miss the omnibus."

Alice shot me a sly smile. She knew exactly how to manipulate Seth's mother and she'd only known her a little over a week. She would make a marvelous daughter-in-law, if only Lady Vickers would allow it. Or if Alice wanted it too, of course. It was difficult to gauge if she had feelings for Seth.

Lady Gillingham arrived shortly after their departure and

greeted me politely if somewhat suspiciously when I informed her that Lady Vickers wasn't at home.

"The masked ball was a lot of fun," I began as I handed her a teacup.

"Yes." She sipped, her soft blue gaze darting around the room over the brim of the cup.

"I do apologize for not speaking to you on the night. It seems strange that we haven't formally met when I know your husband. He comes here for business matters from time to time," I clarified when she didn't answer.

"I know about the ministry."

I cleared my throat. "And I know about you."

She dropped her cup but caught it before much tea spilled. A few drops landed on the carpet but it could have been much worse. Lady Gillingham's reflexes were faster than mine.

Her hands shook, rattling the cup in the saucer. I took the set from her and placed it on the table. "Forgive me," I said, "that must have come as quite a surprise."

"Mr. Fitzroy assured me he wouldn't tell," she whined.

"I didn't leave him much choice." It was a bald lie, but I couldn't have her thinking that Lincoln informed me or the others lightly. He'd told us because it had been necessary, and he knew we could be trusted. Lady Gillingham wouldn't see it that way, however. "I saw the file he'd created for you when I searched the archives for something else. When I pressed him about it, he informed me of the conversation he'd had with you in your bedchamber."

"It wasn't like that," she said quickly.

She thought I suspected her and Lincoln of *that*? "I know."

"Really? You trust him?"

"Of course." I was about to ask her why I wouldn't but decided against it. I didn't want to hear a list of Lincoln's past mistresses.

"You're not yet married, I suppose," she said heavily. "And you're not a...a creature like me." She was thinking of her own husband's transgressions, then, not Lincoln.

"You are not a creature."

"You haven't seen my other form."

She was a pretty woman with fair hair and smooth skin. She wasn't as young as me, but she must be considerably younger than her middle-aged husband. He ought consider himself fortunate to be married to such a lovely woman, but instead he treated her cruelly, according to Lincoln. Lord Gillingham was the monster, not his wife.

"Lincoln didn't tell you about me, did he?" I asked.

"No." She gave me an odd look. "Why?"

"I'm not normal either. I can communicate with ghosts."

She made a small scoffing sound. "Mediums are not all that unusual."

"I can also raise the dead by ordering spirits to occupy corpses."

She stared at me, her mouth forming a perfect O.

"Even decomposed ones that have been in the ground for some time," I added, picking up my cup. "Gruesome, isn't it?"

"Yes. Er, no. Not gruesome, merely...unique."

I laughed. "I can see from your face what you truly think. It's all right. I've made my peace with it. It is gruesome, but it's what I am, and I can't not be a necromancer."

She picked up her cup. "At least you can control it. I can't always."

"Like when you're asleep?"

She nodded. "He saw me, you know, while I slept. And now he...he's not as attentive."

Lincoln had told me how Lady Gillingham's beastly form disgusted and frightened her husband and that he refused to lie with her once he found out. For someone who dearly wanted children, the lack of intimacy devastated her.

"I appreciate you telling me about yourself, Miss Holloway," she said. "What is it you are called?"

"A necromancer. And please, you must call me Charlie."

She smiled. "And you must call me Harriet. My mother-in-law is also Lady Gillingham. I hate it." She giggled, reminding me of just how young she was.

"Tell me how you and Lord Gillingham met."

"I can't really recall. I was just a child. He asked my father for my hand then and there."

"How old were you?"

"Twelve. Father said he would have to wait, of course. And wait he did."

"You had no choice in the matter?"

"None. But I didn't mind. I knew it was a good match. He's an earl."

He was also a snake. This pretty woman could have had any man, and yet she'd allowed her father to marry her off to a horrid beast like Gillingham. The nobility would never make sense to me. What was more, she seemed proud of him, or at least of his position.

"You've probably already gathered that I asked you here for a specific reason," I said.

"Something to do with my shape-changing?" she whispered, glancing at the closed door.

I nodded. "A situation has arisen where a fellow impersonated another. He looked exactly like the other man, but it wasn't him. Nor is it a relative. Lincoln doesn't believe in coincidence. He thought that the imposter may have shifted shape, similar to what you can do, but so much more."

"Into another man's likeness, you mean?"

"Yes."

"That's remarkable—and so sinister. The implications are unfathomable. Such a person could change into anyone. The prime minister or even the queen! The country would be unsafe."

It begged the question, why hadn't the fellow changed into the prime minster's shape? He had more power than the dead prince consort. It didn't make sense. "As it happens, this does affect the royal family."

"My goodness." She pressed a hand to her chest. "How awful."

"Do you know anything that could help us?"

She shrugged one shoulder. "Such as?"

"Have you ever shifted into anything other than your...beast form?"

"No. I wish I could. It sounds like more fun to pretend to be another human. A man, for example. Wouldn't you want to walk in a man's shoes just for a day to see how differently they're treated?" Her eyes shone with the possibilities. I suspected this woman had a somewhat wicked streak.

I certainly understood her enthusiasm, since I had walked in the shoes of a boy. Those five years as a thirteen year old in the slums had opened my eyes to the many ways in which males and females were treated differently. Some were significant, like the freedom with which I could walk into a tavern and not have my backside groped, and others were subtle, like the friendly jokes the other gang members shared with Charlie the lad. I told Lady Gillingham none of this, however. If her husband had informed her of my background, she showed no indication. I suspected they shared very little with each other, not just the marital bed.

"Do you know anyone else like yourself?" I asked.

"No one. I'm quite alone." She peered down at her teacup but not before I saw her eyes fill with tears.

I touched her arm. "You are not alone. I'm here if you need to talk to someone. I understand about being different and feeling as if no one can possibly understand."

"Thank you, Charlie." She attempted a smile. "You're very sweet. I wish I could help you."

"Are you sure you can't? Has anything unusual happened lately? Anything that could be linked to shifting shape? Or anything odd at all, even if you think it may mean nothing?"

She nibbled on her lower lip and tapped her finger against the teacup. She did not hold the cup by its handle but held the cup itself. The china looked delicate in her big hands. "There may be one thing, but it's not something I've seen, but rather a suggestion on how to find the information you need."

"Go on."

She drew in a breath, but Doyle's shout interrupted her. "My lord! Sir, you can't go in there!"

The door opened and Lord Gillingham burst through. His lips peeled back from his teeth and he thrust his walking stick in the direction of his wife. "Get up, Harriet. You're leaving."

"Gilly!" The cup trembled, rattling in the saucer. "I—I was just having tea with Charlie."

"You shouldn't come here," he snarled. "You should never come here. Understand?"

She gave a nervous little laugh and apologized to me. "I don't know what's come over my husband. He's not usually like this."

He seemed to always be a domineering turd with *me*. "Excuse me," I said, rising. "Your wife and I were in the middle of a private discussion. Would you care to wait outside—"

"Don't address me, *witch*." He stalked across the room and for a moment I thought he'd bring the stick down on me as he'd done the first time we met.

But he did not. He grabbed his wife's arm and pulled her

to her feet. She dropped the teacup, spilling the contents on the floor.

She gasped and her face reddened. "Oh, Charlie, I'm so sorry."

"It's all right," I said, as her husband dragged her away. "We haven't finished our discussion," I snapped at Gillingham.

He ignored me and forged ahead, his wife in tow, trying to remove her arm from his grip. "Gilly, you're hurting me."

"Good. You seem to need the pain to remember who your husband is."

"That's silly."

"Is it?" He rounded on her. His face had gone white, his lips bloodless. He shook her and she recoiled, putting up her other arm to protect herself. "Is it? Because I told you never to come here."

"But Charlie is nice."

"Do not talk back to me! Have you no shame?" He lifted his hand to strike her.

I ran toward them, but I knew I would not make it on time. Doyle, too, reacted, but he was also too far away.

But Gillingham did not hit his wife. She caught his arm and lifted him up so that his feet dangled above the floor. His eyes widened. His jaw went slack. Then his wife shoved him backward so hard that he slammed into the doorframe. The entire room shook with the impact.

He crumpled in a heap on the ground, unconscious.

CHAPTER 5

*H*arriet slumped to the floor at her husband's side. "Gilly! Gilly!"

"Doyle, send for the doctor," I said. The butler rushed out just as Lord Gillingham moaned.

"Gilly? Can you hear me?"

He opened his eyes a mere slit then they widened, almost bulging. "Get away from me!" He tried to scramble backward but the wall was in his way. "Stay back!"

"Gilly? It's just me. Harriet, your wife."

"You are *not* my wife. You're the devil! A witch!"

"She can't be both," I snapped, more out of relief that he wasn't dead than a need to defend her. "In fact, she's neither."

He blinked stupidly at me. Perhaps the bump on the head had affected him after all. "Harriet, get in the coach." He stamped his walking stick into the floor and struggled to his feet. His wife went to his aid but he hissed at her and she stayed back, nibbling her fingernails.

"The butler has sent for the doctor," I said.

"I'll fetch my own bloody doctor. I'll have none of your witchcraft forced on me."

"If I were a witch, I'd have turned you into a worm when I first met you and fed you to the birds."

Harriet covered her gasp with both hands and gave her husband a nervous glance. He tugged on his cuffs and stretched his neck out of his collar. "Go, Harriet!"

"You seem to be back to your usual self," I said. "More's the pity."

The small lines around Gillingham's lips deepened. If I'd been Charlie the street urchin, he would have thrashed me with his stick again. But he feared Lincoln's wrath more than he valued his pride so I would be safe. Besides, thanks to my training, I knew I could avoid his strikes now.

I helped Harriet into her cloak and whispered in her ear. "You were about to tell me something. What was it?"

She gave her head a half shake. "I can't."

"What are you two conspiring about?" Gillingham bellowed.

"Nothing!" she said, her voice high.

"Your wife was helping me with ministry business," I said. It was time he knew that she had a value beyond that of pretty ornament.

He spluttered words, but they hardly made any sense. Harriet appealed to me. "Don't, Charlie. He doesn't like discussion about my other form."

"Then it's time he got used to it. Your wife has a unique perspective," I told him. "One that may offer clues about a ministry matter that arose out of Leisl's confrontation with the Prince of Wales at the masked ball."

He went still. "You've been investigating the seer's claims?"

"Of course. It would be remiss of us not to. It led us to a meeting at the palace—"

"The palace! Why have I not been informed?"

"I'm informing you now."

"Not soon enough. The committee must be kept informed as these things arise."

"I'll pass your suggestion on to Lincoln. He is the head of the ministry, after all."

He resumed his spluttering.

"The meeting took a turn toward the supernatural and shape shifting, to be more specific," I went on. "We thought your wife might be able to advise us on the matter, considering…"

"She cannot. She knows nothing."

"I'd rather hear that from her lips, not yours."

"I am her husband! She'll do as I say."

"Yet she is the stronger. Perhaps it's *you* who ought to obey *her*."

A flicker of fear appeared in his eyes before it vanished. His cheeks pinked, however, and he turned away. It must be odd for a man so used to being in command in his own household to suddenly realize he was weaker than his wife. He still held all the legal and financial power, but she had a bargaining chip in their marriage now that she never had before. I wanted him to know it. I wanted her to know it, too.

She simply stared at me, her gentle eyes round. She'd probably never heard anyone speak to her husband the way I spoke to him, let alone a woman.

"Who else knows about her?" Gillingham asked.

"Lincoln, myself, Gus and Seth."

"Seth too?" Harriet groaned.

"Lord Marchbank and Lady Harcourt don't know," I assured her. I thought it best not to mention Alice. "None of us will tattle. Your secret is safe, but we had to tell Seth and Gus now that there's a threat to the crown."

"What is the threat, precisely?" Gillingham demanded.

"It's too early to say. We must investigate more before—"

"Bah! You know nothing. I'll ask Fitzroy."

"Very well."

"A meeting will be called this afternoon, three o'clock. Be prepared."

"I can't be certain if Lincoln will be here."

"Be sure that he is." He turned and walked off. "Harriet! Come!"

She gave me an apologetic shrug and hurried after him.

"But what were you going to tell me?" I called after her.

She dismissed my question with a wave of her hand and raced down the front steps to the waiting carriage.

I sighed and shut the door behind them. I considered myself a non-violent person, but if ever a man deserved to be thrashed, it was Gillingham.

I spent the next little while interviewing the housekeeper that Lady Vickers had chosen before helping Cook in the newly refurbished kitchen until the others returned in time for a late luncheon.

I didn't need to ask how their morning went. The frustration was written clearly across Seth and Gus's faces. Lincoln's was as impassive as ever.

"We were thwarted at every turn." Seth lowered himself into the armchair in the corner of the kitchen and stretched out his long legs. "No one would answer our questions, not even when we paid them."

"That in itself is telling," I said. "Perhaps they're keeping mum because they're afraid of this fellow."

"Or they know nothing," Lincoln said, peering into the pot on the stove.

"Who did you speak to?"

"Anyone we came across," said Gus, pulling bowls out of the cupboard. "Flower sellers, vagabonds, old women who were too slow to run away from us." He set the bowls on the table. "They're a suspicious lot."

"They probably thought you were the police."

"Dressed like this?" Seth plucked at his thick brown woolen trousers. He'd discarded his coat, jacket and cap in the cloakroom upon his return. The three of them had gone out in clothes befitting laborers, not gentlemen, to blend in. It would seem it wasn't enough.

"It is strange that you didn't get a single piece of useful information," I said to Lincoln. "Interrogation has always been one of your strengths."

"Fitzroy should have questioned them more thoroughly," Seth told me. "He's gone sof—" He cut himself off as Lincoln's gaze turned hard.

Lincoln dipped a wooden spoon into the pot and tasted the soup. Cook would admonish either Seth or Gus if they did that, but he didn't even wince this time. "I find my methods of interrogation somewhat restricted these days," Lincoln said.

Because he *had* softened somewhat, most likely because of my influence.

"We'll try again tomorrow," he said.

"In a different area?" I asked. "Using a different approach?"

"Perhaps."

"Why don't I come with you? That way—"

"No!" Seth chopped his hand through the air. "Absolutely not. Whitechapel is not for ladies."

I pressed my fist to my hip. "Have you forgotten that I used to live there?"

"Have you forgotten that you're no longer a scrawny lad but a..." He made the shape of a curvy woman with his hands. "A pretty lady of breeding and education?" He pushed to his feet and snatched up a bowl. "No gentleman in his right mind would allow a lady he cared about to wander through the slums of the East End. Right, Fitzroy?" Seth thrust his bowl at Cook and arched his brows at Lincoln.

Lincoln plucked a bowl off the table too. "If you're not busy tomorrow, Charlie, I'd appreciate your help."

Seth shook his head and muttered something at the ceiling that sounded French.

"She'll be fine," Gus told him, lining up for his soup. "We'll be there to make sure nothing happens to her."

"*I'll* be there," Lincoln said.

"What are we supposed to do while you two go gallivanting through Whitehall after a body changer who may or may not exist?" Seth asked.

"You could take your mother and Alice out," I quipped. "I'm sure they'd both love spending time with you. Do try not to make cow eyes at Alice, though. You know how it riles Lady V."

He screwed up his nose. "Stop being so smug, Charlie. You only won because he can't say no to you, not because it's a good idea."

Cook snorted as he ladled soup into my bowl. "Seth be asking for it now," he whispered.

"The stables need cleaning," Lincoln told Seth. "There's a task for you tomorrow. Gus can take the day off."

Gus beamed. "Thank you, sir."

Seth opened his mouth to protest but must have thought better of it. He simply shot me a glare then tucked into his soup.

"Speaking of tomorrow," I said as I sat beside Lincoln. "Our new housekeeper will begin in the morning. Her name is Mrs. Cotchin, and she has excellent references from a household that Lady V is familiar with. She was a senior maid there and with the housekeeper far from retirement age, she decided she had to leave their employ if she wanted to improve her situation. I think she'll fit in here nicely. Doyle has met her, haven't you, Doyle?"

The butler had entered quietly and helped himself to

soup. He was used to dining with us on the odd occasion, and he no longer held himself in check if Lincoln or I entered the service area.

"I have," he intoned. "She's an experienced woman of good character."

"He means she's nice," I added.

"But will she fit in?" Seth asked. "This household is not an easy one to adjust to. And what do we tell her about the strange comings and goings?"

"We don't tell her anything," Lincoln said. "That side of things must remain a secret for now. Understood?"

We all nodded.

Cook pouted. "I ain't going to see you much no more, am I?"

"You'll see me," Gus said.

"Not me," Seth said. "Downstairs will become strictly for servants only."

"You're a tosspot," Gus told him. "And you ain't no better than me, Cook or Doyle. The last year should've proved that to you."

"Things are different now with my mother and Alice here. The invitations to social engagements are coming in thick and fast. It's time to resume my proper place in society."

"You wish to leave my employ?" Lincoln asked.

"What? No! I need to work. I just meant that I have to fit my work around my newfound popularity."

"I thought you hated the sycophants and gossips," I said.

"I do, on the whole."

"Are you trying to appease your mother?"

"God, no. I'm simply assisting her now that she has Alice to think about. And you, too, of course, Charlie. My mother wishes to take you both out to show you off to her friends. It's only right that I come along to keep an eye on things."

Gus snorted. "You mean make sure no gen'lemen catch Alice's eye."

"Don't be ridiculous." Seth beamed and pushed out his chest. "No other gentleman could possibly interest her when she gets to see me every day. She might go out, but she always comes home to me."

"Toss pot," both Gus and Cook said.

I didn't share their sentiments on this score. Despite his cockiness, a hint of vulnerability edged Seth's tone. He truly liked Alice and wanted to make a good impression. This man, who won hearts wherever he went, was finding it difficult to win the heart of a woman he actually admired.

"What happened with Lady Gillingham?" Lincoln asked me.

I exchanged a glance with Doyle, the only witness to events in the drawing room. "She was about to tell me something that may have been important to our investigation, but we were interrupted by her husband."

The black centers of Lincoln's eyes constricted to pinpoints. His spoon stilled in the bowl. "And?"

"And she threw him across the room."

Gus and Seth set down their spoons. "Bloody hell," Gus said. "Is he dead?"

"No." Cook sat back in the chair and rubbed his stomach. "Next time, we hope."

"He came here to order her to return home with him," I said. "He didn't like her speaking to me. He manhandled her and she lashed out. She's remarkably strong."

"Her senses are acute, too," Lincoln said. "Like an animal's."

"She picked him up and threw him at the wall as if he weighed nothing more than a cat. She shocked herself, I think. He came to and was still furious with her. He wanted to know why she was here so I told him about our meeting at the palace and how we needed her help. I didn't give him any details, though. He still didn't allow her to talk to me, however. She left without telling me what she wanted to say." I looked to Lincoln. "Should I not have told him anything?"

"I would have informed him and the others anyway," he said. "I'll set up a committee meeting."

I glanced at the clock on the mantel. "Gillingham already has. They'll convene here in thirty minutes."

"Cake and finger buns will be served," Cook said, rising. "I'll clean up now and start preparing the tea."

"You want us there?" Gus asked.

Lincoln nodded. "You'll attend all committee meetings from now on. It'll save me repeating everything later."

"They won't like it."

Lincoln lifted one shoulder and stood.

"Does that trouble you?" I asked Gus.

He grinned, revealing two rows of broken and missing teeth. "No. Just making sure it don't trouble no one else."

"Charlie," Lincoln said, holding out his hand. I placed my hand in his and we walked out of the kitchen together. "Gillingham will still be furious with you," he said.

"I know."

He rubbed his thumb along mine, the sensation gentle and soothing. "Do you want me to step in if he berates you?"

"Only if he seems to be getting the better of me. Perhaps just give him one of your deathly stares."

"Deathly stares?"

"The ones that make Gillingham and most others quake in their boots."

He pulled me into the dark recesses beneath the main staircase and held me against his body. My heart thumped so fiercely he must have been able to feel it. "You never quaked in your boots."

"I most certainly did. I just never let you see it."

He pressed his lips to my forehead and sighed. I put my arms around him and rested my cheek on his chest. His heartbeat was loud but steady.

"Did I ever look at you that way when I sent you to the school?" he asked.

"No. You hardly looked at me at all." I held him tighter, wanting him to know I didn't harbor any anger toward him for sending me from Lichfield. His deep regret had diminished my anger upon our reunion, and seeing him vulnerable, after the kitchen explosion, had dissolved it altogether. "I stopped being afraid shortly after meeting you when I realized you only killed in self-defense."

"Nowadays."

"But let's not tell Gillingham that." I pulled away and stroked his cheek. It was rough; he hadn't shaved before going into Whitechapel.

"I can always make an exception for him."

I laughed softly at his joke. At least, I thought it was a joke. "You'd better go and change for the meeting."

* * *

Lincoln's first meeting as a member of the committee began with him reminding them that he was General Eastbrooke's heir and therefore not only inherited his house and wealth but also his position on the committee.

"Yes, yes," Gillingham said with a stamp of his walking stick into the floor. "We all know."

"The general's death is a timely reminder to everyone to have a successor in place to take over their position here," Lincoln said. "Preferably one who knows of the ministry's existence, if not all of the details. Charlie is mine."

"And if she dies before you?" Lord Marchbank asked. If anyone else asked that I would consider it a horrid thing to say to a man about his intended, but not the very practical earl.

"Seth," Lincoln said.

Seth straightened. "Really? Er, thank you, I suppose."

"My son Edward is my heir," Marchbank said. "You all know that, and he's aware of the ministry. Gilly? Julia? Neither of you have children. Who do you appoint?"

"That's none of your affair," Gilly said with a sniff.

"It is. We may need to seek them out when you're dead and tell them about us."

"My wife inherits everything," he said, lowering his chin so that he mumbled into his chest. "She knows about the ministry."

"Andrew is my heir," Lady Harcourt said quietly. She wore deep black today, despite appearing in half-mourning colors in recent weeks. The lustrous sheen of the gown brought out the gloss in her hair and the whiteness of her skin. She was a woman aware of her beauty and knew how to enhance it with clothing and jewels, and black certainly suited her. Yet the sudden change surprised me. Was she mourning the general? Or the death of her reputation and popularity?

"Buchanan?" Gillingham waved off the cup of tea I held out to him. "Why not his brother?"

Andrew Buchanan was the younger son of Lady Harcourt's late husband. Donald Buchanan, the current Lord Harcourt, was the elder and lived with his wife on the family estate in Oxfordshire. Both knew about the ministry, but as the eldest, Donald should have inherited the committee position from his father. Old Lord Harcourt had elected his wife, however.

"Andrew is interested," she said, "Donald is not. Besides, Donald rarely comes to London."

"Then that's settled." Gillingham tilted his chin at the teapot. "Got anything stronger, Fitzroy?"

Seth poured him a brandy at the sideboard. We sat in the drawing room rather than the library. With both Seth and Gus joining us, the larger room suited better. Lady Vickers and Alice had not yet returned from their shopping expedition, and Doyle had been instructed not to disturb us, so privacy wasn't an issue.

Gillingham accepted the brandy glass. "Now," the earl said, "I called this meeting because it came to my attention that the events of the masked ball led to Charlotte and Fitzroy being summoned to the palace."

"The palace?" Marchbank's heavy brows crashed together. "Why weren't we informed?"

"Who did you see there?" Lady Harcourt asked, her features suddenly coming to life. "The Prince of Wales?"

Lincoln nodded. "I was about to call a meeting to inform you but Gillingham got in first."

"How did you learn about all this before us, Gilly?" Marchbank asked.

Gillingham swirled the brandy around his glass. "Mere happenstance."

"It arose out of Leisl's pronouncement that she sensed the Prince Consort's ghost would bring danger to his family," Lincoln said. "On the night of the ball I suggested to the Prince of Wales that we could help him in ghostly matters, so he took me up on the offer and summoned us." He told them how the meeting went and that we spoke to the ghost himself.

"In the presence of the queen?" Lady Harcourt asked. "How did that go?"

"Awkwardly," I said. "But we got answers. He's not haunting his family and has no wish to harm them. But that's not the most interesting part of the meeting."

Lincoln told them about the imposter and his theory that it could have been a shape shifter posing as the Prince

Consort rather than a lookalike. "I'm seeking the counsel of another shifter known to us through the archives," he said, avoiding mentioning Harriet by name.

"Another shifter?" Lady Harcourt asked. "You mean we already know of one? Perhaps he's the imposter?"

"She's not. She can only change into a beast form, not human."

"She?" Marchbank echoed at the same time that Lady Harcourt said, "So she says. Women do not always tell the truth, Lincoln."

"Nor do men," he countered.

She gave him a tight smile over her teacup.

"So what did your shifter have to say?" Marchbank asked. "Did she know of anyone who can do what you suggest?"

"No," I said. "But she may know something of importance. Unfortunately we were interrupted before she could impart anything of use to me."

"You can't rely on one silly female who most likely doesn't know anything." Gillingham said, waggling his empty glass at Gus. "You must extend your inquiries."

Gus dutifully stood and poured him another brandy. "We are."

Gillingham didn't even look his way.

"The palace footman followed the imposter as far as Whitechapel," Lincoln went on. "We're currently making inquiries there."

"How?"

"You don't need to know my methods." Lincoln's ice cold voice matched his eyes. "All you need to know is that they work."

Gillingham gulped his brandy down.

"The involvement of the palace is a bold move on the villain's part and extremely concerning." Marchbank stroked the white scar slicing through his beard. "It means he has no respect for authority, coupled with a brazen nature. A dangerous combination in my book."

"Or it could mean he already bore a remarkable resemblance to Prince Albert," I said.

Everyone turned to me. "Go on," Lincoln said.

"Did the imposter choose the Prince Consort because he already resembled him to a certain extent so the shift wouldn't be too difficult? Or does pretending to be the prince achieve something in particular? If the former, then his motives will be difficult to discover, but if the latter, then it will be easier because it's highly specific. He chose the dead prince for a reason."

Marchbank nodded. "Excellent point, Charlie."

"Not really," Gillingham drawled. "It brings us no closer to learning the imposter's identity."

"It's something to consider," Seth spat back.

"Who asked you? Fill up my glass, there's a good fellow."

Seth ignored him. Gillingham waggled his empty glass, and Gus got up to fill it again, but Lincoln put a hand out to stop him.

"The meeting is concluded," Lincoln said. "I've told you everything you need to know."

"Need?" Marchbank intoned. He nevertheless rose, as did Lady Harcourt. Lord Gillingham did not.

"I'll keep you informed of developments," Lincoln said.

"Will you really?" Gillingham sniffed. "Because it seems to me that you haven't questioned the most logical suspect. Your mother."

It felt as if the air got sucked out of the room as everyone focused on Lincoln. His face remained impassive. "Leisl is not a suspect."

"Why not? She knew about the imposter. Perhaps she knew because she has something to do with the villain."

Sometimes I wondered if Gillingham had a death wish.

To my surprise, however, Lincoln merely repeated, "She's not a suspect."

"Why would she warn the Prince of Wales if she were part of the scheme?" I asked. "Your theory is absurd."

"She may have had regrets." Gillingham shrugged. "She's a gypsy. They think differently to us. No offense intended, Fitzroy, but it's not like you care about the woman who gave you up, is it?"

If Lincoln didn't shut him up, perhaps I would. It was very tempting.

"If she were involved," Seth said, "which I doubt, why would she choose the royal family, and the Prince of Wales in particular? What would she gain?"

"Revenge for past wrongs," Gillingham said before I could stop him.

Seth and Gus both frowned. As the only ones who weren't aware of the relationship between the prince and Leisl, Gillingham's response made no sense to them.

"What wrongs?" Seth asked.

"It's not relevant to this investigation," I said quickly.

"Charlie's right," Lincoln said. "It's not relevant. But Gillingham wants to remind everyone that Leisl and the prince had a liaison some thirty years ago. It resulted in me."

Seth and Gus stared at him, utterly speechless. Then Seth burst out laughing. "Is that a joke?"

"I don't joke."

Seth's laughter died. "Right. Er, Charlie, did you know about this?"

I nodded.

"Blimey," Gus muttered. "Does that make you a prince? Do you outrank everyone here?"

Gillingham snorted. "Simpleton. Illegitimacy has no rank. He would have to be publicly acknowledged and a title bestowed upon him. That sort of thing doesn't happen, nowadays."

"Ain't no one here who can say their pa is a prince."

Gillingham had no response to that and Gus sat back with a smug look on his face.

"Are you quite sure we can rule out revenge?" Marchbank asked. "It's a simple yet effective tactic—scare him with a strange vision about his dead father, and embarrass him in a public place."

When Lincoln didn't answer, I said, "I may have only just met her, but she seemed sensible and not at all inclined for revenge. Besides, why now after thirty years?"

"Ask her. We expect you to, Fitzroy, regardless of your personal feelings on the matter."

"I have no personal feelings on the matter," Lincoln said. "If I decide to question her, it will be because I think it's relevant, not because you or anyone else does. Is that clear?"

Marchbank held up his hands in surrender. "If you say so."

"We should vote," Gillingham said.

"No." Lincoln pulled the bell pull to summon Doyle and opened the door. "Doyle will see you out."

They filed out and headed down the stairs. Lincoln remained by the door, not following. I slipped my hand into the crook of his arm.

"Lady Harcourt seemed glum today," I whispered.

He bent his head to mine and smirked. "You're building up to something. What is it?"

"Am I that easy to read? Never mind answering that. Yes, you're right, I am building up to something. I want you to ask her what the matter is."

"Why?"

"Because she looks sad, and she'll speak to you and not to me."

"That doesn't answer my question."

I gave him an arched look. "Because I'm curious. There. Does that satisfy?"

His smile was positively sly. "Seth would be a better choice than me."

"No, he would not." Because she loved Lincoln, not Seth. She respected Lincoln more, too, and had relied on him in the past for help. I suspected she'd open up to him. "Go on, ask her."

"You won't get jealous if she flirts with me?"

"Of course not. I'm not the jealous type."

"Pity." He strode off.

I smiled at his broad back as he retreated down the stairs. I wouldn't be jealous of Lady Harcourt if she flirted with him. I knew that to my bones. The only thing that would make me jealous would be if *he* flirted with *her*.

I waited in the drawing room with Gus and Seth, a sherry glass cradled in my hands. Seth handed a brandy to Lincoln when he re-entered a few minutes later. "Well?" I asked. "What did she say?"

"Not much," he said, standing by the fireplace. "I gather her unhappiness is a combination of living with Buchanan and the way her friends are now treating her since discovering she was a dancer."

"Living with Buchanan would be enough to drive anyone to despair," Seth said.

"Or drink," Gus added, saluting with his glass.

"At least she got an invitation to the ball," I said. "Not all of her friends are shunning her."

Seth shook his head. "Lady Hothfield told me she only invited Julia at the request of one of the prince's friends, a Sir Ignatius Swinburn."

"I fail to see how that is a problem."

"Swinburn is a fat, old cad with foul breath and disgusting manners. He treats women like whores, discarding them when he tires of them, and he quickly tires. Most ladies of quality steer well clear of him, but some widows are desperate enough to make themselves available, hoping it will put them in the prince's path. It never does. The prince already has his favorites and doesn't care for his friends' discarded mistresses."

"How'd you hear all that?" Gus asked.

"It's amazing what some women will tell you when they believe themselves in love with you." He glanced at me. "Don't tell Alice I said that."

Gus shook his head. "You toffs are a strange lot. Glad I weren't born into your class."

"My class is glad of it, too."

"So we can assume from what you say that Lady Harcourt is desperate enough to throw herself at Swinburn," I said. "That's why he specifically requested her presence."

"I think so."

"And perhaps he tired of her already."

Seth lifted one shoulder. "Or he didn't take any notice of her the night of the ball, despite asking for her to be present. The fellow is a turd. It's possible he wanted to see her there so he could toy with her; dangle a carrot in front of her face, so to speak, then take it away. I wouldn't put it past him."

"He sounds utterly despicable."

"He is."

"I feel sorry for Lady Harcourt."

"Don't," all three men said.

Lincoln finished his brandy and set the glass on the sideboard. "I have the general's paperwork to look over tonight. Send someone up with food and I'll eat as I work."

I almost followed him but hung back, warring with myself.

"Charlie?" Gus asked. "You still thinking 'bout Lady H?"

"No. About Leisl."

They both looked to the door through which Lincoln had just exited. "You going to talk to him about her?" Gus said.

"Yes. Someone should, but do either of you dare?"

"Blimey, no."

Seth nodded at my sherry. "Drink up. You're going to need it."

CHAPTER 6

*L*incoln opened his door before I knocked. He leaned against the door frame, his arms folded, a small smile on his lips. He looked devilishly handsome, with his hair unbound and his jacket and tie discarded, and I suspected he knew it.

"It's disconcerting that you know when I'm about to knock," I said, touching his tie and pretending to straighten it when I really just wanted to touch him.

"And knowing what you want to ask me?" he said.

"You do?" It was a good sign then that he was still smiling. Perhaps he'd decided he needed to talk to Leisl.

"It's either because you want to ask me to press Julia to be more specific, or you want to ravish me." His smile widened ever so slightly. "I know which one I prefer, but I suspect it's the other."

"Actually, you're wrong." I pressed my hands to his chest, enjoying the hardness of his body, the flex of muscle, and the slight uptick in his heart rate. "But they are both excellent suggestions, and a good indication of how your mind works."

His gaze wandered past me, down the hall. He drew my hands away. "Doyle or Bella may come past at any moment."

"Actually, I'm not here to ravish you or discuss Lady Harcourt," I said. "I want to talk about Leisl and why you won't visit her."

Surprise momentarily brightened his eyes before they darkened again. "You're wasting your time."

"Don't dismiss the idea immediately."

"I haven't." He stepped aside and allowed me to enter, then shut the door behind me. "I thought about it then dismissed it. Charlie, there's no point seeing her. She told us everything about her vision on the night of the ball. She said she has no more information for us, and I believe her."

"I don't want you to discuss her vision. I simply want you to talk to her, as a son to his mother."

He lowered his head. "Charlie, I have nothing to say to her, and I doubt she has anything to say to me. She would have approached me if she had."

"Perhaps she didn't know how to find you." I clasped his arms above the elbows and rubbed. The act soothed me but did nothing to smooth away the crease in his brow. "Perhaps she doesn't know how to begin."

"Nor do I."

"Lincoln, do you remember when I met my mother? Her ghost, I mean. It went better than I expected. It was wonderful to meet her, and know that she'd cared for me. The experience soothed an ache within me. Perhaps talking to your mother will help you in the same way."

"I don't need help, and I don't need a mother." The strain in his voice warned me that his temper was close to snapping.

I pressed on anyway. "Perhaps *she* needs *you*."

"Then she can come here and see me."

"I'll invite her for tea."

He tilted his head and lifted his brows.

"I'll take that to mean you'll get cross if I do," I said.

"I know the idea of us sitting down to tea together appeals to you." He stroked my hair off my forehead, his gaze following the sweep of his hand. "I know you miss your own mother, both your real one and adopted one, and I know you think this is an opportunity to gain a family member. But you have to leave the idea alone. I don't want Leisl to come here and be disappointed that I can't be a proper son to her. Do you understand?"

My throat felt tight and I could feel my eyes filling. "Why can't you be a proper son?"

"I'm not capable. It's not in me."

I cupped his face in my hands. "You didn't think yourself capable of loving anyone a few months ago, and now look at you."

"There's only enough for one." He kissed the end of my nose and cut off my protest. "Now go before I say something I'll regret later."

"This discussion is not over."

"Yes, Charlie, it is." He pulled away and opened the door. He glanced up and down the corridor before stepping aside and allowing me to exit. "Be ready early in the morning. Wear your old boy's clothing." He closed the door before I could protest.

I stood by the door, waiting for him to reopen it. He must know I was still there.

But he did not. After a moment, I went to my rooms to retrieve the trousers, shirt and jacket I'd worn in the slums. It was going to be an interesting day; one I wasn't looking forward to. I thought I'd seen the last of my old haunts and the gangs I had befriended. My life felt so far removed from those days now. Revisiting the slums would bring back memories that had only recently stopped haunting my dreams. Memories I'd wanted to put behind me forever.

* * *

LINCOLN and I didn't go to Whitechapel, but to the rookery of Clerkenwell. London harbored dozens of slum pockets where the middle and upper classes dared not enter. The slums scaled from bad to worse, with Clerkenwell being on the bad end and Whitechapel, where the Ripper murders occurred, at the worst. Daylight did nothing to improve the dark, damp lanes and yards. In fact, it only served to reveal the filth the darkness hid. The tenements groaned like old men in the stiff wind. Broken windows, peeling paint and grimy façades could be easily fixed, but the rotting timbers and dangerous leans signaled deeper problems that nothing less than demolition could improve.

We didn't speak as I led the way down lanes so narrow I could stretch out both arms to the sides and brush the slippery bricks with my fingertips. I stopped at a crumbling old house that looked as though a child had built it from blocks in the nursery. It felt abandoned, but the telltale signs of life were there for those who knew where to look—the shoe prints leading to and from the boards at knee height, the small marks on the wall where the boards scraped against it.

I hesitated, uncertain whether to knock. A knock might not be answered, so I simply slid the boards aside and crouched at the small opening.

A hand on my shoulder stopped me. I glanced back at Lincoln, at the same moment I heard a whistle inside and the sound of a door closing.

"I can't come in," Lincoln said quietly. He was too big, his shoulders too broad.

"You can be lookout."

Lincoln was never the lookout man. That job always fell to Gus or Seth. He must hate the suggestion, but he simply handed me the canvas sack he'd carried with him. "Be careful."

I nodded and crawled through, dragging the sack behind me. The gap was tighter than I remembered. A comfortable bed and regular meals had fattened me up. I may still be small and slender, but I wasn't a bag of bones anymore.

It took a moment for my eyes to adjust to the dim light filtering through the dirty window but my other senses told me the space was empty. The lookout stationed at the trapdoor had whistled a warning then dropped down to the cellar below. It was standard procedure when a stranger entered through the front door flap.

But I was no stranger. Crouching, I opened the trapdoor an inch. "It's all right," I called down. "It's me. Charlie. I've come back."

Whispers drifted up. I imagined the newcomers asking who Charlie was, the older members telling them about me. If any older members of my last gang remained, that is. It was possible they'd all moved on—or died. Winter was never kind to street children, even ones with a roof over their heads. I shivered and realized just how cold the house was. Not just cold but damp. The sort of damp that turned blood icy and numbed toes.

"I've brought blankets, clothes and food," I said through the gap. "There'll be money too if you agree to help me."

The whispers increased in volume and urgency, then suddenly ceased. I sat back on my haunches, away from the trapdoor. It opened, revealing a set of wary eyes that darted to me then around the space.

"I'm alone," I said. "Stringer, is that you?"

The trapdoor lifted higher. "Charlie? It really is you?"

I nodded and squinted at the face, familiar yet not. "Finley?"

He grinned, revealing a set of teeth, some of them missing, but most still white. "It *is* you!" The boy had changed in the months since I'd lived here. His face had angles where before it had sported the softness of childhood, and his hair was longer. So was mine.

"Is Stringer not here anymore?" I asked.

Another shake of his head. "You came back."

"I did. Are you the leader now?"

He shook his head. "Mink is. Oi!" he called down. "It's Charlie, all right." He opened the trapdoor wider, inviting me in.

I hesitated then followed him through the door and down the ladder. If I wanted them to trust me, I had to show that I trusted them.

The cellar was just as I remembered, with the lumpy mattress pushed into the corner and some blankets piled high at one end. They'd be lice ridden and dirty, but the darkness hid the worst of the grime. The only light came from the glowing embers in the grate. The flames had gone out, the coal almost burned away, although smoke and a little warmth lingered. The pile of blankets coughed, a harsh, racking cough, before quieting again.

"Get back up there, Finley," ordered a reedy voice from the shadows. "Make sure no one followed him here."

"There's a man outside in the lane," I said. "He's my friend. He won't harm anyone, he's just my lookout."

"Why do you need a lookout?" The speaker with the reedy adolescent voice emerged from the shadows. It was Mink, the quietest member of the original gang, and the most serious. He could read, too, unlike the others, and I suspected he was whip smart, although he'd kept to himself so much that it was difficult to gauge how smart.

"He worried that I'd be in danger down here from you lot," I said as Finley disappeared through the trap door.

Mink peered at me through long strands of greasy hair, and for one moment I wondered if he was like me, female pretending to be a boy. But then I remembered seeing him piss once. He was definitely male. "Why would you be in danger from us?" he asked.

I counted three others in the cellar, including the person beneath the blankets. Finley and Mink made five. Their numbers were depleted, unless the rest were out scavenging and stealing. With my training, I could probably fight them off if I had to, particularly with the knife strapped to my ankle and another to my forearm.

"I'm not," I said. "But he worries about me."

Mink's gaze slipped down my length then slowly met mine again. "So you found yourself a husband."

The other lad gasped and the body on the mattress pushed back the blankets to peer at me.

"I'm not married," I said.

"But you are a woman."

"I am. How long have you known?"

The body on the bed swore softly. The other boy, Tick, if I recalled correctly, stared at my chest as if he'd never seen a woman before.

"Not at first," Mink admitted, "but the idea grew on me the longer I knew you. You never pissed or changed in front of us and you liked to be clean. In my experience, only girls like to be clean."

"I always knew you were the clever one." I handed him the sack and watched him open it.

Tick reached into the sack and pulled out a loaf of bread, baked the day before. He tore off the end and knelt on the mattress. A bony hand emerged from the folds and squirreled the bread away.

Mink pulled the blanket from the sack and, to my surprise, smelled it. He breathed deeply, closing his eyes, burying his face in the wool. I knew it had been laundered with a lavender scent, but couldn't smell it from where I stood. The stench of urine and filth was too strong.

"How many are you now?" I asked softly.

He lowered the blanket but didn't let it go. "Just us five."

"There's more than enough food for five of you to eat well for a few days, at least." I nodded at the sack. "There are clothes, too."

He pulled out a shirt and smelled it. "You always did like clean shirts."

"And trousers."

"Dresses?"

"I'd almost forgotten what it was like to wear a dress," I said. "It took some getting used to again. They're no good for climbing, or running." Or fighting.

Mink's face softened and I thought he'd smile, but he didn't. I'd never seen him smile. When the others would howl with laughter over a childish joke, his lips would hardly lift. Sadness dogged him, so deep that he couldn't shake it. In my experience, sorrow like that haunted only those who'd once known love and safety and lost it, whereas those like Stringer could laugh and enjoy themselves because they knew nothing better than the life they lived in the cellar hovel. They were born in the slums and would die in the slums. I suspected Mink wasn't born to this class but had found himself entrenched in its mire at some point.

"You mentioned money," he said. When I listened really hard, I could hear the middle class tone in his voice. He hadn't learned to cover it completely. "How can we get some?"

"My friend and I need ears and eyes in the East End."

He shoved the sack away. "No. We're not dobbers. We ain't risking our lives for your fancy man."

"He's not my fancy man."

"He a pig?"

"No. He works for a secret organization that tries to keep the world safe from..." I sighed. There really was no way to describe what Lincoln and the ministry did without mentioning supernaturals, and he'd strictly forbidden me to tell them that. "Never mind. He's a spy, of sorts, but his network is a little fragmented in this part of the city." Although Lincoln had tavern keepers, police constables, shop keepers and prostitutes in his spy network, he didn't have anyone at the very bottom level. It was impossible to get lower than these child gangs.

"We can't help you," Mink said, folding thin arms over a thin chest. "Take your things and go." He signaled for Tick to give back the blanket. Tick clutched it tighter and watched his leader through narrowed eyes.

"Don't be a fool, Mink," I said. "You need what's in that sack, and you need regular money. My friend can offer you that. Look at me." I held out my arms. "I'm healthy and happy."

"You've definitely changed, and not just your..." He waved at my chest but didn't meet my gaze.

"Pups," Tick said with a grin.

"You used to be real skinny," Mink went on. "And quiet. I thought you were quiet so no one noticed you."

That was exactly why. It had worked until I raised the spirit in the police cell and been taken to Lichfield. After that, there was no point in remaining insignificant. "If no one notices you, no harm can come to you," I said. I watched him, the boy who had been quiet too, but was now the leader, even if of a depleted gang.

"I used to wonder how you got here," he said. "You could

read and write so I knew you weren't from round here."

"I wasn't the only one." How much did he want the others to know? How much did they already know, or had guessed? "What happened to Stringer?"

He blinked quickly at the change of topic. "He died."

"How?"

"Mutiny," Tick said. "He tried to sell Weasel here to a brothel keeper." He patted the blankets and the body—Weasel —wheezed.

"Weasel's a girl?"

"Not that kind of brothel," Mink said. "The kind that takes boys."

"Weasel's got a pretty face," Tick said with a shrug. "When it ain't all sickly like now. Pretty like a girl's, but he ain't. I seen his pizzle stick."

"So the rest of the gang rose up against Stringer?" Thank God I hadn't been around to witness the events, yet I wished I'd been there to help. Ousting a bigger, stronger lad like Stringer must have taken some courage.

"Aye," Tick said. "But Mink worked it all out. He led us coz he's smart."

"What did you do with the body?"

"Sold it to the resurrection man."

"Shut it," Mink hissed. "She'll tell the pigs."

"Your secret is safe with me," I assured him.

"Resurrection man were right glad he didn't have to dig one out of the graveyard," Tick went on.

"That was very brave of you, Mink. Brave and noble. You have a good heart." If one disregarded the murder of Stringer. "You're exactly the sort of person we need." When he didn't answer, I added, "My friend is a good man, too, also brave and noble." Perhaps noble wasn't the right word, but Mink didn't have to know that. "We're not asking you to do bad things."

Mink's lips flattened. He glanced at the two figures on the mattress. "I can't risk it. I can't risk their lives."

"You are, just by refusing my offer. Without our help, not all of you will survive the winter." My gaze settled on the body buried beneath the blankets as another coughing fit racked him. I remember being that sick once, but no one had bothered to take care of me. I'd coughed until I vomited up bile and snot, but no one had cleaned me up. I'd lain in my own filth for a week until I somehow got well enough to get up. I'd left that gang as soon as my legs were strong enough to take me away.

"Come on, Mink," Tick said. "Stringer would of done it, for the money and stuff."

"I'm not Stringer!" Mink snapped.

"Maybe that's why we're hungrier than we ever were," Tick retorted. "Maybe that's why Fleece talks about taking over this place and setting up his gang in here."

"Fleece?" I prompted. I remembered him. A nasty, violent boy of about sixteen who controlled the streets to the east. His gang had chased me many times when I ventured too close to their territory, but they never caught me. It was how I'd earned the name Fleet-foot Charlie.

"He tried to take this place from us," Tick told me, "but we fought him off. Stabbed him in the leg, good and proper like the pig he is, but he says he'll come back soon and kill us all if we don't leave."

"Then leave," I said rashly.

"And go where?"

"I know a place." Even as I said it, I knew it wouldn't be possible. Gus's great-aunt took in girls in need of shelter, but her house was already full and these boys were, well, boys.

"If you could help, why didn't you come back before now?" Mink asked, his top lip curled up. "Why wait?"

It was a good question, and the answer didn't make me

feel proud of myself. "Because I didn't want to be reminded of what I became after my father threw me out of the house."

Tick's jaw flopped open. "You got a father?"

"He's dead now, but yes, I had one."

"What'd he throw you out for?"

"It's a long story for another day, Tick."

He pulled up his knees and hugged them fiercely. "I can't remember my father."

I looked to Mink. The sneer had vanished and he seemed uncertain. "Take my offer," I urged. "It's simply a matter of gathering information, reporting back things you hear. You'd be surprised at what you already know that could be useful to us. We must find a very bad man, someone who may harm the queen and her family."

"Bloody hell," Tick muttered. "Come on, Mink, we got to help Charlie if it'll save the queen's life. It ain't British to refuse."

"I'm in a position to help you now, Mink, and I *will* help you." I pushed the sack back to him with my foot. "I'll return tomorrow for your answer."

"Wait," he said. "Was it you who left us the coat a few weeks back?" He picked up one of the blankets on the mattress. No, it wasn't a blanket. It had arms and buttons. It was a familiar black woolen great coat. I hadn't seen Lincoln wear it since my return from the north. He must have left it here while I was away. "Not me," I said. "My friend outside."

I climbed the stairs and opened the trapdoor. Finley wasn't there. I bit the inside of my lip as I slid aside the boards leading to the street, hoping not to see the lad in Lincoln's grip. Lincoln wouldn't take kindly to being spied upon, and Finley was the bold, inquisitive sort.

I breathed a sigh of relief as I spotted Lincoln leaning one shoulder against the wall opposite, his ankles crossed as if he didn't have a care in the world. Only his sharp gaze gave away his alertness. Finley stood in a replica position beside him, his gaze on Lincoln, not me or the street. He copied Lincoln's pose, right down to the frown and slight nod in greeting as he spotted me. I bit back my smile.

"I see you've found yourself a friend," I said.

"He wouldn't leave." Lincoln pushed off from the wall and so did Finley. Lincoln stepped toward me, as did Finley. Lincoln stopped and turned a flinty glare at the lad. Finley tried to copy it but it lacked intensity.

"Mink's got food for you," I told him. "And warm clothes. Tomorrow, there'll be money too, if you can get him to agree to help us."

Finley's eyes grew wider with each word. The mention of money sent him sprinting across the lane and sliding open the boards. He slipped through like a rat into its hole.

Lincoln and I headed out of the lane side by side.

"Any trouble?" I asked.

"Just the lad."

"He's no trouble, just mischievous."

We walked a few steps in silence and I thought the matter dropped until he said, "Was he mocking me?"

"I think he was trying to be like you."

"Why?"

"Because you're big and powerful and have a commanding air about you. What boy wouldn't want to emulate that? Especially one in such a hopeless situation as he is." I glanced up at the sliver of sky visible between the roofs. It seemed so much grayer here, lower and heavier, even though it was the same sky over Lichfield.

Lincoln rested a hand on the back of my neck, under my hair. "Was coming here a mistake?"

"No. Not at all. I thought it would be horrible, but it wasn't. I'm glad I came."

He dropped his hand away but not before skimming his

fingers against mine. "Did they agree to the plan?"

"Not yet, but I think they will. The old leader would have, but he's dead. I'm not sure how trustworthy he would have been anyway. He would have double crossed us as soon as someone flashed a coin in his face. Mink will be more reliable and loyal, if we can get him on board."

We exited the lane and walked through the streets. No one accosted us or tried to steal from us. We looked like two regular men—or a man and a lad—with nothing worth stealing. No toff wore clothes like we wore or kept hair this long.

Gus waited outside Kings Cross Station where we blended in with the crowd and a coach didn't look out of place. Lincoln settled the blanket across my lap. I drew it to my nose and breathed in the scent, as Mink had done. It didn't just smell of lavender, but of Lichfield itself, somehow.

"The memories pain you," Lincoln said gently.

I blinked, unaware until that moment that my eyes were full. "It's not that. I just wish I could do more for Mink and the others. They have no one, and they're just children. I doubt Mink is much more than fourteen, and he's the eldest. And Weasel is sick."

"I'll send the doctor."

"They won't let him in, even if he could fit through."

He sat back and said nothing for the entire journey home.

At Lichfield, the new housekeeper, Mrs. Cotchin was in the process of putting things into order. She saw me before I managed to change out of my boy's clothes and lifted her brows, but thankfully made no comment.

"I think I'm going to like her," I said to Seth as I passed him on the landing.

"Alice?" He glanced back over his shoulder, looking for her.

"No, Mrs. Cotchin. Why did you think I spoke about Alice? And why are you gazing at her rooms like that?"

"No reason." He tried to move past me but I blocked his path.

"Seth, if you've compromised her, I'll pull out your guts myself and feed them to the horses."

"Horses don't eat human guts." He nodded past me, down the stairs. I turned to see Alice walking below, a book in hand, her attention on the page. "She wasn't in her rooms."

"No, but you were, weren't you?"

His cheeks blazed red. "I had to return something. Needle and thread."

"Then take it down to her. There's no need to sneak into her room."

"Downstairs was too far away." He didn't deny the sneaking part. "You may like Mrs. Cotchin already, but I don't think Doyle does."

"Don't change the subject." I looked down to the entrance hall where Doyle now crossed the tiled floor to answer the knock at the front door. "Why doesn't he like Mrs. Cotchin? He hardly knows her."

"Professional jealousy." He shrugged. "Either that, or he needs a woman, if you gather my meaning."

"Your meaning is crystal clear, particularly when you add a wink like that. Is it all you can think about?"

"No," he said, sounding distracted. "I can also spare a thought or two for our indomitable leader." He nodded at the door which now stood open, revealing the figure standing there in a long, black cloak, the hood pulled up. "For example, I wonder what he'll say to his mother now that she has come to visit him."

Leisl removed her hood and pitched her gaze directly at me. I felt like I'd been speared by it.

"If you'll wait here," Doyle intoned, "I'll fetch Mr. Fitzroy."

"No." Leisl lifted her crooked finger and pointed at me. "I come to see her."

CHAPTER 7

*L*incoln had Leisl's eyes. I'd noticed their dark pitch the night of the ball, but now, in the light of day, I spotted the intelligence in their depths as she met my gaze.

"Come with me," I said, directing her to the informal parlor on the ground floor. "Doyle, please bring refreshments."

Leisl quickly took in the furnishings before choosing to sit on the sofa. She tucked her skirts close to her legs, as if afraid of taking up too much space. She clasped her brown hands in her lap and sat with her ankles together. The prim pose was utterly English.

I'd met a gypsy seer some months ago, when Lincoln and I visited a Romany camp at Mitcham Common. She'd been a lively presence, whereas Leisl had more reserve.

"I'm glad you came," I said to begin the conversation since she did not. She continued to glance around the room, her gaze settling on each vase or object before flicking to the next. If she were hoping to gain some measure of Lincoln by the way the room was decorated, she wouldn't learn much. Doyle and I had dressed it together without Lincoln's input.

"You are his woman," she said finally.

"Lincoln's? We're not married."

"You will be." She said it so off-handedly that it took me a moment to respond.

"Is that the seer talking or the mother?"

Her knuckles whitened. "I have not been a mother to him."

"No, but I'd wager the connection is still there between you."

"You think this? Why?"

"My mother gave me up soon after I was born, too. I called her spirit when I learned her name and...and a connection existed between us. She hadn't forgotten me."

Leisl leaned forward a little as I told my story. "Your mother...did she choose to give you up or were you taken?"

"She gave me up for my own safety, and to give me a happy future." I didn't tell her that it hadn't quite turned out as well as my birth mother hoped. That part of the story was for another day.

"I was forced to give up my son," Leisl said.

My breath hitched. I hadn't expected her candor so early in the conversation. A thousand questions swirled in my head, but I got none of them out before she spoke again.

"They came for him the day he was born and I never saw him again."

"My God," I murmured. It must be a mother's worst nightmare. "Did they tell you why?"

"No, but I know why. I see them in my visions. I knew they would come for him."

At least it wasn't a surprise, but still. "You must have been upset."

"Yes and no." Her angular features slackened, but only for

a moment before they once again firmed. Unlike Lincoln, her face was easy to read, the creases folding or stretching according to the direction of her thoughts. "It was for the best. I saw his destiny and knew I could not keep him. He is special. Royal blood flows with Romany through him, but he is not royal or Romany. He was not mine to keep." Her gaze drilled into me. "And he is not yours, Charlie."

I bristled. "I know that. People don't belong to other people." I sounded defensive, but I didn't know why. Of course Lincoln wasn't mine. He wasn't anybody's, just like I wasn't his. We were both free individuals. And yet... "Is that why you came here? To tell me I can't have him?"

Doyle entered with a tray and set it on the table. I poured as he left and handed a cup to Leisl.

"You do not understand," she said. "You will have him as a wife has a husband."

My face heated and I concentrated on pouring my tea. When I looked up, Leisl smiled back with a wicked gleam in her eye.

"You will have his heart," she went on, "but not his soul."

"Nor do I expect to. Souls belong to us alone. I know that much from speaking to the dead."

She gave a firm nod. "Good. I see you are not a silly English girl."

"You thought I would be?"

She lifted one shoulder and muttered something that sounded like, "Eh."

"Now I know why you came here. To see if I was a suitable woman for your son." I laughed softly. I wondered what Lincoln would say if he knew his mother worried about his choice of a wife just as much as Lady Vickers worried about Seth's.

"A little," she said, smiling. "But also, I want you to tell him that I didn't want to give him away, but I knew it had to be so. Tell him the general would not say where he took him so I could not visit."

"General Eastbrooke?"

She shrugged. "I did not know his name, only that he is general. Did he—Lincoln—live with the general?"

I nodded.

"Was he a good father to him?"

Hell. How to tell a mother that the son she gave up endured a terrible childhood? "The general was often absent, but Lincoln grew up to become a good man despite the loneliness."

"You choose your words carefully," she hedged.

"You're very observant." I set down my teacup. "Leisl, you should be telling Lincoln these things, not me. Let me fetch him."

"He will not listen."

"He will if we make him sit here."

She smiled sadly. "He will hear, but he will not listen. Not with this." She tapped her chest over her heart. "Not to me. But to you, perhaps."

"Perhaps."

She put down her teacup. "Thank you, Charlie. You are good girl. You will be good wife."

"Wait, you can't go yet. I still know nothing about you." I handed back her teacup and picked up my own. "Where are you living?"

"A cottage in Enfield."

"Not in a gypsy camp on one of the commons?"

"No. That life is hard, and the general gave me money. I am comfortable."

She was *paid* to give up her son! How could financial compensation ever be enough? I wasn't sure how the arrangement sat with me. On the one hand, money couldn't replace what she'd lost, but on the other I was glad she had a home and was not roaming the streets trying to sell rags or flowers like the other Romany folk.

"The general died recently," I said. "I'll make sure Lincoln continues the payments to you. What of your family? Do you have a husband? Other children?"

"I married but he died eight years ago. We had two children, a boy and girl."

"Lincoln has a brother and sister!" I pressed a hand to my rapidly beating heart. What would it take to get him to meet them?

"They know nothing about him, and I do not wish them to know."

"Oh."

"My past with the prince...it is painful." She tapped her chest again and her face fell.

Painful because he'd forced himself on her or painful because she still loved him? "How did you meet him?" I asked gently.

"At a fair." She smiled wistfully. "He was so young, so handsome and charming. I tell him his future."

"You can tell someone's future at will? Did you read the lines on his palm?"

"No. I need to have vision." She held up a gnarled finger. "Do not trust gypsies at the fair, Charlie. They cannot read your palm or your tea leaves. Understand?"

"Thank you for the warning. So did you have a vision about the prince?"

She nodded, smiling again. "I knew that we would be together as soon as he walk into my tent. I saw our child when I touched him. I knew our baby would grow up to be an important man, but a troubled one, too."

"Did you tell the prince any of that?"

"No. He would think me mad, or using him for money." Her smile turned sad. "I tell him what he want to hear—that he will be king one day, he will be a good king, and have children and many mistresses."

"How did he take that?"

"He laughed and said I wasn't reading his future but his present. I laughed too. It was enough."

"Enough?"

"To catch his eye. I was beautiful then, Charlie. Men liked me."

"I don't doubt it. You're still very beautiful."

"Bah. I am old and wrinkled."

"You have the bones of a beautiful woman, Leisl, and the bearing. The lines on your face tell the story of a life well lived. Don't wish them away."

"So wise and kind for one so young." She suddenly sucked in a sharp breath, and set down her cup again with a clatter in the saucer. "I must go." She quickly rose and headed for the door before I could stand. She was spritely for her age.

Lincoln filled the doorway, blocking her exit. He wore his expressionless expression, the one that told me there was far more going on behind that façade than he wanted anyone to see. But he forgot that I knew him well now, and that he couldn't dupe me into thinking he was unaffected.

"Leisl," he said with a slight nod.

She glanced at me. For assistance? To carry the conversation? I hesitated. I didn't want to help her—or him. I wanted them to converse without my interference.

"I am leaving," she said.

He stepped aside. "Good afternoon."

"Good afternoon." She hurried to the door, her head bowed. Doyle assisted her into the cloak.

"Wait!" I marched past Lincoln, grabbed his hand, and tugged him after me. I felt his reluctance with every step. "You can't leave yet. Lincoln, say something to her."

Leisl pulled the edges of her cloak together at her throat. "I must go."

"Doyle," Lincoln said, "have Gus drive Leisl wherever she wishes to go."

Doyle bowed and left. Good. It would take a few minutes for the coach to be ready. That would give them time. They needed help to begin, however.

"Lincoln, Leisl was telling me about the day you were born," I said. "How the general—"

"Now is not the time or place." His voice rumbled with simmering anger.

I drew in a deep breath. It was worth risking his ire for this. "There is no better time or place."

His gaze turned flinty. "I know the general took me from her. He told me." To Leisl, he said, "The general's allowance will continue, with an increase."

"You do not need to," Leisl said, her gaze lowered. "It is enough."

"Prices have risen over the years. It's only fair that your annuity does too. In the event of my death before yours, the payments will continue."

"Thank you."

I looked from one to the other. How could mother and son speak of money after so long apart? Why weren't they asking more important questions? I didn't expect them to embrace, but this formality felt wrong.

"Lincoln." I pressed my hands on my hips. "Did you know you have a half-brother and sister?"

His nostrils flared. "I have them on my father's side too. They don't know I exist, and I have no interest in meeting them. Now, if you'll excuse me, I have work to do."

He turned and stalked off. I went to run after him, but Leisl caught my arm.

"Leave him," she said quietly. "One day, perhaps, we can talk, but not today."

She was far more forgiving of his rudeness than me. "If that's what you want."

"Thank you, Charlie. You are a good friend to him, I see." She took both my hands in her bare ones. She had not worn gloves despite the cold. "You love him and he loves you."

I bit the inside of my lip in case it wobbled. I nodded.

She patted my hands and looked up at the chandelier dangling above our heads. "Then it must be difficult to live here together and not be married, eh?" She chuckled. "Very difficult."

"We're, er, waiting for...for me to know my own heart on this matter. Our past together has been full of ups and downs."

"Aahhh. You wish to punish him for wrongs?"

"No!" Not really. Perhaps. I tried to smile, but it felt forced.

She patted my hand again and made a noise in her throat that I think meant something, but couldn't decipher what. She let me go and flipped her hood over her head. Outside, wheels rumbled on the gravel.

"Goodbye, Charlie."

"Wait, Leisl! Will we meet again soon?"

"If you wish it."

"You can't see whether we do or not? In a vision?"

She laughed. "No. I cannot choose to have a vision. They come when they want, not when I want."

"How inconvenient. Well, I'd like you to know that I do wish it. In the meantime, I'll work on Lincoln."

"Good luck." She tapped her temple. "He is stubborn. Romany men have hard heads. It takes a strong woman to be a good match. You are a strong woman, Charlie. Never forget that."

I waited until Doyle shut the carriage door behind her then headed up the stairs. I knocked on Lincoln's door and held my breath, unsure if he would even receive me.

He opened the door, crossed his arms, and scowled. "No."

"You don't even know what I'm going to say."

"You're going to ask me to visit her. The answer's no."

"You're wrong." I pushed him in the chest, not hard, but he stepped back anyway and allowed me to enter. I kicked the door shut and scowled back at him. *Be strong*, Leisl had said. I would do my best. "I haven't come to *ask* you to do anything, but tell you how rude you were to her."

He turned away and strode to his desk.

"Lincoln! Don't walk off on me. Disregarding the fact that she's your mother, she was your guest today, and you ignored her."

He sat at his desk, his back to me. "I spoke to her."

"That is hardly the same as having a conversation."

"You know I'm not very good at small talk. You said so yourself. Besides, you were doing fine without me. Better, I'd wager."

"That is not the point. The point is, she came here to see her son."

"I am not her son!"

"Lincoln—"

"Don't, Charlie." He half turned and glared at me over his shoulder. "I don't want to argue with you, so don't press me on this."

I fisted my hands at my sides and forced my nerves to settle. "I don't understand you. If I had the chance to meet my mother, my real mother, in the flesh, I would be so happy and eager."

He turned away again. "Not everything I do or say is supposed to make sense to you."

"Explain it to me then. Help me understand how you feel."

"I feel nothing toward Leisl. I told you that."

"I don't believe you."

His body rose and fell with a silent heave of breath. "Go before I say something I regret."

Anger and frustration flared in the pit of my stomach, but I doused it. I wasn't going to win this battle today, and certainly not like this. I came up behind him and circled my arms around his shoulders. The engagement ring I'd flung back at him sat in its box, waiting for me to slip it on my finger. I'd promised him I would put it on when I'd decided to marry him. He must see it every day, a reminder of the mistake he'd made in sending me away.

I kissed the top of his head. I wasn't prepared to apologize for pushing him to speak to Leisl, but I wanted him to know that I harbored no ill will toward him over his refusal.

His body relaxed and he tipped his head back against my chest. "I don't want to fight with you," he murmured.

How could I remain angry with him after such a plea? "We won't."

"Promise you won't bring it up again."

"I can't make that promise."

He drew me around his side and sat me on his lap. He gave me an arched look. "Promise, Charlie."

"I cannot."

He regarded me closely. "What can I do or say to make you promise?"

I pulled away from him and frowned. "You mean you want to bribe me?"

"I wouldn't have put it like that, but yes."

Well then. If he wanted to use underhanded methods, then so would I. I nibbled my bottom lip and undid the second top button on his shirt since the top was already undone.

"There is something that I want, as it happens," I said in

what I hoped was a seductive voice. "Something that you can give me to extract my promise." I popped open another button and kissed him lightly on the lips.

He broke the kiss. "What are you doing?"

"Being bribed."

I reached into the gap of his shirt and stroked the hard muscles of his chest. His heartbeat quickened against my palm. With my own pulse throbbing, I leaned closer and kissed his throat.

He plucked me off his lap and stood suddenly. The chair tipped with his violent shove, thumping on the floor. "That's not fair," he growled, his voice ragged. "You know I won't."

"And you've always played fair?"

He raked his fingers through his loose hair. "You win, Charlie."

"It's not about winning. It's about me not making a promise I can't keep." I went to do up one of his buttons, but he stepped to the side and did it up himself. Both of them.

"You have to go before I decide I can't wait."

I kissed my fingers then touched them to his cheek. "I'll leave you to your work."

He grunted and saw me to the door. He shut it between us, but not before I saw him drag his hand through his hair again.

WE VISITED Lady Gillingham late in the afternoon. Lincoln had insisted on coming with me in case Lord Gillingham put up an argument. He sat beside me in the gently rocking coach, our shoulders bumping. He set a satchel on the other seat.

"We can't force our way in to see her," I said. "It's his house, and she must do as he says. If he forbids us to speak to her then we have to abide by his rules." I shook my head. "Men like him are beasts. I wish the law didn't state that women had to obey their husbands when they're being turds."

When Lincoln didn't respond, I glanced at him, only to see him watching me intently. "I would never forbid you to do or say anything, or to see anyone."

"I know." I took his hand in mine and squeezed.

"Then...?" He shook his head and looked out the window.

"Why haven't I picked up the ring?"

"You're not ready," he said. "I understand."

Did he truly? Sometimes, I wasn't sure why I hadn't put the ring on either. I loved him and I knew he loved me. I wanted to marry him. But I didn't want to rush. No matter how much he said that nothing would change between us, I knew it would. Legally, I became his property. I'd been free and independent for so long, the step into marriage seemed enormous.

Yet he'd already given me a cottage, in my name, and had it written into legal documents that no husband could take it from me. Were those legal documents binding? I felt stupid for not knowing. The property contract might as well have been written in Latin, it was so complicated, and I'd never even been into a bank, let alone had an account in one. A woman had to utterly trust that her future husband had her best interests at heart before she put his ring on her finger.

"It's growing dark," he said.

"Yes. So?"

"If Gillingham forbids us to see his wife, we'll wait until it's completely dark and climb in through her window."

I stared at him. "You're serious, aren't you?"

"It's how I got in last time."

"You expect me to go too?"

"You're capable. I've seen you scale walls and climb trees no matter how you were dressed."

"Yes, but I'd wager her rooms are not on the first floor, and probably not even the second, and a house is not a tree."

"There are foot holds on the window frames and plumbing pipes. Your legs should reach them. I brought rope to tie you to me, just in case. If you slip, you won't fall far. But I don't think you'll slip."

"You are serious." I laughed, despite my apprehension. "But my dress will get in the way."

He handed me the satchel. "Your boys clothes are in there."

I pulled out the trousers and shirt. "You're mad."

He suddenly grinned. It made my stomach do a little somersault in delight. "I know you like to climb," he said.

The prospect of climbing again did thrill me. I enjoyed being outdoors, up high, where no one bothered to look and the view took your breath away. "This is a strange way to bring us closer together," I said. "Most men go courting with flowers and tickets to the theater. You bring rope and trousers."

"I'm not like most men."

We asked the butler if Lady Gillingham was at home, and were met with guilty silence then a stumbling, "Er, well, she's indisposed at the moment. That is to say, she's out. Taking in the air, sir."

"She's gone for a walk?" I inquired, all innocence.

"Yes. Hyde Park."

"Excellent. Perhaps we can join her."

His eyes widened. "No!"

"Why not?"

"I just remembered, she's not at Hyde Park." The butler chewed the inside of his bottom lip until I urged him to go on with a nod. "Her ladyship is...somewhere else. She didn't tell me where she was going."

"Is Lord Gillingham at home?" Lincoln asked.

Why did he want to speak to that horrid man? I thought we wanted to avoid him.

"His lordship is in his study, sir," the butler said, relief flooding his face. "Would you like me to announce you?"

"No." Lincoln turned away and waited for me to go before him down the steps.

"Why did you ask after Gillingham?" I said as he opened the coach door. "Did you simply want to know if he was there?"

He nodded. "Gus, drive somewhere until it's dark then bring us back, but not here. A street or two away will be sufficient. Charlie and I can walk from there."

"A half hour ought to do it," Gus said with a glance at the sky.

"I'll turn my back while you change," Lincoln said as we drove off.

"You expect to be climbing to her room after all?" I asked.

"I do. The butler was lying. She's at home."

"I know. But what if she goes out for the evening?"

"Then we'll wait for her return in her room."

"But a maid might see us in the meantime."

"If you don't wish to go, I can do it alone."

"And sit with Gus in the cold carriage and wait for you? No thanks. I'm coming."

He gave me a satisfied smirk. He'd known all along that I wouldn't allow him to go without me.

He turned his back and I changed into the boys' trousers and shirt. In the confines of a moving carriage, it wasn't the smoothest change I'd done, or the quickest, but I managed.

"You can look now," I said, doing up the top button of my shirt. "Help me on with the jacket."

I lifted my hair and he slipped the jacket around my shoulders. His fingers skimmed my bare skin. The touch was fleeting and impersonal, thanks in part to his gloves. I sighed inwardly, wishing for more.

I slid across the seat until my back rested against his chest. I grasped his arm and positioned it around my waist. He tensed and his fingers hovered above my hip, not touching.

After a moment, I felt his body relax, as if he'd given up the fight to remain unaffected by our closeness. He kissed the top of my head.

"Will you leave your hair up?" he asked.

"Down, I think. I could tuck it into my clothing." I reached up and began plucking out pins. "The darkness will hide its length, and hopefully my feminine curves."

The vibrations from his chuckle rippled through me. "Sometimes I wonder how you fooled me back then. I had no inkling. I must have been blind."

"I was as thin as a rake with no feminine curves to speak of. You weren't blind, you simply didn't expect a girl so you didn't see one."

"Julia suspected."

I knew she'd been the one to first put it to him that I might not be a boy. I'd hated her for it then. Sometimes, I still hated her but for different reasons. But that hatred was no longer as strong as it had been. Perhaps because she held no hold over Lincoln, or perhaps because I felt a little sorry for her nowadays.

"Whatever her faults," I said, "she is very astute when it comes to understanding people."

"Not all people. She has underestimated someone badly." He meant the person who'd gone to the newspapers with the story of Lady H's past as a dancer.

I collected the hairpins and tipped them into my reticule.

Lincoln removed his gloves and set them on the seat beside me.

"What are you doing?" I asked.

He responded by raking his fingers gently through my hair. "It's so long now," he murmured, fascination edging his tone. "Much longer than mine."

"You had a trim only last week."

"I might cut it off altogether."

"No!"

I felt his grin against the top of my head. "You need time to get used to the idea."

"A lot of time. I like it the way it is."

He massaged my scalp. I closed my eyes and sighed. We sat like that for a long time, not speaking. I didn't feel the need to fill the silence, and it seemed he didn't either. When the coach jerked forward, I opened my eyes.

"We're moving," I said, reluctantly breaking contact.

His eyes, half hidden beneath hooded lids, followed me as I slid along the seat away from him. "Are you ready?"

"Of course. I'm looking forward to it."

We stopped again in a street I didn't recognize but had townhouses similar to those in Mayfair and Belgravia. Lincoln alighted first and did not lower the step or assist me down. I jumped.

"Come on then." I skipped off, beckoning for him to follow.

He caught up to me, the satchel slung over his shoulder. "You need some practice first," he said.

"You want me to scale one of these walls as practice?" I asked, waving at the nearest house.

"Not quite." He led me down a lane and then into a yard surrounded by stables. "Climb that far wall."

I looked at the wall. It was well above my height but the three crates stacked nearby told me we weren't the first to climb over it. It was dark now and we were alone in the courtyard, except for a horse snuffling in one of the nearby stalls. I arranged the crates and scrambled up. I could just reach the top of the wall with my fingertips if I stood on my toes. Using my shoes for grip against the brickwork, I hauled myself up.

It was a lot harder than the last time I scaled a wall. I was heavier, for one thing, and the muscles in my fingers were out of practice. It took me three attempts.

I dropped silently to the other side. Lincoln landed beside me a moment later. He got over the wall with his first try.

"Good," he said simply. "A fair effort."

"Fair? It was bloody good," I said, slipping into my street cant.

"It was *fair*, Charlie. You used to be better."

"Huh. I see you're as brutally honest as ever."

He stopped suddenly. There was just enough light from the hissing streetlamp for me to see his frown. "Did I hurt your feelings?" he asked. "I thought I was making a simple observation."

"I know, Lincoln, and no, you didn't hurt my feelings. But if you ever observe that I've gotten fat, you should lie."

"I'll keep that in mind."

I rolled my eyes but he wouldn't have seen in the dark. "A better response would have been: 'You'll never get fat, Charlie. Yours is the sort of figure that couldn't put on a lot of weight.'"

"I'll keep that in mind too."

I laughed. I was no longer sure if he was serious or teasing me. "Come on. Let's visit the princess in the tower."

We waited across from Gillingham's house and watched as Lord Gillingham left in his carriage. Light edged the drapes in one of the third floor windows. The curtain briefly fluttered, revealing Lady Gillingham, before closing again.

We waited another hour in the shadows for the passing coaches to thin. Being winter, no one was out walking, and the street grew quiet. Lincoln tied the rope around both our waists and we silently approached the house. With a quick glance to see that we weren't observed, he used the external plumbing pipe to scale the wall. My eyes had grown used to the darkness, and I was able to see where he placed his feet and hands. I easily followed him. Neither of us spoke, and my body settled into a rhythm, as if it remembered how to move up a vertical surface. It was exhilarating and more satisfying than I could have imagined. I paused only once as he took a moment to look down and check on me.

"Keep going," I whispered.

We reached the third floor faster than I expected. Lincoln tapped on the window where we'd seen Lady Gillingham—Harriet—earlier. By the time I located holds for my fingers and feet, the window sash flew up. Harriet's face appeared. She smiled at Lincoln, then saw me and gasped.

"Charlie! When I heard the knock on my window, I suspected it would be Mr. Fitzroy, but not you. My goodness, come inside before you fall."

"She won't fall," Lincoln said.

I smiled at his faith in me. He helped me through the open window and didn't let go until I planted both feet flat on the floor. He untied me from the rope coiled around his waist.

"I enjoyed that," I said, dusting off my hands. We hadn't worn gloves, the better to grip onto pipes and ledges.

Harriet's bedchamber was very large and pink. From the dusky rose shade of the curtains to the bolder cerise of the bed cushions, it matched the woman's girlish nature. The room was cold, however, with no fire in the grate. Our breaths frosted in the air. Fortunately, I was warm from the exercise.

"You're braver than I," Harriet whispered, glancing at her door.

"We saw your husband leave," Lincoln told her. "You're safe."

"Yes, but the servants…they spy for him."

"Spy?" I blinked. "What sort of husband spies on his wife?"

"The sort married to an ugly beast." She plopped down on the bed, her pretty face a picture of misery.

I sat next to her and went to take her hand to squeeze it as a show of support, but stopped myself. Her station was far above mine. As friendly as she was, she might not like me touching her. "The servants know nothing of your shape shifting, do they?"

She shook her head. "Gilly told them that I'm unwell and must remain in my rooms tonight. Even if I ask to leave, they're not to allow it."

"He's keeping you prisoner in here?"

"I'm sure I'll be allowed out in the morning." She lifted one shoulder before it slumped further than before.

"He's the beast," I muttered. "Not you."

She blinked tear-filled eyes. "Thank you, Charlie."

"For what? I haven't done anything. And to be perfectly honest, we're here because we want something from you, although if I'd known you were being kept prisoner, we would have come sooner—and perhaps brought something to make your imprisonment less dull."

"Sherry?"

"I was thinking of a deck of cards."

She giggled into her hand. "Thank you for cheering me up a little. But please, don't blame Gilly entirely for this. He is only doing what he sees as right."

"Right?" I blurted out. "If he sees *this* as the proper way to treat a woman, he needs spectacles to improve his vision. It is never right to have your freedom curtailed."

"Gillingham will hear from me in the morning," Lincoln said.

"No!" Harriet sprang up but sat down again just as abruptly, as if she'd surprised herself with her vehemence. "Please don't mention you were here. It will only make things worse."

I looked to Lincoln and shook my head. His flattened lips were the only sign he'd comply with her wishes.

"Better times are ahead of us," Harriet said, her childlike voice full of hope. "If only I can have a baby. All I have to do is convince him to…" Her hands screwed into her skirt, and she studiously avoided our gazes.

"Right," I said. "Well then. The reason behind our visit. We want to know what you were about to say to me when your husband interrupted us. You said you might know of something that could help us learn who the imposter is."

"Yes, of course." She plucked at her skirts. "It's not much, and I hope I haven't brought you here under false pretenses. You see, it may not work."

"Work?" Lincoln asked with a small frown.

"I know so little about what I am, but there is someone who knows more. Much more. He may have the answers you seek."

She knew of another like her? She had claimed not to. Had she lied, and there was a family member, after all?

"I see," Lincoln said simply. He turned to me and I blanched at the odd look in his eyes. A worried look.

What did I have to do with any of this?

And then I understood. Harriet meant her *father* could help us. He was the only other person she'd ever known who could change shape like her. But he was dead.

I drew in a deep breath to steady my suddenly pounding heart. "It's fortunate that I came."

"Will you do it?" Harriet nibbled the skin on her top lip and glanced between us. "Will you summon his ghost here?"

"It seems like a good idea," I said. "Indeed, it's the only idea we have at present. What's his full name?"

"Wait." The single word dropped from Lincoln's lips like a stone. "He's a supernatural."

"A shape-changer, nothing more," I assured him.

We'd once encountered a midwife capable of breathing temporary life back into the newly deceased using a spell. Her magic had allowed her spirit to ignore my commands when I directed it back into her body. If she'd been a cruel, hateful woman, she could have done enormous harm to the living in those few hours. We did not want a repetition of that incident.

Lincoln crouched before me and rested his hand on my knee. He didn't speak or offer counter arguments. But I knew from the look in his eyes that he was remembering the midwife too.

I placed my hand over his and touched the amber orb tucked beneath my clothes. It throbbed in response. "He's a shape-changer," I said again. "Not a necromancer or whatever Estelle Pearson was."

"Good heavens, no," Harriet said. "Why would you think that?"

Lincoln swallowed then gave a single nod. He stood and glanced at the door then the window—deciding which to guard, I assumed. He chose the window.

I turned to Harriet. "What's your father's name?"

CHAPTER 8

The heart of the imp inside my amber necklace beat steadily, albeit faintly. It held no fear of the spirit coalescing into the shape of a tall, solidly built man with an equine nose and untidy mutton chop whiskers. I wasn't afraid either, merely uneasy. But until I knew that the bare-foot man wearing a nightgown was harmless, my gut would continue to churn and I wouldn't let go of the orb.

"Good evening, my lord," I began.

Harriet's gaze darted around the room. "Where is he?"

I nodded at the figure, an imposing man, even in death. The mist shimmered, as if the spirit couldn't quite keep his form, then steadied.

"Harriet?" he murmured. "What are you doing here?" Then, louder, "What is the meaning of this?"

"You're dead," I said quickly.

"I know that. Are you? Is…is she?"

"No, she's alive. We three are, but only I can see you."

"I'm alive and in excellent health, Daddy," Harriet said cheerfully. "Don't worry about me."

Lord Erskine's wooly brows drew together. He studied

his daughter and then Lincoln, standing impassive by the window. "Who're you? And who's he?" I put up my hands to stop his questions, but he ignored me. "What are you doing in my daughter's bedroom? And why has my rest been disturbed? Where's Gillingham?"

I introduced myself and Lincoln, and explained about my necromancy. "It was your daughter's suggestion that we summon you," I told him. "You see, we need your help. We need to understand more about how you and your daughter are able to change form."

The spirit shimmered again and clasped his hands behind his back. He studied Harriet, sitting primly on her bed, a look of expectation on her face. "I don't know what you're talking about," Erskine growled.

He reacted as I expected, but it still irked that I had to win his trust when his own daughter believed us. "Harriet has told us everything she knows, but it's not enough. We need to know if there are others like you, and if it's possible to change into anything other than a...a wolf-like creature."

The mist drifted away then suddenly swept around the room, darting over furniture, up to the ceiling, and plunging to the floor.

"My lord," I said. "Please, settle down and I will answer your questions. Firstly, Lord Gillingham has gone out and left instructions that his wife not be allowed out of her rooms."

The spirit stopped suddenly, his scowling face directly above mine. "He did *what*?" he bellowed.

"Don't worry about Gilly, Daddy," Harriet said. She couldn't hear or see her father's displeasure, but she must have guessed my statement upset him. "I can manage my husband." She gave me an arched look and I decided to leave the topic alone.

"Mr. Fitzroy and I are friends to your daughter, my lord.

We wish her no harm. Indeed, we protect people like her and myself. People with supernatural abilities."

His nostrils flared. Up close, they were cavernous. "Being her friend doesn't make me inclined to speak to you of her affliction."

I didn't expect her father, a man who could change shape too, to call it an affliction. I was glad she couldn't hear. She had enough disappointment to bear with her husband's disgust.

"Please, sir," I begged. "If there's anything that can help us, you must tell us. There is no one else."

"You may be my daughter's friends, but I don't know you. I do know that Harriet is too trusting of others. She's gullible and inclined to think well of people who might not have her best interests at heart."

"We don't wish to harm her. Indeed, she's like me. Neither of us are normal."

"And him?" He jerked his head toward Lincoln. "What is his affliction?"

I paused but dared not glance Lincoln's way. "An inability to understand people."

Out of the corner of my eye, I saw Lincoln shift his stance.

"Daddy, you must help." Harriet got to her feet and put out her hands, as if searching for something in the dark. I nodded in his direction and she turned toward the spirit. "The royal family is in trouble."

Erskine cocked his head to the side. "In what way?"

"Someone impersonated the Prince Consort," I told them. Harriet hadn't known the particulars, only that the royal family was affected.

"But he's dead," both Harriet and Erskine said at the same time.

"You see why we're searching for answers."

Harriet sat heavily on the bed again. "Indeed."

Erskine paced the room as a living person would, except his footsteps made no sound on the carpeted floor. After crossing the room three times, he stopped in front of Lincoln. "Why you?" he said to Lincoln's face.

Lincoln didn't answer, of course. He wouldn't even know Erskine was there.

"The Prince of Wales tasked us with the investigation," I told him. "We belong to a discreet organization working for England on matters such as this. Matters that can't be explained with reason or logic."

"Supernatural matters."

"Yes."

He half turned to look at me. "A government organization?"

"Semi-official. Mr. Fitzroy is our leader. Lord Gillingham is on the committee."

"Is he? Then why isn't he here, urging me to help?"

"Because he doesn't like his wife being involved, or his wife's family."

He must have understood my meaning because his nostrils flared again. His misty form shot toward me, his chin thrust out in all its noble glory. "If it's for the queen, then I am obliged to assist in any way I can."

"Thank you." I let go of my necklace. "He agreed to help," I informed the others.

Harriet clapped her hands quietly. "Thank you, Daddy. It's very important."

He sat on the bed beside her. "You wanted to know if I am aware of others like us?" He placed his hand over hers, but she didn't move. I could see that she'd inherited her father's large hands. Feet, too. "There *are* others, as it happens."

"How many?"

"I don't know. All I know is they do exist. I grew up

thinking I was alone, you see, that nobody like me existed. My parents died when I was young, so no one ever told me what I was. I could control my changes easily, and none learned what I could do. Not even my wife. Not until..." He looked sadly at Harriet. "Not until Harriet changed from a baby into her other form as she slept. My wife went mad from the shock. She screamed whenever the nurse tried to give Harriet to her. I had to pay the nurse handsomely to keep her quiet about my daughter's condition, and I had my wife committed to an asylum."

An asylum! The poor woman. Poor Harriet, although I was quite sure she didn't know her mother's fate. She'd told Lincoln her mother had died.

"Harriet doesn't know the truth," he said, following my thoughts. "You have my permission to tell her, if you think she can cope with it. Otherwise, please keep it to yourself."

I nodded, somewhat numb. "Go on."

His large chest rose and fell, as if he took in a deep breath, although he no longer needed air. It would seem that breathing wasn't a habit easily broken. "I thought Harriet and I were the only ones in the world who could change, but then I read a newspaper article about some wolves seen in London."

"Wolves?"

"Wolf-like, was how they were described by the witnesses. They ran on all fours, had fur, a muzzle, claws and teeth. According to the article, they didn't harm anyone, just ran through the streets at night, sometimes howling."

He paused and I repeated what he'd told me for Lincoln's benefit.

"Did they appear at a specific time?" Lincoln asked, speaking for the first time since Lord Erskine's spirit arrived.

"One of the witnesses said only at a full moon, but others made no such comments," Erskine said.

I repeated this for Lincoln.

"Animals roaming the city's streets isn't unusual," Lincoln said.

"No," Erskine said. "But what was unusual was that they simply disappeared. When witnesses chased them, they came across only other people. Naked people. When asked if they were attacked by wolves, these people claimed they were not and showed their unmarked limbs to prove it. They laughed off their lack of attire as if it were nothing."

"Extraordinary," I said, and told Lincoln what Erskine had said. "You think these people were the wolves, back in their human form?"

Erskine nodded.

"Were any names given?"

"No, but I inquired at the newspaper office. The reporter gave me addresses of the witnesses and I sought them out. They laughed it off as a silly joke, a trick of the light, and claimed they must have been mistaken. They said the newspaper sensationalized the incidents and that it was really nothing."

"Why would they laugh it off? Didn't they believe their own eyes?"

"It was dark, for one, and the lamps in that part of the city often don't work, particularly in those days. But it was largely because of the people they came across after chasing the wolves who convinced them they were deluded. They were well known in the area, you see. The witnesses believed them without question."

Again, I repeated his story for Lincoln.

"Did you investigate further?" Lincoln asked.

Erskine said he did. "I tried not to think any more of it after speaking to the witnesses, but I couldn't stop. Then the more I thought about it, the more I became certain these people were like me, capable of changing shape. The notion consumed me. I *had* to find them and know for myself. So I returned to the slums and asked the witnesses for names of the people they'd seen that night. I then went to speak to them, but was met with silence and threatening glares at every turn. I wasn't sure if they wouldn't speak to me because I was an outsider or because they had a secret to keep. Their silence frustrated me." He spread his hand over Harriet's then curled it into a fist. "I couldn't stand it anymore, so I told one of them that I could change shape too and that I was searching for others like me."

Revealing himself had been a risk. "And what did he say?"

"He gave me the name of a man, a leader of their group, I suspected. I visited him and he didn't dismiss me immediately, at least."

I shifted forward on the chair, my gaze riveted to Erskine. "Go on."

"He asked me to prove that I could change. So I did."

"He wanted you to change in front of him? Without proof that *he* could do so first?"

Harriet made a little sound in her throat, part horror, part surprise. She must have guessed her father's answer.

Erskine nodded. "It was the only thing I could do to get him to open up."

"And did he talk to you?"

"Once I returned to my human form, he became quite excited. He was eager to ask me about my changing, and we compared notes, as it were. I learned that he could also change into a wolf-like animal at will, but he was learning to change into other types of creatures."

"How could he learn to change into other things?" I asked, repeating his words for Harriet and Lincoln.

"From his friends. Some could change into other animals. There was a pack of them, you see. A pack of shape-changers, all learning off each other. According to this fellow, however, none succeeded in changing into anything other than their main form. He'd had the only success."

My voice, as I repeated this for Lincoln, sounded stunned.

"The group," Lincoln said, "where do they live?"

"Whitechapel."

The palace footmen saw the impersonator disappear into Whitechapel. The impersonator must be one of the men Erskine stumbled upon, if not the leader himself. "His name?" I asked.

"King," Erskine said, "but I'm unsure if that's his real name. He didn't strike me as the sort of fellow to give it out to a stranger, even one like him. If I had to guess, I'd say he and his friends weren't always law-abiding, like most folk from Whitechapel." His nose wrinkled, as if he could still smell the unwashed slum dwellers. "Although I sensed my every move was being watched from the moment I entered that Godforsaken rookery, I came to no harm, and I suspect I had him to thank for it. He didn't strike me as an uncivil man, either. Indeed, he spoke quite eloquently, and I didn't feel threatened in his presence."

"Where did you speak to him and where can we find him?"

"At the Cat and Fiddle. Whether he still drinks there, I wouldn't know, but someone ought to know him. He was a popular figure."

"How long ago was this?"

He glanced at Harriet. "She was still quite young, not yet a woman. About eleven or twelve years ago."

"Can you describe this Mr. King?"

"Receding brown hair, mid-twenties at the time, moustache and side whiskers. He was quite tall and powerfully built, very broad in the shoulders. Large hands and feet, too, which in hindsight, I think might be a trait of our kind."

"What do you mean?"

He glanced at his hand, still covering his daughter's. His was extraordinarily broad, the fingers thick and the knuckles bulging. Hers too, for a woman's hands. There was nothing delicate about them, although she wasn't a big woman on the whole.

"The first fellow I spoke with had big hands too, as do Harriet and I." He thrust out one bare foot. "And big feet too. Poor Harriet. She always had gloves and shoes made to fit. She couldn't find any readymade feminine ones in shops."

I repeated what I'd learned about Mr. King for Lincoln and Harriet. It gave me time to digest it all, and consider any further questions to ask Erskine. But I could think of none.

Lincoln, however, wanted to know more about Erskine's own family. "What of your relatives?" he asked.

"I have none. I knew nothing of my parents, and was brought up by a governess then tutors who oversaw my day-to-day welfare. The family lawyer who managed my affairs until I was of age. If they knew anything about my form changing, they never said and I never asked."

I repeated this for Lincoln.

"Daddy was very much alone," Harriet said. "That's what he always told me. It was just him and me. That's why he wanted to make sure I married a man older than myself, to care for me properly after Daddy was gone. Someone of solid stock and good family."

Erskine's form shimmered. "Just in the nick of time as it turned out," he said. "Not that I expected Gillingham to lock her away like this. Tell me, Miss Holloway, what's the story there? Ought I be worried?"

Harriet blinked her innocent eyes at me, waiting for me to repeat her father's words back to her. She was so naive and seemed to actually care for her husband. Or, at least, care enough to want his child. I decided to keep quiet about the particulars and my opinion of Gillingham. Lord Erskine could do nothing in his present form to make his son-in-law pay for his treatment of Harriet. It would only frustrate him.

"No," I said. "Mr. Fitzroy and I are seeing that her husband treats her well."

"Good. Good. Is there anything else?"

"Do we have any more questions for his lordship?" I asked Lincoln.

"Have you seen King since that day?" he asked.

"No," Erskine said. "Having met him and ascertained that there were others like us in the world, I had no need to see him again. Knowing that we weren't alone was the important point. I didn't want a friendship with the fellow."

I passed on his answer to Lincoln, then added my own question. "King never sought you out?"

"I never gave him my title or place of residence. That would be foolish. The man's a slum dweller. He may be like me in that we can both change our form, but we are nothing alike in any other way. I didn't dare risk giving him a clue as to where to find me."

"One cannot trust slum dwellers." He did not seem to detect my sarcasm. "Thank you for helping us, but it's time for you to leave now, my lord."

"He's going?" Harriet whispered, her lower lip trembling. "Oh, Daddy, I wish I could embrace you one last time."

"So do I." He nodded at me to repeat his words. I did. "Goodbye, my dear Harriet. Be a good girl and obey your husband."

I couldn't bring myself to repeat his last words, but I passed on his fondest regards and wishes. They both seemed satisfied with that.

Then I sent him back.

* * *

"CHARLIE!" Lady V's screech had everyone shuddering and Seth putting his hands over his ears. It was as painful as nails down a blackboard. She certainly knew how to make an entrance that could garner the attention of the room. "What are you wearing?"

I sat sprawled in an armchair in the parlor, a glass of sherry in hand. Lincoln and I had just finished telling Gus, Seth and Alice about our conversation with the spirit of Lord Erskine, but we hadn't had a chance to discuss the implications or devise a plan before Lady V arrived.

She was dressed for dinner in what I now knew was her only evening gown, a black velvet and lace dress with the large bustle that was a few years out of date but nevertheless looked regal on her tall figure. Bella had attempted to do her hair but, having been employed by Seth because of her pretty face and curves rather than her hairdressing skills, the arrangement already looked in danger of collapsing like a tent in the wind.

"I had a need to wear boy's clothes today," I said simply.

"What could you have possibly been doing that necessitated boys' clothing? Climbing trees?"

"Not trees," I said into my glass.

Gus smirked and Alice bit down on her lip, but it curved at the edges into a smile despite her efforts. Lincoln remained as impassive as ever by the window, a glass of brandy dangling from his fingertips.

"Leave Charlie alone, Mother," Seth scolded. "She is the lady of the house, after all, and can do as she pleases."

"Not yet," Lady V quipped.

I saluted her with my glass. "Quite right."

Lincoln set his glass down and placed both hands on the window sill at his back. I kept my gaze studiously ahead on Lady V, but I felt very aware of his sudden alertness.

"A small sherry before I go, please, Seth." Lady V sat on

the sofa beside Alice. "And even if you were mistress of Lich-field, Charlie, you must be prepared to receive callers at all times, and that means dressing appropriately. In women's attire," she added, as if I might mistake her meaning.

"We rarely have callers," I said. "Except the committee members, and I don't particularly care for their opinions."

Lady V clicked her tongue. "I see we're not going to have a sensible conversation about it."

I sighed. "I promise to wear women's clothing at all times around the house, unless a particular situation arises where I must change. Does that suffice?"

She gave me one of her queenly nods. "Thank you. Now, will you please *sit* like a lady, at least, and not like an apprentice in his cups?"

I straightened my back and pressed my knees together. I felt just like Harriet, a good girl who did as others bade her, even when it meant the loss of her liberty. In her situation, I would have climbed out the window and run off. But I was not like her, not even now that I lived in a grand mansion with respectable people.

I crossed my legs and downed my sherry in a gulp. If Lady V disapproved, she gave no sign.

"Now, tell me what you've been doing that necessitated..." She looked me up and down, her nose wrinkled. "...*that*."

"I paid Lady Gillingham a visit, if you must know, and her husband is keeping her locked in her room for the night as punishment for coming here—"

"Locked away! Punishment!" She looked as if she would march to Gillingham's house and wring his neck. "That man's a monster. The poor girl must have been terribly upset."

"She's bearing it with more tolerance than I would."

"That's because you're like me, Charlie, and such behavior from our husbands would never be tolerable." She angled a sharp glare toward Lincoln.

He lifted a brow and I had the feeling he was challenging her—*daring* her—to accuse him. Then his gaze darted to mine, and a small crease appeared between his brows.

Doyle entered and announced the arrival of Lady Dalhouse's coach, Lady V's ride for the evening.

"Goodnight everyone," she said, rising. "Don't wait up." She kissed the top of her son's head, much to his embarrassment.

We all watched her leave and then a collective sigh filled the room. "Your mother never fails to create a stir wherever she goes," I said to Seth.

"Why do you think I drink so much?" He got up to refill his glass, and refilled Gus's too, but Cook and Lincoln refused. "Another sherry, ladies?"

"No, thank you," I said.

"Not for me, either," Alice said. "I've had quite enough for one evening."

Seth set down the decanter. "Poppycock."

Poppycock? Since when had that word dropped into Seth's vocabulary?

"What now, Fitzroy?" Gus asked. "Want us to go to the Cat and Fiddle tonight?"

Lincoln nodded. "We three will head there shortly."

"To a Whitechapel tavern!" Alice blinked owlishly at Lincoln. "Is that wise?"

Lincoln's eyes narrowed ever so slightly. "Yes."

"They'll be fine," I assured her before she protested. "They've done it many times. Lincoln has even been into the Cat and Fiddle before, and no one has troubled him."

"Not after he smashed some heads together that night," Gus said with a chuckle. When he noticed no one else chuckling with him, he sobered.

"You're right to worry," Seth said, coming to Alice's side. He squatted beside her and patted her hand. "Whitechapel is a dangerous place, but we're well trained in the art of pugilism." He tapped his chin. "I'm used to taking a few blows in the process of gathering information. A bruise here and there never bothered me, and the other fellow always winds up worse off."

Cook rolled his eyes, and Gus shook his head.

Alice frowned prettily, albeit dramatically. "You're so brave! To venture into a rookery with only your fists as weapons, when the thugs will possess knives and possibly even guns. You're a hero, Seth. A true warrior."

Gus snorted a laugh and Cook grinned. "I like you more 'n' more, Alice," he said.

Seth laughed too, and didn't seem at all perturbed to have been mocked. "Yes. Well. We'll be armed with more than just our fists, of course." He backed away and plucked his glass off the table where he'd deposited it. "The thing is," he said to me, "how can we be sure Erskine isn't talking complete...poppycock?"

Poppycock again. Good lord, if he was going to act and sound like a toff around Alice, we were going to have to have conversations without her present. "I think he spoke the truth," I said.

"He had no reason to lie," Lincoln added. He set down his glass and strode across the room. "Get ready. We leave in thirty minutes."

Seth and Gus followed him out, and Cook rose to leave too.

"Just a moment," I said to him. "How is Mrs. Cotchin working out? Are you two getting along?"

He scratched his bald head. "She be too busy to bother me. I told her straight up that the kitchen be my space and the rest of the house be hers. So far she ain't caused no problems."

"Good, I'm glad everything's settled."

"She did look at me odd when I came in here and looked to be about to say something, but then Doyle spoke to her. I 'spect he'll tell her what's what with us."

"I hope he doesn't tell her too much. Not yet, at least. We don't want her fleeing with fright and telling tales."

"She be a robust sort, I reckon, but Doyle won't tell."

"What of the new kitchen?"

"It ain't all done yet. The builders be back tomorrow. It'll be grand when it be finished. The new cooker be a dream to work." His face lit up at the mention of the cooker. He was a complex, interesting man, yet his joys were simple. He loved to cook.

He left, leaving Alice and I alone. "I think I'll stay in my boys' clothing a little longer," I said, sitting like a man again with my knees apart. "It's rather liberating sprawling in an armchair like this."

"Perhaps I'll try it one day when no one's about."

"Or you could try it when everyone is about, if you'd like to shock them."

"I'd prefer to avoid Lady Vickers' censure, thank you. I get quite enough fierce glances directed my way when she sees me with Seth."

"Speaking of Seth, you shouldn't tease him. He handles your barbs well, but he is trying very hard to impress you."

"I wish he wouldn't," she muttered, looking away.

"I've never seen him try so hard, in fact," I went on. "He's used to women falling at his feet no matter what he says or does. You confound him."

Her fingers twisted in her lap and she still didn't meet my gaze.

"It's all right, Alice. If you have no feelings for him in *that* way, then there's nothing for it. He'll recover, I'm sure. I'd wager his belief in his own appeal is in more danger than his heart."

She looked relieved. "I'm glad to hear it, because...I don't know what to make of him, to be honest. I'm not one for falling at the feet of handsome, charming men just because they're handsome and charming."

"I don't think we'd be such good friends if you were."

"There must be something more in a man to interest me, something of substance," she said.

"Seth does have substance. It just takes time to find it beneath the attractive exterior. He's terribly loyal, for one thing, and fiercely determined to right the past wrongs of his father." He'd worked hard to pay his father's debts, taking any work he could find. Some of that work was dubious, however. "Is it his lack of money and property?"

"No! He's gainfully employed here, and that's quite enough for me."

"Lady V, then? I know she doesn't think it a good match, but she'll come round once she gets to know you."

She sighed and slumped into the chair, her spine finally relaxing for the first time since sitting down. "That's the thing, Charlie. I hardly know him and he hardly knows me."

"I admit he's probably dazzled by your beauty, as most men are, but you do at least have substance beneath your pretty face, and if he doesn't know it yet, he will. He surely knows I wouldn't be friends with a silly twit." I laughed, but she merely smiled, and half-heartedly at that. "What is it, Alice? What's troubling you?"

"He's not being himself around me, is he? I can tell from your reactions and that of the others."

"I don't understand."

She hesitated, choosing her words carefully. "He seems very upright, never saying or doing anything foolish or confrontational. He agrees with all my opinions, even when I deliberately say something absurd."

"You've been testing him?"

She winced. "It's awful of me, I know."

"Actually, I was thinking how clever of you. As to him agreeing with you, I'd play along. I wish Lincoln would agree with all my opinions."

"No, you don't."

I sighed. Perhaps she was right. Lincoln was his own man. A sycophant wouldn't do for me at all, and not for Alice either.

"Tell me, is Seth usually the sort of person who says poppycock?" she asked.

I smiled. "No. He tends to use much stronger words, although he does temper it a little in his mother's presence. Sometimes. And he'd never say a crude word in front of a woman. He treats me like a sister, so I don't count."

"I suppose."

"Do you want me to talk to him?"

"If you like, but I don't want him to think that it makes me interested in him in *that* way."

"I'll try to word it so he understands."

"It's just that I don't know him yet, not the real him without the act. So how can I tell if I will like him in *that* way?"

"Noted." Good lord, I sounded like Lincoln. "I'll speak with him tomorrow. Now, I'm starved. Do you want some supper?"

"Good idea."

"Ring for Doyle while I get changed. I don't want to send Mrs. Cotchin into a spin if she sees me dressed like this."

"You're remarkably calm considering Lincoln and the others are heading into Whitechapel at night."

"They can take care of themselves. All joking aside, they're very capable."

"Yes, but..." She sighed. "Sorry, I'm simply thinking the worst."

"Try not to." I gave her a flat smile, but as I headed up to my rooms, the familiar icy fingers of dread curled around my bones.

Instead of going straight to my rooms, I stood in the corridor outside Lincoln's. He emerged almost immediately, having probably sensed my presence. He'd already changed into coarse flannel trousers and a graying shirt. His feet were bare and he held a yellow neckerchief with frayed ends in one hand. His hair was still tied back. I knew from previous excursions into the East End that he'd untie it and ruffle it up a little.

He handed me the neckerchief. "Would you mind?"

I took the scrap of fabric and fixed it around his neck. Then I reached behind his head and untied his hair. It fell to his nape, but didn't have the desired crumpled effect, so I dug my fingers through it, scrunching and tangling it. We stood very close; closer than was decent for an unmarried couple. I tilted my face up to see him better, only to notice him already watching me. Heat smoldered in his half-closed eyes. He lowered his face to mine and my heart did a little somersault in anticipation of his kiss.

Then he suddenly pulled away and clutched my arms, holding me at bay. "I must finish getting ready," he said, his voice a low hum.

I cleared my throat. "I'll see you when you get back."

"There's no need to wait up."

I gave him an arched look. "I won't be able to sleep until I know you're home safely."

He nodded. "I'll see you then."

"Be careful, Lincoln."

"I'll do my best."

It was hardly a reassuring answer. He wasn't one for caring much about his personal safety, but I knew he couldn't promise me anything more. I might accept that fact, but I didn't have to like it. I wouldn't sleep until I saw him home, safe and sound, and Gus and Seth too.

* * *

Supper with Alice was interrupted by Doyle.

"You have a caller, miss," he intoned. "Mr. Buchanan."

I groaned. "At this hour?" It was late for callers, but not *too* late, particularly for a cad like Andrew Buchanan. He slept until noon most days and stayed up most nights, gambling, attending parties, and probably making a general nuisance of himself.

"If the fire's still burning in the parlor, I'll receive him in there," I told Doyle. "Will you serve drinks, please."

"Of course. Would you also like me to stay?"

"I'd appreciate it."

"May I join you?" Alice asked. "I'd like to meet this fellow."

"You'll want to scrub yourself clean after speaking to him," I warned her.

"Now I definitely want to meet him, just to see what you mean." Her eyes sparkled with humor.

I laughed and we walked arm in arm to the parlor.

CHAPTER 9

"M r. Buchanan," I said smoothly. "This is a surprise."

Andrew Buchanan spun around, bowed, lost his balance and almost tumbled over. He grabbed onto the back of a chair and steadied himself. *Ugh.* The man was drunk and it wasn't even nine-thirty. He tugged on his jacket hem and cleared his throat.

I shook my head slightly at Doyle as he glanced up questioningly from where he stood at the sideboard. Instead of pouring drinks, he returned to the doorway and stood with his hands at his back.

"Pleased to see you again, Miss Holloway." Buchanan may have been greeting me, but he didn't take his eyes off Alice.

I made the introductions.

"Everheart," he repeated. "I don't know any Everhearts."

"You do now," Alice said.

He smiled a charming smile that would disarm most women. Fortunately I knew Alice wasn't like most women. "You don't sound like a Londoner," he said.

"I'm from Dorset."

"Is that so? Dorset's a lovely county."

"Oh? Which part have you been to?"

"Er…" His fingers drummed on the back of the chair. "The seaside part."

"All of it?"

"Yes," he said emphatically. "All of it." He swayed a little, but quickly righted himself.

"Perhaps you'd better sit down," I said, indicating the chair. "Did you come to see Mr. Fitzroy?"

Buchanan sat in the chair by the fire. "Your butler said he's not here."

"He's not."

"Lucky for me because I get to see you two charming ladies instead." Anyone could be mistaken for thinking he only wanted to speak to Alice since he didn't look at me.

Alice and I sat side by side on the sofa. "What did you wish to speak to Mr. Fitzroy about?" I asked, attempting to hurry him along.

He waved a hand. "I'll get to that in a moment. Miss Ever-heart, tell me about yourself. How do you know Miss Holloway?"

"We met recently," she said. Alice knew not to tell anyone about the School for Wayward Girls in Yorkshire where we'd met. The fewer people who knew where Lincoln had sent me, the better. One day I might need to find refuge there.

"Yes, but where?" he pressed.

"That's none of your affair," I said bluntly. Alice may be too polite to speak plainly to him, but I wasn't.

Finally, he looked at me. His pupils didn't quite focus, but he saw me well enough through his drunken haze. His top lip lifted in a sneer. "So we're back to that, are we?"

"I have no wish to quarrel with you, Mr. Buchanan."

"Then don't. Not in front of your lovely friend, anyway." He flashed her a toothy smile.

She didn't return it, but he didn't seem to notice. His smile didn't waver.

"What do you want?" I asked.

"Now, now, let's slow down and get to know one another, shall we? We've hardly spoken, really, not like this. With Fitzroy and his clowns absent, its a perfect opportunity to see if we can be friends."

"We won't be friends."

He pouted. "Why not?"

"Friends don't arrive drunk at one another's houses—"

"I beg to differ. The very best friends always turn up with a gullet full. It's a mark of…something. I forget what. Besides, I'm not drunk."

"Then why are you swaying, slurring your words, and flirting with Alice?"

He dug his fingernails into the armchair. "I'm neither swaying nor slurring. As to the question of flirting…" He flashed another grin at Alice. "I'm simply being friendly. If you don't know the difference, Miss Holloway, then it's most likely no one has ever flirted with you."

Alice's breath hitched. She stared at Buchanan, her face a picture of shock. In her world, men didn't speak so cruelly to ladies. The only horrid words she'd probably heard in her life were those that fell from the lips of Mrs. Denk, our headmistress, and perhaps those of her parents when they'd sent her to the school.

"On the contrary," I said breezily, unruffled by Buchanan's poor manners. "Mr. Fitzroy has flirted with me on several occasions. For instance, just yesterday he allowed me to punch him in the stomach. He doesn't let just anyone do that."

His jaw dropped open.

"It was rather sweet," I went on. "He tensed, of course, and

I felt like I was hitting a brick wall, but it was a very flirtatious offer. Don't you agree?"

He shook his head over and over. "The man's courting rituals are unusual. It's no wonder he's not yet married."

"But he does have extraordinary luck with women," I added, wanting to bite off my own tongue and yet also wanting to see my barb hit. Lincoln and Lady Harcourt had been intimate before he met me, and Buchanan had feelings for her. It must gall him that she still cared for Lincoln, and yet seemed to have no interest in her stepson.

Their complicated relationship always made me feel cold and a little revolted. Not because they had been intimate before Lady Harcourt married Buchanan's father, but because they seemed to want to hurt one another. I wasn't sure if they still shared a bed, or just a house, and I didn't want to know.

The muscles in Buchanan's face twitched. The veins in his throat throbbed above his collar. I thought he'd shout at me, perhaps leap out of the chair and threaten me, but he did not. He barked out a laugh.

"I wish I knew his secret," he said simply. "Well, since we've stripped away all polite façades, let me get to the point of my visit."

"Please do."

"I'm glad it's you here, actually, and not Fitzroy."

"Why?"

"Because I find him intimidating to speak to, Miss Holloway. I also think he'd refuse my request before I even finished speaking it."

"And you think I'm more likely to listen?"

"Oh, I know you are. Do you want to know why?"

"Please enlighten me."

He leaned forward and rested his elbows on his knees. "Because you feel sorry for me."

I burst out laughing.

He sat back with a pout on his lips. After a moment, he recovered himself and attempted another smile. "Very well, let's just say that you're intrigued. You're far more curious than Fitzroy. He wouldn't care why I was here. You, however, want to know."

I nodded. "You have me there. Go on, then. What is it you want?"

"I'll speak to you alone."

"Thank you, Doyle, that will be all."

Doyle left quietly and shut the door.

"And the lovely Miss Everheart too." Buchanan lurched to his feet and held out his hand to Alice.

She looked to me.

"She stays," I said to Buchanan.

"Not if you want to hear what I have to say." When I didn't move or ask her to leave, he added, "Oh, come now. What harm am I going to cause you in here alone? For one thing, you're a quick little whippet and could probably dart away from me in my present state. For another, I'm afraid of Fitzroy. And finally, if I'm going to ravish anyone here tonight, it'll be your friend." He winked at Alice.

Alice made a sound of disgust in her throat. "I'm not leaving you alone with him," she told me.

"It's all right," I assured her. "He doesn't mean it. Besides, he knows Lincoln would kill him in the most painful way imaginable if anything happened to me. Either that or castrate him."

Buchanan winced. "You do have a way with words."

"Are you sure?" Alice asked me.

I nodded. "I'll be fine."

"I'll be just outside. Call if you need me."

"You can wait with Doyle, and probably Cook. I'm sure they're both hovering, most likely with one of Cook's kitchen

154

knives. While you wait, you should ask him to show you how to throw them. He's an excellent knife thrower, as it happens. Very accurate." I smiled at Buchanan.

He sneered again. "Most amusing, Miss Holloway."

Alice left, but not before opening the door wide enough so we could both see Doyle and Cook who were indeed hovering. Cook made a great show of wiping a very large meat cleaver on his apron.

"You have the most remarkable staff," Buchanan said, helping himself to the brandy.

"What do you want?" I snapped.

He sat down heavily, sloshing the brandy around the glass, but not spilling any. "I want your help with Julia. I want you to invite her to things."

I cocked my head. "Invite her to what? We don't have dinners or parties here, and if we do, it's usually because the committee members have invited themselves. She's part of the committee. So really, what more do you require of us?"

"I require…" He let out a breath and set his brandy down, untouched. With nothing to hold, his hands became animated. He placed them loosely together and pointed them at me. I was reminded of the parishioners in my adoptive father's church, praying, and of the beggars in the street, imploring passersby for food. "I need you to be kind to her now. To be a friend to her."

"You ask too much."

"Please, Charlie," he said, using my Christian name for the first time since arriving. "Just make her feel wanted. Let her know that she isn't alone in the world." I'd never seen Buchanan look so earnest. He'd been here when the general created havoc before Christmas, and he'd actually been of use that night. But he hadn't behaved like this. I felt like I was seeing the real Buchanan, the man he used to be before Lady Harcourt broke his heart all those years ago.

"Why can't *you* make her feel special?" I asked. "You're family, after all. She isn't alone when she has you and your brother."

A shadow passed across his eyes and he slumped back in the chair. "It's not the same. There's familial obligation, and then there's voluntary friendship."

"I'd wager *your* friendship is voluntary."

His jaw hardened. "She won't accept my friendship," he bit off. "She loathes me despite…" He jerked his head to the side and stared into the fire. "Despite everything we are to one another. Yes, Charlie, *are*. It's not over."

Well, that was more information than I expected.

"Sometimes she wants it to end, until I convince her otherwise." He nibbled his thumbnail, drumming the fingers of his other hand on the chair arm. "I know you think what we have is sordid. Perhaps it is. Perhaps neither of us knows how to love properly and this is our twisted way of showing that we care. Or perhaps we should both be committed to an asylum." His fingers stopped drumming but he continued to stare at the glowing coals. "The thing is, it's not enough for her. What we have…she wants something else. Something more. *Someone* more." His head jerked back to face me. "Do you understand?"

I flinched at the hollow, haunted look in his eyes. "I think so. She wants a husband, but only if he's titled or rich, or both." Seth had said as much about Lady Harcourt. He'd been intimate with her, although she'd never professed to love him like she loved Lincoln.

"You're an astute judge of character for one so young." He no longer slurred his words, but the familiar lazy drawl was back, as if he couldn't be bothered to even open his mouth. "So you'll help her get back on her feet, so to speak?"

I considered my answer carefully. "As I said, we don't host dinner parties."

"But you do get invited to some. Perhaps mention her name and secure an invitation for her too."

"She seems quite capable of securing her own invitations, despite the gossip. She was at the Hothfields' masked ball, for instance."

His face twitched again, as if the muscles danced of their own accord. "She was, and she made a fool of herself."

"That must have been after we left. What did she do?"

"She gambled it all on the prince and lost. She did pick up the consolation prize of one of his friends, however, a rather smarmy member of parliament by the name of Swinburn." He pulled a face. "Upstart," he spat. "He's in shipping, of all things."

I remembered Seth mentioning him after the New Year's Eve ball. "He's not titled?"

"He's a nobody."

"Does it matter, if he's rich? He must have some influence with the prince if they're friends."

"You don't understand, Charlie. Swinburn is hardly even a gentleman. His grandfather was a sailor. His father began the shipping firm but it was only modest in size by the time he died. Swinburn built it into the empire it is today."

"My God, how beastly of him!"

He rolled his eyes. "You're not amusing, you know."

"So he's a self-made man. Is that all you have against him?"

"No. I have…a feeling. He drinks, gambles, and treats women abominably, discarding them after he's had his fill." He downed his brandy in a single gulp. "I'd wager he's quite without morals, although he can be charming enough to one's face."

"He sounds a lot like someone I know."

Half his face lifted in a smirk. "Perhaps it takes one to know one. The thing is, Charlie, it's all right for someone my age to gad about, but not a fellow of his age. He must be mid-forties, at least."

"If you're worried that Lady Harcourt will lose her heart to him, then why not tell her your concerns? I'm sure she'll appreciate you worrying about her."

"I doubt it," he mumbled. "She'll accuse me of having an ulterior motive."

"Don't you?"

His gaze slipped away. He pushed himself out of the chair and sauntered to the sideboard. I was faster, however, and got there before him. "You've had enough to drink."

"Come, now, Charlie," he slurred, a bitter smile on his lips. "I have to drown my guilty conscience or it'll drown me."

I narrowed my gaze. A sick feeling settled into my stomach. "What do you have to be guilty about?"

He sniffed and stared down into his empty glass. "Can't you guess?"

"Yes," I whispered, horrified. "I think I can."

His gaze lifted to mine. It was filled with remorse, all the usual arrogance stripped away.

"You notified the newspapers about her past, didn't you?" I said. "It was *you* who told the reporters she used to be a dancer at the Alhambra."

He lifted one shoulder then nudged me aside. I lost my balance but caught on to the sideboard and recovered. I let him help himself to another brandy as I digested his confession. This man, who professed to love Lady H and seemed to care for her, had betrayed her in the worst possible way. Her reputation was everything to her. She'd buried her past as thoroughly as she could, only to have the man closest to her dig it up and tell the entire world. I'd never felt sorry for her —until now.

I watched him pour himself a brandy, drink it in one gulp

then slam the glass down on the sideboard. By some miracle, it didn't shatter.

"Go on, then," he said with a detachment that I didn't believe. He cared far more than he was letting on. "Tell me what you think of me."

I shook my head. "You regret it. That's something, at least."

He blinked a slow, drunken blink. "I wish you weren't so god damned *noble*."

It struck me that his plea to invite Lady Harcourt was a ruse, a vehicle to allow him to confess. "Did you come here to unburden yourself? To somehow assuage your guilt?"

"Nothing can assuage my guilt. But I had to tell someone my dirty little secret or I'd go mad."

"Why me?"

"Every man must have a confessor, and I've decided that you're mine. Don't look at me like that, Charlie. Who else have I got? Aside from Julia and Douglas, you're the only one who knows all my faults."

"Why not tell your brother then?"

"He's a self-righteous cock and would lecture me until I knocked all his teeth out. You're not so bad. In fact, I even like you."

I reached for a glass and poured myself a brandy. He snickered as I sipped. "Let's be clear, Mr. Buchanan."

"Call me Andrew."

"No. Let's be clear—we are not friends."

He held up his hands in surrender. "I abhor friendship. It comes with expectations that I'm not prepared to meet."

"I am not someone you can tell all your disgusting secrets to. I don't want to know them. This one was quite enough, thank you."

"Oh. Pity." He pouted. "I feel better already for telling you."

"You shouldn't. You did a despicable thing."

"Yes, but let's be honest, she's a despicable person. Doesn't that cancel out what I did?"

The man was truly awful. How could I have ever thought he might have been a nice person before Lady Harcourt destroyed his innocence? I doubted he was ever an innocent. "I think you ought to leave now."

"If you insist. But you will consider my request, won't you?"

I blanched. "You were serious about me asking her to parties where she'll meet other gentlemen?"

"Of course."

"But why do you want to do that? Is it simply because you feel guilty?"

He screwed his eyes shut and squeezed the bridge of his nose. When he pulled his hand away and opened his eyes, he suddenly looked much older than his early twenties. "What I want is to extract Julia from Swinburn's clutches and place her into those of a man less likely to discard her. She wants marriage, but Swinburn won't marry her. If she must hitch herself to the marriage wagon again, then I want her wedded to some dull, dusty old lord she can't possibly fall in love with. Swinburn's got swagger. He's got charm and is influential, not to mention he has the prince's ear and leads an exciting life. That's the sort of man Julia could fall in love with. That, Charlie, is a nightmare I'd like to see avoided."

His little speech left me stunned. If it were anyone else, such devoted love would be the stuff of poetry, but with those two, it was too sordid for even the penny dreadfuls. "I...I'll think about it. We're busy with an investigation now and we have few staff. Dinner parties are not on our list of priorities."

"But they will be, if I know Lady Vickers." He went to kiss my cheek, but I moved away. He snorted a laugh then patted my shoulder instead. "Thank you, Charlie. You won't utter a word of this to anyone, will you?"

"I don't keep secrets from Lincoln."

"He's hardly the gossiping sort." He lifted one shoulder. "You can tell him, if you like, but no one else."

"You have my word."

"Good. Excellent." He eyed his empty glass. "Perhaps just one more before I go."

"Doyle!"

The door swung open and Doyle rushed in, Cook and Alice behind him.

Buchanan held up his hands in surrender. "Bloody hell, Charlie, call off your dogs. I was just leaving."

Cook and Doyle escorted him out.

"Are you all right?" Alice asked, frowning into my face.

I nodded and wrapped my arms around my body. "I need a bath."

* * *

I WAITED in the library alone, my feet tucked under me, the fire and a blanket keeping the chill at bay. Alice and the servants had gone to bed an hour ago. I tried to read but worry for Lincoln, and thoughts about Buchanan and Lady Harcourt, distracted me.

Soft footsteps and murmured voices after midnight had me throwing off the blanket and leaping out of the armchair. I met Lincoln in the doorway. Behind him, Seth and Gus retreated up the stairs, their steps weary.

I released a long breath. "You're back," I said simply.

Lincoln inclined his head and searched my face. "You look tired."

"I'll go to bed after you tell me how it went." I took his hand and led him to the fireplace. He ought to be cold, but he wasn't. Nor did he look tired. He was fully recovered from the explosion then, thank goodness.

He sat after I did, our two armchairs facing across the hearth. He stretched out his legs and crossed his feet at the ankles. "There's little to tell," he said. "Our inquiries were met with silence, despite offering a financial reward. We even gave assurances that we only wanted to talk to him, nothing more, but we received no answers."

"It's a dead end then. Speaking of dead, perhaps King is. It was years ago that Lord Erskine spoke to him."

Lincoln shook his head. "We spoke with old timers, and none claimed to know him. I think they lied."

"How do you know?" Lincoln wasn't all that good at understanding people, but he usually knew when someone lied to him.

"Small signs. The lack of eye contact, for one, and the quick dismissal of our questions altogether. Seth and Gus reported the same strange behavior."

"You split up?"

He nodded. "We entered the Cat and Fiddle separately and left the same way. We questioned discreetly. Even I was discreet," he added with a wry smile.

I laughed softly. "So they're all protecting this man, King. How interesting that he inspires such loyalty."

"I wish I knew his secret."

"You inspire loyalty, Lincoln."

"Perhaps now, but certainly not before you came here. *You* inspire their loyalty, not me. At least I no longer expect to wake up to someone standing over me with a knife."

I laughed again, even though I knew he spoke the truth, or close to it. The men hadn't particularly liked him when I arrived at Lichfield, and I certainly hadn't. I'd even planned to kill him in his sleep, although I knew now that I never could have carried out that plan. "You would never let anyone get that close," I said lightly. "So now what?"

"Now we take our questions outside the Cat and Fiddle. Perhaps we'll find someone less loyal."

"We'll return to Mink's hideout tomorrow," I said. "Hopefully he'll be prepared to spy for us." I yawned, covering it with my hand.

"Bed," he said, rising and holding out his hand to me.

I took it and stood. "I have to tell you something. Buchanan was here tonight."

"Did he cause trouble?"

"No more than usual." At his frown, I added, "He wanted to talk to me about Lady Harcourt, as it happens."

"Why?"

I stifled another yawn and he tugged me toward the door, plucking the lamp from the table.

"Tell me tomorrow," he said.

He led me up the stairs to my room. I leaned back against the closed door and placed my hands on his shoulders, gently drawing him to me. His hand cupped my waist and he lowered the lamp.

"Orange blossoms." His whispered breath tickled my ear.

"Hmmm?"

"You smell like orange blossoms."

"I had a bath."

His lips brushed the skin of my neck. He drew in a deep breath then suddenly stepped away. I grasped his shoulders tighter in an attempt to keep him there.

"Kiss me," I murmured.

He hesitated. "We shouldn't."

"I don't care."

He glanced along the corridor and leaned toward me. His face was near mine. His eyes were two dark wells, as he stared at me.

"Kiss me," I said again, circling my arms around him.

He pecked my cheek. "Goodnight, Charlie."

I sighed and considered making a scene to get my way. But that was something the old Charlie would do, not this one. This one was more patient, more mature, and knew that she wouldn't get her way on this. "Goodnight, Lincoln."

* * *

"I can't make my mind up about him," I said to Lincoln as we drove toward Clerkenwell. He and I sat in the cabin while Seth and Gus sat on the driver's seat so we could discuss Buchanan's visit in private. "Is he a selfish, unscrupulous prick or is he trying to do the right thing by Lady H?"

"Don't try to understand either of them," Lincoln said. "They're driven by forces unlike any that drive you or I."

He'd listened impassively while I told him how the conversation with Buchanan had evolved. He didn't even seem surprised when I told him that Buchanan had been the one to notify the papers.

"You knew he did it, didn't you?" I asked him now.

"He was on my list of suspects, but not at the top."

"Did you warn her? Did she even know you had a list of suspects?"

"No. I wasn't investigating, merely surmising. Not for any particular reason," he added. "The exposure of her secret means nothing to me."

"I know." My heart lifted a little to hear him deny it, even though I already knew there was nothing between them now. "Shall we invite her to dinner parties we may have in the future? I suspect Lady V will wish to have a dinner for her friends, with eligible gentlemen on the guest list for Alice and ladies for Seth."

"If you want to invite her, then do so."

"I don't. Not really."

"Then we won't."

He wasn't being very helpful. "I'll worry about it when we decide to host something."

We stopped outside Clerkenwell and walked to the hole in the wall that led to the hideout. I slid the planks of wood aside and wriggled through.

"It's me," I announced to the guard on duty. "Charlie."

Finley grinned back at me, his gap-toothed smile just visible by the dull light. "You come for your answer?" he asked without preamble.

"Have you got one for me?"

"Depends." He hammered on the trapdoor.

"On what?"

"On what answers you give Mink."

The trapdoor flipped back and Mink's greasy head appeared. He peered at me through the curtain of hair and rested his elbows on the floor. He gave me a thorough inspection then climbed all the way through.

He glanced at the exit. "Your man out there again?"

I nodded.

"He's protective."

"He is."

"Does he treat you well? Or does he...?" It was impossible to see if he blushed, but from the way he dipped his head and wouldn't meet my gaze, I suspected he did.

"Fuck you?" Finley finished for him.

"*Finley!*" Mink sounded mortified.

"Pimp you?" Finley offered with a shrug.

"Bloody hell, you're an idiot."

I laughed to show him I didn't mind. A few crass words didn't shock me. "Lincoln treats me well. He employed me as a maid when I first lived with him, and now I work for him in the ministry."

"Ministry?" Mink asked. "That's who we're working for?"

"So you've accepted?"

"Depends. What's in it for us? Be specific."

"Regular food, warm clothes, money and blankets."

Mink scratched his neck. "We want medicines, too, for when we're sick."

"Yes."

"And supplies to fix this place up." He shoved his big toe, protruding from his boot, into the wall. Plaster sprinkled from the ceiling like snowflakes. "It's getting real old."

"You need to move out of here," I said, eyeing the ceiling. "It might collapse."

Mink snorted. "And go where?"

"You can come and live with us," I blurted out without thinking it through. What would Lincoln say to five extra residents, and adolescents at that? At least we had room. Gus's aunt did not.

Finley's face lit up. "Really?"

Mink put a hand on Finley's arm. "Depends on how this arrangement turns out," he said. "You trick us, we'll cut you up. You got it?"

I nodded, even though I didn't think Mink or Finley were capable of cutting anyone up. They might be desperate, and would protect themselves with violence if necessary, but Stringer was the cutting up for revenge sort, not these two.

"You can trust me," I said. "You know me."

"Aye, but can we trust him?" Mink jerked his head at the hole in the wall.

"Yes, you can. In time, you'll see that I'm speaking the truth. Do we have an arrangement?"

Finley and Mink glanced at one another. They exchanged no words or nods, but must have communicated in some way because they both turned back to me.

"We do," Mink said.

Finley spat on his palm and held it out to me.

Mink brushed him aside. "She's a girl now, remember?"

Finley wiped his hand down his shirt. "Right. Forgot." His gaze dipped to my chest.

"Come outside and meet Lincoln Fitzroy," I said.

"He the one with the money?" Mink asked.

I nodded and went out first. Finley followed. He blinked at the sudden brightness, even though it was another dreary day. Mink came through next, hesitating when he saw Lincoln leaning on the wall opposite.

Lincoln nodded a greeting. Mink nodded back and looked to me. Since Lincoln made no move to approach them, I led the way.

"This is Mr. Fitzroy," I said. "Lincoln, this is Mink, and you already met Finley."

Finley crossed his arms as Lincoln did and puffed out his chest. Mink remained a few feet away, warily assessing. Lincoln put out his hand and took a step forward. Mink paused then shook it.

"We have a task for you," Lincoln said.

Mink glanced up and down the lane, but we were alone. The wind, cold and threat of rain kept the streets quiet. "Something that'll get us into trouble with the bobbies?" he asked.

"No. Information gathering. There's a man known as King from the East End, most likely Whitechapel. He'll be mid-thirties, receding brown hair, and has large hands and feet."

Finley snorted a laugh. "You want us to look at every old man's hands and feet?"

"Mid-thirties is not old."

"You would say that."

"What else can you tell us about this King?" Mink asked.

"He inspires a great deal of loyalty in his friends," Lincoln said.

Mink waited. When Lincoln didn't go on, he said. "That's it? That's all you can tell us?"

"He drinks at the Cat and Fiddle, or used to."

"That ain't much."

"It's all we have," I told them.

Lincoln handed Mink a pouch of money. The coins clinked musically as Mink tore the drawstring open. Finley grinned. "Cor, I ain't never seen so much ready before."

Mink pocketed the money and once again glanced up and down the lane. "It might take a few days."

Lincoln nodded. "Be discreet."

"Be careful," I added. "If anyone seems to get suspicious, stop asking. Don't put yourselves in danger. And don't let anyone know who you work for." I suddenly regretted giving them Lincoln's name in case they were forced to reveal it.

"Never thought you were one for rules, Charlie," Finley said with a chuckle.

"I've changed."

He glanced at my chest again. "Aye."

"I live at Lichfield Towers in Highgate on the edge of the Heath," Lincoln said. "It's the big estate with iron gates on Hampstead Lane. Come there if you have anything to report."

We watched Finley and Mink return to their hideout then we turned to go. "You shouldn't have told them where we live," I said.

"You don't trust them?"

I glanced back over my shoulder. The plank of wood had stopped swinging, hiding the door completely. "I don't know."

* * *

168

LINCOLN HAD some informants he wanted to question alone, so Seth, Gus and I returned home without him. We arrived at the same time as the post.

Alice met me on her way to the library, a book in hand. "There's a letter for you," I said, passing it to her.

She tucked the book under her arm and opened the letter. She read it once then re-read it. The color leached from her face. "I can't believe this," she said, shaking her head over and over. "The nerve of them!"

"Of who?"

"My parents." She looked up at me, her eyes full of tears. "They're demanding that I return to the school immediately. If I don't, they'll have Mr. Fitzroy arrested for abducting me."

CHAPTER 10

"They can't do that!" I accepted the letter she handed to me. "They disowned you." Alice's parents had refused to pay her school fees any longer and ordered her not to return home. She'd had nowhere else to go but here.

She folded the book against her chest and looked as if she would burst into tears. "I don't want to bring trouble here or to Mr. Fitzroy. You've all been so kind to me, and you have enough worries."

I shook my head as I read. It said they regretted their hasty decision to cast Alice out and traveled to the school to take her home for Christmas. There they learned that she had fled here after receiving their message, and they now worried that Lichfield was a den of sin and that Lincoln is a whoremaster. "Good lord, it's so outrageous as to be laughable," I said.

"I'm not laughing, Charlie, and neither are they, I'm sure. My parents always think the worst of strangers."

"If they were that worried, why not come here themselves? Why send a letter?"

"Because they don't really care what happens to me. They simply want to be *seen* to be doing the right thing." At my frown, she added, "Me being here makes me look wayward. If any of their friends found out, they'd be horrified. My parents care more about the opinions of their acquaintances then my wellbeing."

"In that case, the threat to have Lincoln arrested is just that, a threat. Going through with it would bring them notoriety they don't want."

"They would be horrified," she agreed. She blew out a breath and looked relieved beyond measure. "Hopefully you're right and it's just an empty threat."

Doyle appeared from the shadows at the back of the entrance hall which led to the kitchen and service area. "My apologies, miss, I didn't hear you arrive home," he said.

I handed the letter back to Alice and removed my coat and hat. Doyle took them, and I walked with Alice to the library.

"Write a polite response," I said. "Tell them you're simply visiting me and will, of course, return home if they wish."

"But I don't want to go! They hate me."

"I doubt they hate you. It's more likely they're afraid of you." I hooked my arm through hers. "Afraid of your dreams."

"I suppose," she said heavily. "But they might make me go back to the school. Charlie, what if they insist I return to the school *forever*?"

It had been something that I'd feared too when I'd been sent to the school in Yorkshire. Sometimes, students with nowhere else to go after their graduation were employed by Mrs. Denk as teachers. Those women never left, and were unlikely to. The thought filled me with hopelessness.

"We'll cross that bridge when we come to it," I said. "For now, just tell them that Mrs. Denk didn't want you to return. Lincoln can write to your parents, too, and reassure them that you're welcome here and that you're a good companion to me, his...ward."

"Not fiancée?" she asked.

I removed my arm from hers. "His letter requires a delicate and amiable touch. Perhaps I should draft it. I'll end it with an invitation for them to visit and see our household for themselves." There. That ought to ward off any more threats of arrest.

Alice, however, didn't seem quite so convinced. "It's something, I suppose."

I spent the rest of the morning discussing housekeeping matters with Mrs. Cotchin, including the employment of more staff. Lady V sat in on the meeting, but didn't interfere unless I asked her opinion, which I did frequently. I had a lot to learn. Running a household the size of Lichfield was not an insignificant task. Mrs. Cotchin and Doyle had already discussed how many extra servants were needed, and had settled on two maids and a footman, with extra ones to be employed on a temporary basis for balls or dinner parties. Mrs. Cotchin already had candidates in mind.

If deferring to me and not Lincoln or Lady V struck Mrs. Cotchin as odd, she didn't say. It didn't occur to me until after she left how it must appear. I was not the senior lady of the house, I wasn't engaged to Lincoln, nor was I officially his ward, yet everyone treated me as if I was in charge in his absence.

I had a mind to sneak into his rooms and try on the ring, but his return after luncheon put an end to that idea. I got the opportunity to see the ring again when he called a meeting in his study over luncheon.

Doyle brought in a tray of cold meats and salads, but I was momentarily distracted from the food by the ring box. It had moved. It no longer sat at the back of the desk, but near the front. Had he moved it? Had Doyle? He was the only servant allowed in, to clean and make the bed each morning. Mrs. Cotchin hadn't yet earned Lincoln's trust. But surely Doyle knew not to move anything, or if he did, to put everything back exactly as it was.

I eyed Lincoln to see if he'd realized that I'd noticed, but he concentrated on his plate of food.

"I have a lead," he said after a moment. "There's definitely a man named King in the area, but I can't pin him down. One lead tells me he lives in Pelham Street, another says he's in the vicinity of Swallow Gardens, and another claims there's a King in Lower Chapman. I did find the man named King in Pelham, but it's not the right one."

"Wrong age?" Seth asked.

"Wrong hands. They were smaller than mine. He was also blond."

"Did you go to Swallow Gardens and Lower Chapman?" I asked.

He shook his head. "I want to watch the areas, not ask more questions. Too suspicious. To watch both places on my own is too time consuming."

"You need us," Gus said, his mouth full of ham. "Want to go now?"

"Finish your lunch. We'll take a cab. You two watch Lower Chapman, one positioned at either end. I'll watch Swallow Gardens alone. There's only one exit."

"He might not be at either," I said.

"He might not. There was also a report that he's not in Whitechapel at all, but moved out of the district a few years ago. My source didn't know where."

We finished our luncheon, and the three of them prepared to head out, but I asked Lincoln to remain. "A quick word before you go," I said, turning my back to his desk and the mystery of the moved ring box. "It's about Alice. She received a letter from her parents demanding she return to the school. They're worried she's fallen prey to your charms and has become your mistress."

His brows flew up his forehead. "They have good imaginations for a couple as staid as Alice claims them to be."

"She's already written to them and explained the situation, but I think you ought to write too. Be friendly and agreeable, and reassure them that she's here merely to keep me company. Then invite them to stay."

"More visitors?"

"Alice doesn't think they'll come. She thinks they're doing this for show, and they won't follow through on their threat."

"I'll write to them this evening."

"Or I could draft a response on your behalf, since you're so busy and I have nothing better to do. You can copy it later, or change it, if you like."

"I like your plan."

He went to leave but I caught his hand. "Be careful today. It's not all that long ago that you were confined to bed with exhaustion and a head injury."

"I'll be more careful than usual." He pressed a warm, soft kiss on my forehead.

"You will?"

He drew away. "You make me want to be careful." He strode off, leaving me more certain than ever that there'd been times in his life when he hadn't cared about his own safety. That had changed.

After they left, I sat at my escritoire and drafted the letter from Lincoln to Alice's parents. I was just re-reading it when Doyle announced two visitors.

"Names of Finley and Mink," he said, wrinkling his nose. "They're waiting outside at the back of the house."

I invited the boys into the kitchen, keeping to one end, away from the painter and his apprentice putting the finishing touches to the wall. Cook handed each boy a bowl of hearty beef and vegetable soup. Finley blew on it then sipped straight from the bowl. Mink used the spoon. Despite the steam rising from the soup, they managed to consume it all in under a minute.

"Do we have anything else?" I asked Cook. "Some cake, perhaps?"

"Cake!" Finley's eyes almost popped out of his head. "We can have *cake*?"

Cook chuckled. "Aye, if you like fruitcake." He headed into the pantry to retrieve the leftover Christmas cake.

"Just a small portion," I said. "If you eat too much of anything you'll be sick." I'd eaten too much too quickly when I first came to Lichfield and thrown it all up in the corner of the tower room. Those days seemed so long ago now, but a mere seven months had passed. It felt like a lifetime.

Cook unwrapped the cake and cut off two small pieces and handed them to the boys on plates. Finley ate his in two bites, but Mink nibbled more carefully yet no less enthusiastically.

"Mmmm," Finley said around his mouthful of fruitcake. "This is the best thing I ever tasted. Eh, Mink? You ever had somefing as good as this?"

Mink didn't respond. He simply looked away, but not before I saw tears in his eyes. I'd wager he had tasted Christmas cake before, and the taste brought back memories of a happier time, perhaps Christmases spent with a loving family.

Doyle, Mrs. Cotchin, Cook and I watched them eat and drink. Finley finished first and got up to warm himself by the range. When Mink finished, he picked up his plate and cup.

"Where's the scullery?" he asked.

"I'll take them," Mrs. Cotchin said with a motherly smile.

"Come with me to the parlor," I said. "The fire's burning."

"Wait!" Doyle rushed out ahead of me, not running, but

doing an odd fast walk. He headed into the store room and emerged a moment later with sheets. He handed one to each of the boys. "Sit on these. Mrs. Cotchin doesn't want your smells penetrating the furnishings."

"Be off with you, Mr. Doyle," Mrs. Cotchin chided. "They don't smell so bad." She did not, however, ask him to remove the sheets.

She was right and the boys didn't reek. They both wore the new clothes I'd given them the first day we'd gone to their den. A strong smell still wafted from them, but it was from their bodies, not the clothes.

I led Mink and Finley into the parlor. They both stopped inside the doorway and stared in wonder at the luxurious furniture, the thick curtains, and the expensive vases and other knickknacks. I'd been equally overwhelmed when I first saw the room.

Finley moved first. He set his sheet on the rug in front of the fireplace and sat down cross-legged. He stretched his fingers toward the heat. Mink followed but laid his towel out on one of the armchairs. He sat and stretched his feet and hands toward the fireplace.

I scooped some coal from the scuttle and added it to the fire.

"You done well for yourself, Charlie," Finley said quietly. "Real well. You sure you ain't his doxy?"

Mink kicked him.

"I'm quite sure," I said with a laugh.

"How'd it happen, then?" Finley asked. "How'd you get so lucky? Last I remember, you was being chased by some big men."

Although he asked the question, it was Mink who eyed me closely. He was as interested in my answer as Finley. Perhaps more so.

"It's a long story," I said. "The short version is that I was in possession of some information that Mr. Fitzroy wanted. He brought me here to extract it, and once I realized the importance of the organization's work, I agreed to stay and help."

"But his men roughed you up," Finley said, now giving me his full attention.

"Not as badly as you would think." I'd been terrified of Lincoln and his men in the beginning, but he'd never raised a hand to me, or allowed anyone else to. He may have put me into a precarious situation to win me to his side, but he'd later acknowledged that had been a mistake, and I'd forgiven him. It had taken much longer for Lincoln to forgive himself.

"Bet they was surprised when they noticed you was a girl."

"Surprised is an understatement, Finley." We both laughed. Mink continued to watch me, but the wariness was gone from his eyes. He seemed awed, surrounded by fine things and me, the woman who used to be a boy in his gang. Awed and a little sad.

"So tell me," I said, "you have something to report already?"

"We do," Mink said, becoming businesslike. "We decided not to ask for the man by name. Instead, we asked people if they knew someone with really big hands."

"Real big," Finley echoed. "Gi-normous."

"That's clever," I said. It would separate them from Lincoln's own inquiries. Too many people asking about a fellow named King would raise suspicions.

"We only asked other gangs," Mink said. "Orphans, like us."

Another wise move. Mink was careful.

"Cross's gang knew someone with big hands." Finley took up the story. "Big feet, too. He sniffed out their hideout one day 'bout a year ago."

"Sniffed out?" I asked. "What do you mean?"

Finley shrugged. "That's what Cross said, sniffed out. He

stole a fresh baked loaf of bread from the baker and took it back to their den. He says next thing he knew, the big hand man came. Cross says he was sniffing, like he followed the smell of the bread there."

"He must have found it another way," Mink cut in. "He must have followed Cross there."

"Cross says he didn't, and I believe him. He couldn't have just found the den, neither. It's hard to find, like ours. You gotta know its there. So he must of smelled the bread."

"I believe you," I said. If the man shifted into an animal then he would have an excellent sense of smell, like Harriet. "So what happened then? Did he try to steal the bread?"

"Nope," Finley said. "He wanted them to work for him."

"Doing what?"

"Running messages, spying, that sort of thing. He said his gang needed some children to work for 'em."

"His gang?" I echoed. Could he be referring to the group of wolf-like shifters reported in the newspaper a year ago?

"Cross refused," Mink said. "When he asked the man why he needed children, the man said it was because young 'uns don't get noticed when they're little. It's not 'til they're older and bigger that they get caught. That got Cross worried. He's real careful, and he protects his gang. It sounded like the man wanted them to do something dangerous, or something that'd get them in big trouble with the pigs, so he refused."

"And what did the man say then?"

"Nothing," Finley said. "He left and didn't ask again. Cross reckons he found another group of children. Plenty of 'em in London, and most ain't careful like Cross."

Very true. Cross sounded a lot like Mink. His name wasn't one I recognized from my days living on the streets. "Did he describe the man's appearance to you?" I asked.

"He did better than that." Mink's lips stretched into a small smile, the first I'd ever seen on his face. It made him look even younger, like the child he was, instead of the adolescent he was pretending to be. "He said he often sees the man around, but he's always at the same place at the same time, every day like a clock."

I sat forward on the chair. "Where?"

"Butcher in Smithfield. Cross reckons they have a regular arrangement. The man with the big feet goes to the butcher's at the end of the day, after the market's all closed and everyone's gone. He gets any bones that's not sold and are starting to go off."

"How late in the day?"

"Dusk."

I glanced out the window. The rain had held off, but it was still cloudy. Dusk arrived early in January and must be about two hours away.

"Lincoln should be back by then," I said. "In the mean time, who would like a bath?"

Finley looked horrified. "What we want to do that for?"

"I can get kerosene for the lice," I said as Mink scratched his head. "Or we could shave your heads. Yes, let's do that first, and then you can have a bath. Mink?"

"S'pose," he muttered.

Finley sniffed then wiped his nose on his sleeve. "Not me. I like my dirt, and my lice."

"You do not," I said with absolute certainty. "I heard you complain about the lice a thousand times when I lived with you."

"I did not!"

"You do," Mink said.

"Come on then," I said cheerfully. "Let's do it outside in the courtyard." I rose and so did Mink, but Finley stayed stubbornly on the rug.

"I ain't moving," he mumbled.

Alice walked in, but stopped when she saw the boys. "I'm

sorry, I didn't realize you had company." She smiled at them. "Are these friends of yours, Charlie?"

Finley jumped to his feet and wiped his hands down his trousers. He bowed to hide his red cheeks. "Name's Finley," he said. "Pleased to meet you."

"Finley, Mink, this is Miss Everheart," I said.

"Everheart," Finley repeated. "Pretty name." He grinned.

She smiled back.

"I was just taking the boys outside to give them haircuts. Lice," I added.

She pulled a face. "Do you want me to fetch Bella?"

"Thank you."

She headed up the stairs while I led the boys back to the service rooms. Finley came meekly, his cheeks still a little pink.

"You think there'll be time for baths after?" he asked, glancing back over his shoulder.

I smiled. "Of course. You can go first, if that's all right with Mink."

Cook set up a chair in the courtyard while Mrs. Cotchin fetched warm water and clean towels, and Doyle looked for scissors and a razor.

Alice returned, shaking her head. "Bella refused, and Lady Vickers stood up for her," she said. "She doesn't want Bella catching their lice and giving it to her." She drew in a fortifying breath and began rolling up her sleeves.

"I'll do it," Doyle said.

"There's no need, Doyle," I told him.

"I don't mean any disrespect," he said, removing his jacket. "But have either of you used a razor before?"

Alice and I looked at one another. "Perhaps you're right," I said. "We'll assist you."

Finley sat down and meekly allowed Doyle to shorten his hair with the scissors first then shave the rest off. Afterward, he ran his hands over his bald head. "Do I look like him now?" He nodded at Cook.

Cook scrubbed his head.

"You've got eyebrows and lashes," Mink told Finley.

Mrs. Cotchin had gone to draw the bath and came out to announce that it was ready. She took Finley upstairs while Mink sat for his haircut. "When we get home, we're getting rid of all the blankets, the mattress, all of it," he said.

"I'll see what I can find here to replace them," I told him. "Are you sure you don't want to spend the night? We can fetch the other boys."

He didn't answer straight away, and I suspected this was something they'd discussed after we left this morning and a decision had not yet been made. "Not tonight," was all he said. "Maybe later."

So they were waiting to see how this arrangement turned out, and if we could be trusted. I didn't blame him. I'd find it hard to trust people being so kind to me, too, even if one of them was an old gang member.

After his haircut, Mink went up for his bath. Finley helped Doyle gather all the spare blankets and a few pillows that we could find. He turned out to be quite a handsome lad, despite his crooked teeth, but not as handsome as Mink. Without the greasy, lank hair covering Mink's face and the dirt on his skin, he appeared older. I guessed him to be about fifteen, although it was difficult to tell, as thin as he was.

"You both scrub up well," Alice said, inspecting the boys like they were about to lead a parade. "I'm very impressed."

"The blankets are stored in the coach," Doyle announced. "When would you like them and the boys delivered to their home?"

"Not yet," I said. "The boys will go out with Lincoln when he returns." I checked the clock. It was nearing four. If he didn't get home soon, it would be dark and the opportunity gone. "Perhaps we'll have tea while we wait."

"There's no time for tea." Mink looked out the parlor window at the sky. "If we don't go now, we'll miss him. You'll have to wait for tomorrow."

Another day would only drag things out. I bit my lip and looked at the sky. Lincoln would hate me going without him. He'd worry.

But Smithfield wasn't Whitechapel, and the fellow meeting the butcher hadn't harmed Cross or any of the others.

"Doyle, I'm going to a butcher's in Smithfield. The boys will come with me. Will you drive us?"

"Won't the market be closed now, Miss?"

"We're not there to shop. Please ready the carriage. Ask Cook to help if you need it."

"Hang about," Finley said, going pale. "We're going to *drive* there?"

I nodded. "Alice—"

"I'm coming with you," she said before I could ask. "You're not going alone."

I smiled. "I was hoping you'd say that. It'll be quite safe. We won't even need to get out." She fetched coats, hats and gloves and we waited for Doyle to bring the coach around.

Cook handed each of the boys a woolen cap. "You'll be needing these now. Mind you put up your collars. You be noticing the wind on your necks more."

The boys put on their caps and pulled up their collars. "Thanks Mr. Cook," Mink said, holding out his hand.

Cook shook it.

Finley was too busy staring at the horses and coach, approaching from around the side of the house, to shake hands. He gulped audibly.

"Are you afraid of horses?" I asked him quietly.

"No. I ain't never been in no coach before."

"You'll be quite safe." I put out my hand, but he didn't take the hint.

Mink, however, did. He crooked his arm and I took it. He led me down the front steps to the coach. I looked back to see Finley catching on and offering his arm to Alice. She smiled sweetly and accepted it. His blush disappeared into his cap.

"Call out when you're ready, miss," Doyle said from the driver's seat.

"Just a moment, I've got an idea. Doyle, please take us to Lord and Lady Gillingham's residence in Mayfair first. I want to ask Lady Gillingham if she'd like to join us."

"Why?" Alice asked once we were settled on the seats, the spare blankets intended for the boys' den piled on our laps.

"Because she needs the adventure, and to do things her husband doesn't want her to do." It was, perhaps, a fool's errand. She'd most likely refuse to come with us, preferring to abide by her husband's wishes. Of course, she may not even be home, or he might be, and then my plan would come to naught. But the devil inside me wanted to try, wanted to encourage Harriet to stand up to her husband in this small way.

Fortunately, Harriet was home but her husband was not. She was allowed to receive callers and go out. "But not with you," she added, greeting me in the entrance hall. "Gilly said if you came here, you weren't to be allowed past the entrance." Hence why I spoke to her on the threshold with the door open.

I eyed the butler. He stood to one side, attempting to be unobtrusive, yet we both knew he would report every word of our conversation to his master. It wasn't going to be easy to convince Harriet. Indeed, how hard did I want to try? She wasn't integral to our plan.

Yet I wanted her to come with us, and I had an idea on how to go about it. "The thing is," I said, "we're going to see someone about a glover who makes special gloves for ladies with large hands. I thought you'd like to come along and see the gloves for yourself."

She looked offended and tucked her hands behind her back. Then it was as if the clouds cleared and she understood the true meaning of my words. *Yes*, I wanted to tell her. *I've found someone like you.* "You do want to meet him, don't you?" I asked. "There may never be another opportunity."

"Yes," she whispered, her eyes two huge pools. "Very much." She studied her hands then curled them into fists. "I'd like to meet a new glover." She turned to the butler. "Fetch my coat, please, Owen. I'm going out."

"Er...my lady..." The poor butler didn't know what to do. "Perhaps you ought to wait for his lordship to return."

"No. I'm going out, with or without a coat."

He did not move. His face grew paler by the second, his eyes anxious as they darted past me, perhaps praying his master would suddenly appear and take charge.

Harriet simply gave a small shake of her head and ushered me out the door. She closed it herself and took my arm. "I don't need a coat anyway." Her senses may be acute, but she didn't feel the cold.

"Will your butler get into trouble?" I asked.

"Probably. I don't care. I don't like him."

We hurried to the coach and climbed in. Mink folded up the step then joined Finley and Doyle on the driver's seat. Harriet eyed Alice warily, even after I introduced them.

"Alice knows about you," I said.

Harriet blinked back tears. "You told her?"

Alice smiled warmly. "Don't be cross with Charlie. She knew I'd understand. My nightmares come to life, you see. A few weeks ago an entire army chased me. If it weren't for

Charlie, I'd still think I was a madwoman. I'd also be alone in the world."

Harriet's hands had been buried in her skirts to hide them, but she now settled them on her lap, hesitantly splaying them to reveal their full size. "An entire army? How frightening."

I laid my gloved hand over her bare one. "We all have each other now. We're not alone."

"Charlie, are we truly going to speak to someone like me?" Harriet asked. "Someone who can change shape?"

I nodded. "The boys told us about him."

"Have they seen him change?"

"No, but he has gi-normous hands and feet, according to Finley."

"Where is Mr. Fitzroy? Shouldn't he be here?"

"He wasn't at home, but I couldn't let this opportunity slip away. I'm sure the man is harmless. Besides, I thought you might have some questions to ask him, and I suspected you'd want to meet someone like you."

"Oh yes. Very much."

The sun retreated behind the buildings and the muted colors of dusk descended. Lamp lighters began their rounds, blowing on cold fingers before lifting their long poles to the lamp casings. We didn't stop out the front of the Smithfield Market, but drove through to the central avenue dividing the market into two halves. The great iron supports holding up the louvered ceiling yawned overhead, and individual butcher's stores occupied both sides. The market was quiet, having closed to the public hours ago. A few butchers lingered, sweeping away dirt and straw by the light of the lamps, or mopping blood from floors and walls. Enormous hooks swung gently in the breeze. Overnight, carcasses would be brought up from the underground railway and hung, ready to sell in the morning.

The last time I'd been in a butcher's shop, dead bodies had hung from the cold room hooks, put there by a mad doctor employed by General Eastbrooke. I shivered at the memory and pulled the edges of my coat tighter.

Our carriage slowed and finally stopped. I went to open the door, but Alice stayed my hand.

"Shouldn't we merely look?" she asked.

"I can't see him from in here," I said. "It'll be all right. Stay here, if you want."

She didn't get a chance to answer. Harriet pushed open the door and climbed out without waiting for the step to be lowered. I followed her. The smell of blood and meat seemed to come from the very walls themselves. It wasn't powerful, but it would likely never entirely disappear. Up ahead, two men stood talking. The butcher, dressed in a worn leather apron, handed a parcel wrapped in paper to a large man with rounded shoulders. He bobbed his head courteously to the butcher and took the parcel with hands much larger than a normal man's.

"Excuse me," Harriet called out, rushing ahead, her neat bustle bobbing with her brisk steps. She didn't care that her hem skimmed the dirty floor.

"Harriet, wait!" I lifted my skirts and rushed after her. "We need to be cautious."

She didn't stop. "Excuse me, sir, may we speak with you?"

The man glanced over his shoulder, took one look at us and our coach, then turned and ran. Damnation! I ran after him, but he was too fast. I'd never catch him.

"Stop!" Harriet's clear voice echoed along the avenue. "Stop, I say! I want to speak with you. I'm like you! Look at my hands!"

The man's pace slowed. He once again glanced back at us, then he stopped altogether. He did not approach, but Harriet strode up to him.

"Wait, Harriet," I said. "We need to exercise caution."

"I don't think she wants to be cautious," Alice said, breathing heavily as she drew up alongside me. Doyle urged the horses forward in a walk.

"Stay back," the man shouted, shoving the parcel of meat down his shirt. "Don't come near. What do you want?"

"I want to talk to you," Harriet said, her voice full of wonder. She held up her hands, to show him their size again. "I want to talk to someone like me."

CHAPTER 11

The man's bristly black whiskers and bushy crop of hair hid much of his face and gave him a fierce countenance. Together with his muscular build and quick, assessing gaze, it wasn't difficult to envisage him as a wild animal. He edged closer, cautious yet curious.

"Blimey," he murmured. "But you're..."

"A woman?" Harriet offered.

"A toff. Ain't never seen a toff one of us."

"Us?" Her voice quavered with barely contained excitement.

"Aye."

"Where do you all live?"

"Here and there." The man stopped approaching as if he suddenly realized he was too close. He remained vigilant, his gaze darting from us to the coach and back to Harriet. He didn't trust us, but I couldn't blame him—I hadn't trusted anyone searching for me last summer either. "You can't have it," he said. "It's mine. I ain't sharing."

"Can't have what?" Harriet asked.

He crossed his arms over the bulge at his chest where he'd tucked the parcel. The butcher had disappeared.

The horses shifted, rattling the harness. I glanced at Doyle and the boys, sitting rigid on the driver's seat. Finley gripped his knees, his knuckles white, and Mink looked as if he would dive off the coach at the first sign of trouble. The light from the carriage lamps glinted off the metal of a pistol in Doyle's lap.

"We don't want your meat," I said to the man. "Keep your food."

Harriet sniffed the air, her nose twitching like a dog's on the scent of a rat. "Lamb?"

"Mutton," he said. "I paid for these bones. They're mine. Ask the butcher."

"My friend spoke the truth," Harriet said. "We don't want your meat. We just want to talk."

"What about?"

"I have so many questions." She lowered her voice, perhaps so Doyle and the boys couldn't hear. If I'd stood as far away as the man, I wouldn't have heard her, but he seemed to hear perfectly.

"What's your name?" I asked before Harriet could get her questions in.

"Gawler, miss."

Not King, then. "My name is Charlotte," I said, "and this is Alice and Harriet." I didn't want to use surnames or titles. Those could be easily traced. If I'd learned anything over the last few years, it was best to exercise caution when it came to identities. "Harriet is curious about you," I said. "She knows no other shifters, you see, so when we heard about you—"

"How'd you hear?"

"We heard of body shifters living in the area years ago, so made some inquiries."

"You made inquiries? Are you mad?"

"About hands," I clarified. "We asked about someone with big hands, not about a shifter."

My answer mollified him somewhat. He nodded at Harriet. "There are six, including me."

"And you all roam through the East End?" I asked. "In a group?

"Not anymore," Gawler said, his top lip lifting in a way that reminded me of a dog snarling. "Our pack broke apart."

"Why?" Harriet asked.

"There was a fight. Me and the pack leader." He hunched and tightened his arms around his chest, as if protecting his parcel of mutton bones. "I got tired of him telling us what to do, see. Tired of him making all the decisions, 'specially when he made the wrong one."

"But he won," I said heavily.

He sniffed and wiped his nose on his sleeve. "He won."

"A fight?" Harriet whispered. "That sounds dangerous."

He pulled his jacket and shirt aside at the shoulder to reveal three ugly scars. I didn't need to ask to know they were made by a claw. So they'd fought in their animal form.

Beside me, Alice smothered a gasp.

Gawler covered the scars. "You're better off in your toff house," he said to Harriet. "It's dangerous out here, for regular humans and for our kind. You stay safe and pretty where you are and don't mix with us. You married to a human?"

Harriet nodded.

"Good. Breed it out, I say. One day, there'll be none of us left."

"Why would you want to do that?" I asked.

He tapped his scarred shoulder. "If our numbers grow, there'll be more fights. We males can't help it. Fighting is in our nature, but the humans will fear us if they see. They'll lock us away. I been locked away one night for being drunk, and that were enough for me. You put me in a cage forever and I'll die."

I understood completely. One night in a holding cell was enough for me, too. "Where's the rest of the pack now?" I asked. "With the leader?"

"He moved out to Bloomsbury." He hawked a glob of saliva onto the floor where the dirt and straw soaked it up. "The others still live in the East End."

"I don't understand. If he's the leader, why aren't they with him?"

"We don't live together, miss. We're friends, not mates. Not husband and wife. They see him at his house sometimes, or he visits them, and they run through the streets at night in their other form together."

"And you?" I asked quietly.

His top lip lifted again, revealing normal, human teeth. "I run alone."

"I'll run with you." Harriet spoke in a rush, as if afraid she'd change her mind if she thought it through first. "I'll be in your pack."

"Harriet," I warned.

Gawler shook his head. "Stay away from us. This ain't no life for you."

"But I *want* to run," she said. "I haven't run anywhere since I was a little girl, but I desperately want to. Sometimes I dream about racing through the fields on our estate, the wind tangling my hair, the earth beneath my feet. I imagine it to be liberating."

Gawler grunted. "You go and run in your fields where it's safe and no one can see." He nodded at Doyle, sitting on the driver's seat with the pistol in his lap. "It's dangerous for our kind, especially here where there's more witnesses. You stay away from us. From *him*."

"The leader?" I asked.

He nodded.

"What's his name?"

"He likes to be called King."

Alice's hand tightened on my arm.

"I've known him since I were thirteen," Gawler said. "That's when he came to London. Don't know where from. We did everything together—played, laughed, even kissed the same girls. Running through the streets with King was liberating, like you say, ma'am. We felt like we ruled the East End. He *was* the king, and I were the prince, I s'pose. Maybe that's why he called himself that." Gawler sounded like he missed him as any man would miss a friend after they were gone. I wondered if he regretted fighting for the leadership.

"Why was he your leader?" I asked. "Was he stronger than the others?"

"Aye, but there's more to it than that. A leader's got to be liked. King's liked, all right." He sneered. "Some think he can do anything he wants, and they bow to him like he really is the king sometimes."

"*Can* he do anything he wants? Can he *be* anything he wants?"

His gaze sharpened. He swallowed. I had my answer—King was the man we needed.

"He can shift into all sorts of different shapes, can't he?" I pressed when Gawler didn't respond.

He backed away. "I didn't tell you that. I didn't say nothing."

"Where can we find him?"

"I have to go."

"No!" both Harriet and I cried.

"Please, Mr. Gawler," she said. "I have so many questions. Are there any women in your pack?"

"I told you, they ain't my pack no more."

"But you're still friends."

He lifted one shoulder.

"I want to speak to them," she said, striding up to him. She reached for him, but he shrank back and she let her hands drop to her sides. "Please, where can I find them?"

He glanced toward the exit. "Best you don't come looking. We don't want no attention." He tilted his chin at me. "Most of us don't want no trouble."

"What about Mr. King?" I asked. "Does he court trouble by shifting into the shape of others?"

His nostrils flared and he sniffed the air. Drawing in my scent and committing it to memory? "King ain't my concern no more. I don't care if he gets into trouble. I don't want none of it, you hear?"

"What has he done?"

He paced backward but kept his gaze on Harriet, matching him step for step. "Please," she begged, her voice shaking. "Please, I want to meet the others."

"Mr. Gawler," I snapped. "This is important. The royal family may be in danger."

He stopped. Stared at me. His throat worked but he didn't speak. He could only shake his head, over and over. Then he turned and sprinted away.

"Wait!" Harriet cried. She did not, however, try to run after him.

I took her hand and she allowed me to lead her back to the coach. She sat in the cabin, blinking back tears. "I can't believe he would run off like that," she muttered. "What am I to do now?"

"Nothing," Alice said. "Mr. Gawler spoke of the dangers, and I see his point. You must protect yourself and stay away."

Harriet hunkered in the corner, a pout on her lips and a hollowness to her eyes. We emerged from the market and rolled along the street. As miserable as Harriet was, I couldn't be unhappy. We had a name *and* a place now. Gawler had mentioned that King lived in Bloomsbury. Lincoln had been looking in the wrong area, that's why he couldn't find him. And from Gawler's reaction, I knew King was the man we needed.

We deposited Finley and Mink back at their Clerkenwell home along with the blankets. They both looked rather pale by the light of the coach lamps. They couldn't have heard our conversation with Gawler from where they sat, but they'd seen Doyle's pistol and the scars on Gawler's shoulder. They must have guessed the meeting could have turned dangerous.

"Will you be all right?" I asked them as I carried an armful of blankets to the boards covering the entrance to their den.

"Course," Finley said. "Weren't nothing to be scared of."

Mink lifted the boards with his foot and threw the blankets inside.

"Mink?" I asked as he reached for the stack in my arms. "What about you?"

He took the blankets, but I didn't let go. He narrowed his gaze. "Tell Mr. Fitzroy we won't be doing any more spying for you."

"What?" Finley blurted out. "And miss out on more of this?" He indicated the blankets. "Mink, we can't afford not to spy for 'em."

"You're an idiot, Finley, if you think they care for us. Don't let these blankets fool you."

"Of course we care," I said. "We don't want to see you put in harm's way. I understand if the meeting tonight scared you."

"We ain't scared," Finley said, puffing out his chest.

I held Mink's gaze until he looked away. "I got to think of the young 'uns," he said. "I got to keep them safe."

"Then come and live with us. We have room. Mr. Fitzroy won't mind."

"And do more spying for him?"

"Not if you don't want to. He won't ask you to do anything you're not comfortable doing."

Mink shook his head. "He'll ask. That type always want something in return."

"They do not," I said, indignant. I let go of the blankets. "You're wrong about him, Mink, but I understand if you feel overwhelmed and unsure right now. You know where to find us if you change your mind, or if you simply need something. Don't go hungry anymore. It's not necessary."

His lips flattened, and I could see he understood the benefit of coming to us on occasion. I suspected if it was just him, his pride would stop him accepting something for nothing, but he genuinely seemed to care for the others in his charge. He wouldn't see them starve if there was an alternative.

I rested a hand on his shoulder. "Be careful."

He nodded.

Finley sighed. "Be seeing you soon, Fleet-foot Charlie." He touched the brim of his cap then disappeared through the hole in the wall.

Mink followed without a backward glance.

I returned to the coach, pausing at the door to give Mink an opportunity to change his mind, but the boards remained in place, unmoving. With a sigh, I climbed inside and Doyle drove off.

"You look troubled," Alice said quietly. "Are the boys all right?"

"Mink's rattled. He feels responsible for them all, and he worries that there'll be trouble now. He thinks Lincoln will ask for more from them, and expose them to danger."

"You reassured him, didn't you?"

"Yes, but he won't take my word for it." I sighed again. "It's a lot for young shoulders to bear."

"You bore it too, once."

195

"Not leadership. I never took on that task. I never wanted it." I didn't think Mink wanted it either, but it had been thrust upon him after Stringer's death. I wished I could do something for him, for all of them. I could, if only Mink would accept my help.

Alice squeezed my hand and I looked up at her. She gave a small nod in Harriet's direction, sitting opposite. Harriet stared out the window into the inky black streets of Clerkenwell. She wasn't very good at shielding her emotions, and her misery was written clear on her face.

"Harriet?" I asked softly. "Don't be too upset."

"How can I not be?" Her lower lip wobbled and she sniffed. "That was the first opportunity I've had to talk to someone like myself and he wasn't interested in talking to me."

Alice pulled a handkerchief out of her reticule and passed it to her. "I'm sorry, Harriet."

Harriet dabbed at her eyes and nose. "So am I. I wanted to ask a woman shifter for advice."

"What sort of advice?"

"You wouldn't understand. Neither of you would. I mean...*look* at your lovely delicate hands!" She looked down at her thick, knobby fingers, twisting the corner of the handkerchief. "They're ugly. I'm ugly."

I swapped seats to sit beside her and put my arm around her shoulders. "You're beautiful. Look in the mirror. Everyone says so."

"Who?"

"Seth, for one." Too late, I realized my mistake. I'd hoped to cheer up Harriet, since she seemed to hold a torch for him. But Seth wouldn't want his name connected to Harriet's, or any woman's, in front of Alice.

Alice's spine stiffened, but I couldn't be sure if that meant she cared or she was simply adjusting her posture. "You are the prettiest, most elegant woman I've ever met," she said to Harriet. "Indeed, your face and figure are so feminine that I'm sure no one even looks at your hands."

"Oh." Harriet dabbed at her eyes and gave Alice a watery smile. "You're very sweet."

I smiled at Alice and mouthed, "Thank you."

"Perhaps Mr. Gawler didn't realize how important it was to me to meet the others in his pack," Harriet said. "I know he only wanted to protect me, but if he knew what it was like to never have met another, he would have invited me to do so, I'm sure."

"The East End really isn't for ladies," I said, patting her hand. "Perhaps I shouldn't have brought you."

"No, Charlie, don't think that!" She grasped my hand in hers, enveloping it almost entirely. "I feel so much better for having met Mr. Gawler. I do, honest. I don't care that he's from the slums. Indeed, he wasn't the violent, debauched sort I was expecting. He was quite civilized."

"You sound as if you were expecting a barbarian."

"It's what I've always been led to believe about men who live in the East End."

"They're not all criminals. Some are, but most are poor working men trying to earn enough to feed their families. It's a wretched existence, I'll give you that, but that doesn't mean they're wicked people."

"I see that now. If only he'd taken me to visit his friends, I wouldn't have minded walking through the streets at all. Look, my hem is dirty and I don't care a whit."

I eyed Alice opposite and she bit back a smile. Harriet was as silly and innocent as a child, sometimes. Gawler had done the right thing in refusing her. I'd hoped she'd have been satisfied simply to meet him, but it seemed I'd miscalculated. She wanted to speak to a woman. Perhaps after this was over, we could ask Gawler to negotiate a meeting with one. I wouldn't mention it to Harriet until I was sure it would go ahead. I didn't want to disappoint her if it didn't.

We deposited Harriet at her home and I was thoroughly grateful that Lord Gillingham was still out. I didn't want to battle with him.

"Will you be able to persuade your butler not to talk?" I asked as she stepped down from the carriage.

"Unlikely," she said. "I expect Gilly will lecture me on the dangers of associating with you when Owen tells him."

"Will he insist on locking you in your room again?"

"Not if I tell him I'll simply climb out while all the neighbors are watching and cause a scandal. I've seen you and Mr. Fitzroy do it, and I'm sure I can too. Gilly hates scandal."

I kissed her cheek through the window. "Good luck."

We didn't have to wait long after our arrival at Lichfield for Lincoln, Seth and Gus to return. I didn't need to ask how their afternoon had been. Frustration was written all over Seth and Gus's faces. Lincoln's was as unreadable as ever.

"Cook is putting together something for supper," I told them. "We'll take it in the parlor in front of the fire. Alice and I have news."

They'd been about to head upstairs to wash up, but they paused at my announcement.

"You've been out," Lincoln said. I tried to gauge his thoughts so I knew how to answer, but couldn't quite read him. I suspected he was holding back on something but I couldn't tell what or why.

"How do you know?" Alice asked.

"Your hems are dirty. Some of it's blood."

"Blood!" Gus and Seth cried.

Gus knelt and inspected my hem. "Bloody hell, Charlie, what've you been up to?"

Now I understood why Lincoln was holding back. He'd noticed the blood and had been waiting for me to broach the subject rather than asking me outright, or demanding that I tell him, which he would have done in the past.

"We could have simply gone for a walk around the garden," I said.

"Your defiance in the face of my simple statement that you've been out would suggest not."

"Damn," I muttered. "Next time I'll answer with as much indifference as you."

"Is there a reason you're reluctant to tell me where you've been and why you have blood on your dress?"

"Yes," Seth chimed in, hands on hips. "Isn't that why you want to talk to us in the first place?"

"It is, but I was hoping to approach the subject in such a way that wouldn't worry you, or anger you, or cause this sort of reaction." I waved a hand at Lincoln.

"What sort of reaction?" he asked. "I thought I was being very calm, considering there is blood on your dress." He crossed his arms defensively.

"We're quite unharmed."

"So I see."

"So there's nothing to worry about."

"I'll be the judge of that."

"Charlie!" Seth shouted. "Just tell us!"

Gus grabbed my elbow and marched me into the parlor. I glanced back over my shoulder at Lincoln. He merely arched his brow and followed. This wasn't going at all how I planned it in my head. I had planned to repeat what we'd learned from Gawler first then tell the story from the beginning, in the hope they'd be so grateful for the breakthrough they'd stop being overbearing.

"Sit," Gus said, directing me to a chair. He looked far more rattled than Lincoln. Perhaps because Gus wasn't very good at hiding his thoughts whereas Lincoln was a master at it.

Seth and Alice strolled into the parlor like a couple

heading into the dining room, her hand on his arm. She sat too. All the men remained standing.

"Sit down," I told them. "You're being so *male*."

All three sat.

"The blood isn't human, it's animal," I told them. "We've been to Smithfield Market."

Seth blew out a breath. "Is that all? Why didn't you say you went marketing?"

"Smithfield's closed by midday," Gus told him. "They weren't marketing."

"You're correct," I said. "We went to meet a man there by the name of Gawler. He's one of the shifters that Lord Erskine read about years ago."

Gus and Seth fired questions at us while Lincoln merely sat and waited. He leaned his elbow on the chair arm and stroked his lip with the side of his finger. He didn't take his gaze off me. He looked like he had all evening to hear my answers. I suppose he did.

Alice and I answered each question until our story was complete. "I'm sorry we didn't wait for you," I said. "But if we waited any longer, we would have missed him today, and tomorrow could be too late."

"I disagree," Seth grumbled. "It wasn't safe to meet a strange man, a shifter no less, in a meat market, of all places."

"Aye," Gus agreed.

"Charlie's right," Lincoln said, to my utter amazement.

"Have you gone mad?" Seth shook his head. "Anything could have happened!"

"They're grown women, free to do as they please. Both are sensible."

"You are mad."

"Seth," I warned him. "No woman likes to be told what she can and can't do." I jerked my head in Alice's direction, but I wasn't sure he got my meaning. He did, however, remain mercifully quiet.

"As to the matter of taking Lady Gillingham with you," Lincoln said. "I'm not so sure that was wise."

"Nor am I," I said on a sigh. "In hindsight, perhaps I shouldn't have. For one thing, I'm worried I've landed her in further trouble with her husband, and for another, she didn't seem too happy when Gawler ran off."

"She wanted more," Alice told them. "She wanted to meet the others. Meeting him wasn't enough."

"You weren't to know that," Lincoln said. He gave me a small smile, and I smiled back. It seemed quite impossible, but we'd reached the end of the discussion unscathed with neither of us storming out or shouting. That conversation would have tested our relationship in the past.

I told Lincoln as much after the others retired for the night. "Once upon a time you would have been cross with me for going out without you," I said, coming to sit on the arm of his chair.

He rested his hand on my hip and looked up at me. "And you would have disagreed with me when I said you were unwise for taking Harriet, even though you knew I was right."

"I was never that stubborn."

He arched a brow.

"Fine, I was, but so were you." I stroked his loose hair and admired the way his eyelids drooped in pleasure. "We've come a long way," I added quietly.

He took my hand and pressed the wrist to his lips. My blood pulsed. "We've both matured," he murmured.

"Goodness, any more mature and you'll be an old man."

He tilted his head to look at me. He wasn't laughing. "Do you mind that I'm so much older than you?"

"Ten years is not that much, Lincoln. Look at Lord and

Lady Gillingham. There must be twenty years between them, at least."

"That's not the same. *They're* not the same as us."

"True." I cupped his face in my hands and stroked my thumbs over the rough stubble on his jawline. I locked my gaze onto his. "No, Lincoln, it doesn't concern me, and before you say that it might one day, let me assure you that it won't. It never will."

He went very still. "Does that mean…" He swallowed. "You've decided?"

I drew my hands away. He caught them, then had second thoughts and let go.

"Charlie?" he asked, huskily.

"I need a little more time." I'd been prepared to tell him yes, but thinking about Harriet locked away in her room at her husband's command had given me pause. Not even the servants would help her, since he was their lord and master and paid their wages.

I couldn't tell Lincoln any of that. He would only try to reassure me that he would never do such a thing. And I believed him. I truly did—now. But what if he changed again? What if he thought he was doing the right thing and keeping me safe? He might have acted calm and agreeable earlier when Seth and Gus had been cross, but I couldn't be sure if he believed his own words. It was entirely possible he was merely saying what he knew I wanted to hear. After our history together, Lincoln knew the thing I hated and feared the most, aside from losing my home, was losing my freedom.

"Anyway," I said. "It's nice like this, isn't it?" If he heard the longing in my voice, he didn't say.

He merely nodded. Then he leaned forward, circled his arms around my waist, and rested his cheek against my chest. I cradled his head and kissed it. We stayed like that until he pulled away with a sigh and announced he had to go out.

"To find King's house?" I asked.

He nodded. "You're not surprised?"

"I knew you'd go tonight since I mentioned Bloomsbury and how Gawler had reacted when I asked him if King could shift into other shapes."

"King's the man we need. I'm sure of it now, thanks to you."

"But you don't know precisely where he lives."

"Bloomsbury's not large and I have contacts there. If he's ever drunk at an inn, bought tobacco, or been to a whore, I'll find him."

"You're going to speak to a whore?"

"You have nothing to worry about." He kissed my cheek as he rose. "She's not a patch on you. You have all your teeth."

I caught his hand as he walked off. "Be careful, Lincoln."

He kissed me again but on my mouth this time. It lasted until my bones turned to jelly and my heartbeat skipped. "Goodnight, Charlie."

I did not bid him goodnight as I planned on being awake when he returned.

However, my body had other ideas. I must have dozed off in the parlor. I awoke to a dark, cold room, the fire having gone out. A noise had startled me and I rose to look for Lincoln.

"Where is she?" came a thin, youthful voice I didn't recognize.

My heart pounded once then halted. My mouth went dry. It was too dark to see the intruder, but the voice came from the doorway. The shadows there moved.

Oh God! What did he want? Had Gawler sent someone to attack us? Could he see me, sitting on the sofa?

"Where is she?" he said again, but harsher, more desperate. "We're running out of time. Look!" The figure burst out of the shadows, brandishing a pocket watch.

But it wasn't the watch that caught my attention. And it wasn't a man holding it. He was a...creature with a white hairy face, long ears and cat-like whiskers. No, not a cat; a rabbit. He was fully clothed, and rushed toward me on hind legs like a human.

I screamed louder than I've ever screamed before.

CHAPTER 12

The rabbit stopped and pulled down its long ears. "Cease that infernal racket!"

I leapt off the sofa and grabbed the fire iron in one hand and my imp's orb in the other. "Don't come any closer."

The rabbit checked the watch again and clicked its tongue. "We're wasting time. She must come with me *now*."

I brandished the fire iron but kept my distance. The rabbit didn't seem to want to attack me, but I wasn't going to let down my guard. "Who are you? What do you want?"

"Charlie!" came Gus's shout, followed by pounding footsteps down the stairs.

"Charlie?" That was Seth.

"In here!" I called. "There's an intruder!"

The word was hardly out of my mouth when Gus and Seth barreled through the door. Gus hurled himself at the rabbit. They crashed through an occasional table. Wood splintered, and the lamp sitting on it broke apart when it hit the floor. Fortunately the lamp casing rolled away, the glass intact.

Doyle entered, carrying a candelabra. He stopped short upon the sight of the rabbit on the floor. "Oh my!"

Gus gave an uncharacteristic yelp of surprise as the light fell across the rabbit's face, but he didn't get up. He sat on its chest, pinning its wrists to the floor. He did lean back and eyed its large teeth warily.

"Bloody hell," Seth said, studying the rabbit. "What the devil is *that*?"

Cook peered over Seth's shoulder. "Want me to turn him into stew, Charlie?"

The rabbit squirmed, but it was no match for Gus. "Let me go! There isn't time for this! We're going to be late."

"For what?" I asked, rather stupidly.

"An important appointment with an important person."

"Explains the fine clothes he be wearing." Cook looked down at his own nightshirt, tugging it over his protruding stomach. Doyle and Gus also wore nightshirts, whereas Seth was bare chested, his trousers riding low on his hips.

"Are you one of them shifters?" Gus asked. "One of Gawler's mates?"

"I don't know who or what you're referring to," the rabbit said in a crisp upper class accent. "But I'm here to collect Alice for her appointment. If you don't—"

"Alice!" Seth snapped. "What do you want with her?"

"I told you—"

"Oh!" I cried. "Alice!" She wasn't here. My scream hadn't woken her up, although it had woken everyone else. Mrs. Cotchin and Bella stood by the door, clutching candles, but Lady Vickers ordered them to return to bed.

I pushed past her, but she hardly noticed me. She was staring at the creature on the floor trying to wriggle out from beneath Gus. "Now I've seen everything," she muttered.

"Doyle, your candelabra, please," I said.

He handed it to me and I raced up the stairs, taking two at

a time. I pounded on Alice's bedroom door, but she didn't answer. She was a heavy sleeper, particularly when she was having one of these odd dreams. I hoped waking her up would get rid of the rabbit. The last time her nightmare had come to life, back at the school, she'd shrunk herself in the dream and so had become miniature in life too. It had been impossible to find her and wake her.

I pushed open the door and, careful of where I stepped, approached the bed. She was in it and normal size, fast asleep, thank God. "Alice," I said. When she didn't wake, I shook her. "Alice! Wake up!"

She awoke with a start and sat up. "Charlie? What's wrong?" She groaned before I answered. "Oh no. It happened again, didn't it?"

"There's a white rabbit on the floor in the parlor, demanding that you go with him."

"Or I'll be late," she said heavily.

I nodded. "What will you be late for?"

"I have no idea." She climbed out of bed and threw a shawl around her shoulders. "He should be gone now. Oh, Charlie, I'm so sorry."

I hugged her. "It's all right. It's not your fault. Besides, he was harmless enough." Unlike the army who'd tried to capture her at the school. Their weapons had been very real.

A number of footsteps rushed along the corridor. Seth appeared in the doorway, carrying a lamp, Gus behind him. Cook, breathing heavily, joined them.

"Alice?" Seth passed the lamp to Gus and took Alice's hands in his own. "Are you all right?"

"Yes, thank you," she said, speaking to his bare chest. "They don't harm me."

Seth stood a little straighter. "Your dreams?"

She nodded. "I am never harmed. Those around me, however, are in danger."

"The rabbit was well behaved," I assured her. "Particularly after Gus sat on him."

Cook chuckled. "Ain't nothing going to move with that lard arse on top of 'em."

Gus thumped him in the shoulder. "Gave me a bit of a shock once I saw its face. Got an even bigger shock when it just disappeared like magic."

"When I woke up," Alice mumbled. She pulled her shawl tighter. "I'm so glad everyone's all right. Who saw it first?"

"I did," I said. "I fell asleep in the parlor, waiting for Lincoln to return."

"Half of London heard you scream," Gus said. "My ears are still ringing."

"You'll have to forgive me," I said with a wry smile. "It's not every night I wake up to see a white rabbit dressed in a waistcoat and trousers, demanding to see my friend."

"Oh, Charlie." Alice took my hand. "It must have been frightening."

"I think my heart has begun beating at its usual pace again, but I doubt I'll be falling asleep any time soon."

"Come to the kitchen," Cook said. "I'll make hot chocolate."

"I never turn down hot chocolate. Coming, Alice?"

She nodded. "I'm almost too afraid to fall asleep again."

All except Seth headed to the kitchen. He went to see if his mother's nerves had recovered. The square set of his shoulders and his strut were a sure sign that he knew Alice was staring at his back.

Bella, Doyle and Mrs. Cotchin were already in the kitchen, pouring hot chocolate into cups for themselves, and another for Lady Vickers.

"Was there an intruder?" Mrs. Cotchin asked, passing the pot to Cook. "Mr. Doyle says there wasn't, but the way you screamed, Miss Holloway, I could swear there must have been someone."

"You couldn't see?" I asked.

She shook her head, causing her nightcap to slip to one side.

"Me neither," Bella said, a cup in each hand, her shawl draped from the crook of each elbow.

Thank goodness for that. "I was resting in the parlor, waiting up for Mr. Fitzroy, and had a bad dream," I told them. "I must have cried out in my sleep and woken myself as well as everyone else. There was no one there, of course. I am sorry. I hope you can get back to sleep."

Mrs. Cotchin gave me a sympathetic smile. "You poor dear. Don't you worry about us, miss. We'll be fine. You just try and rest now."

"Thank you. Goodnight."

She and Bella left, but Doyle remained. He yawned.

"There's no need for you to stay up," I told him.

He glanced at the door. "The, er, intruder has gone?" he whispered.

"It was a figment of Alice's dream," I told him.

He blinked slowly at Alice. "And will this dream occur again? Should I sleep by the door?"

"I hope that's the last time," Alice said. "But I cannot be sure."

"Perhaps if we discuss why the rabbit appeared," I said to her, "it won't happen again."

She nodded. "Thank you, Doyle. I'm sorry your sleep was interrupted."

He bowed. "Don't trouble yourself, Miss Everheart. It's my pleasure to be of service. If there's nothing else, I'll bid you all goodnight."

We watched him leave then sat at the table while Cook prepared chocolate on the range. It was warm in the kitchen, which was rather fortunate since I was the only one dressed properly. Seth had found himself a shirt, but hadn't buttoned it all the way up, while Cook and Gus sported woolen stockings that sagged at their knees and ankles. Their nightshirts didn't look nearly warm enough.

I fixed Alice's shawl to cover her neck. She smiled and drew her long hair around her shoulder, out of the way. "Thank you, Charlie."

"Seth," I said. "Is your mother all right?"

"She's less ruffled than I am." He patted Alice's hand. "Tell us what troubles you, Alice. Why did this dream come to life?"

"The letter," she said with a sigh. "I received one earlier today from my parents." She looked to me and I nodded at her to go on.

She told them what her parents had written, and how it had made her feel—both frustrated and angry, the triggers needed to bring her dreams to life.

"It ain't surprising you had a bad dream about it," Gus said. "I'd have done, too."

"You mustn't worry," Seth said gently. "Fitzroy's too powerful for anything like that to touch him. He and the committee will see that nothing comes of the threat."

"I know." Alice sighed again. "But I worry anyway."

"They can't treat you like this. It's outrageous."

"They can do as they please. The law is on their side. God, I feel awful for bringing my problems here. I should never have come."

Cook placed a cup of chocolate in front of her with a grim smile. "Maybe Fitzroy could visit them."

"I wouldn't want him to go all that way just to talk to them. I doubt it would do any good."

I scowled at Cook. He hadn't meant for Lincoln to visit them to *talk*. I didn't want Alice to grasp his full meaning.

Lincoln himself wandered in, wet from head to toe from the rain. He paused in the doorway. "You're having a meeting without me."

"Not exactly a meeting," I said. "More like a midnight party."

"It's well after midnight, and parties should be amusing. No one looks amused."

Cook handed him a cup of chocolate. "You look like you be needing this."

"I'm *needing* an explanation." He stood with his back to the range and arched his brow at me.

"Alice's nightmare came to life," I said.

He'd been about to sip but lowered the cup. "Is everyone all right?"

"We're all fine. The household woke when I screamed." I put up a hand when he stepped toward me. "I'm fine, as you can see. I fell asleep in the parlor after you left and awoke with a white rabbit looking in on me. He asked after Alice and insisted they had a pressing appointment. There were no armies, guards or weapons involved."

"Unless you count the fire iron you threatened him with," Gus said with a wink at me.

Lincoln didn't speak for a moment, something for which I was glad. I suspected his first thought had been to admonish Alice or perhaps send her away. Neither of which would be helpful to our situation, or for Alice's peace of mind.

"We've assured her that you're taking care of the situation with her parents. They won't come for her or accuse you of anything."

"Charlie's right," he said. "If a letter doesn't suffice, a personal visit will."

Cook looked pleased. "Told you."

"They will be made to understand that you're better off here," Lincoln went on.

"How?" she asked.

Cook, Gus and Seth studied their cups. I tried to think of something to say that would reassure her but not alarm her. She knew Lincoln was a dangerous man to cross, but I suspected she didn't know how dangerous. Not that he would kill innocent people, but it was best not to frighten her.

Lincoln caught my gaze. His mouth flicked up on one side before flattening again. "I'll tell them about the ministry. I'll assure them the ministry protects people like you. Charlie can vouch for it, and me. Won't you, Charlie?"

"Oh, yes." I smiled at Alice. "It's an excellent idea." And unexpected.

"If you say so," Alice said.

"Did you find King?" Gus asked Lincoln.

Lincoln's clothes had begun to steam. He removed his jacket and placed it over a stool near the range. "He has rooms in Rugby Street."

"That's quite a change from Whitechapel."

"Where'd he get the money from?" Gus asked.

"A good question," Lincoln said. "One I cannot answer yet."

"Did you speak to him?" I asked.

He shook his head.

Seth leaned forward, elbows on the table. "You need more evidence before you confront him."

"I got the evidence I need tonight, but I didn't want to confront him alone."

Seth and Gus exchanged frowns.

"If he's anything like Lady Gillingham, his senses are finely tuned and will warn him of my presence. According to her, he is probably also much stronger and faster than me. Forgive me for getting soft as I age, but I want you two there when I confront him."

"To help," Seth said with a nod of approval.

"As bait."

Gus spat out his chocolate, spraying it over the table.

Lincoln crossed his arms. "That was a joke. Yes, I want you there to help."

Cook handed Gus a cloth. "Warn me, next time," Gus said, wiping the table. "I ain't used to your jokes."

I bit back my smile. Gus didn't look at all amused, and Seth looked surprised that Lincoln had attempted a joke at all. Sometimes I forgot that they didn't know him like I did.

"How did you find out he's the man we need without speaking to him?" I asked. "Did you see him change into the form of the late prince consort?"

"Nothing as definitive as that, but I'm sure he's the one. I watched him from the street. He left at twenty minutes to one, so I entered the building and looked through his things."

Alice gasped. "You robbed him?"

"I merely broke in. A robbery is when you take something."

"What did you see?" I asked before they got into an argument about the ethics of his actions.

"The photograph of the queen and prince consort recently stolen from the palace."

Seth nodded in approval, then caught Alice's stunned stare and added, "It's quite all right to break into someone's house if they're a thief."

"Particularly someone who stole from the queen," Gus added, winking at Seth.

"Coupled with the way Gawler reacted when I asked about King's shifting abilities, I'd say you have the right man," I said. "Will you confront him in the morning?"

"Yes. Get some sleep," he said to Gus and Seth. "I want to catch him before he goes out."

We finished our chocolates but I insisted on remaining

behind to help Cook wash the dishes in the scullery. Lincoln, however, ordered Cook to leave and he helped me instead. Once Cook's footsteps faded, and aside from the occasional creak of a floorboard, the house fell silent.

Lincoln tipped a pail of water into the basin. "You've recovered from your shock?" he asked.

"I have. The rabbit really was harmless." I smiled. "It was dressed in a blue waistcoat and buff trousers and it carried a watch that was as big as my hand. He was very worried about being late. You ought to have seen it, Lincoln. It was quite funny, really."

He handed me a cup but didn't let it go. "I am not laughing."

"So I see."

He released the cup.

"I do see your point," I said.

"I didn't make one."

"No, but you're thinking it."

He huffed out a laugh. "Are you sure you're not part seer?"

I angled a glare at him. "You're worried about Alice living here."

"I have a lot of people under my care now," he said. "A rabbit is one thing, but an army is another."

"I know." I handed him back the cup to dry and he passed me another. "But we can't let her live anywhere else. Who would know what to do? Certainly not Mrs. Denk, and her parents sound like awful people. I can't imagine they know how to handle a normal girl with a mind of her own, let alone one like Alice."

"Agreed."

"So she stays?"

He leaned a hip against the bench and regarded me levelly. "Charlie, there was never any question as to whether she stays or goes. Not in my mind."

"Oh. I see." I concentrated on washing the cup, feeling awful that I'd misjudged him. "Then we must do our best to allay her fears to ensure there are no more nightmares."

"Do you think we did tonight?"

"I hope so. She looked relieved when you said you'd take it in hand and pay her parents a visit. Telling her that you'd mention the ministry certainly went down well."

"I thought it a nice touch."

"Will you tell them, if it came to that?"

He lifted one shoulder. "I don't know. I have to think through the repercussions."

We continued to wash the cups in silence. When I finished, I dried my hands on the cloth he used. Our fingers brushed. Our gazes connected. I waited, half expecting him to take me in his arms and kiss me. He did not.

"Lincoln," I murmured.

"Yes?"

"I'm glad you didn't confront King alone. I don't like it when you deliberately put yourself in danger."

He hesitated a moment then said, "Then I'll be careful." Had he expected me to say something else? Perhaps give him an answer about the engagement ring? "Go to bed, Charlie. You look tired."

He offered me his arm and I allowed him to escort me to my room. With a brisk kiss on the cheek, he bade me goodnight, then walked off without a backward glance.

* * *

"Someone's coming up the drive," Alice said as she entered the dining room where Gus, Seth, Lincoln and I ate an early breakfast. The men planned to leave soon to speak to King and I'd been about to tell Lincoln that I ought to go too.

"But it's not even eight," Seth protested with a glance at the clock.

Lincoln rose, not waiting for Doyle to announce the visitor. I followed him out, both curious and apprehensive. No one made calls this early unless it was very important.

Lincoln opened the front door as the large coach pulled by two magnificent , high-stepping horses came to a stop. I recognized the escutcheon of serpent coiled around a sword and groaned. Gillingham.

My faint hope that it would be Harriet and not her husband was dashed when he opened the window. He was alone.

"You!" Gillingham pointed the head of his walking stick at me. "What have you done?"

"All manner of things," I said, trying to keep calm and sound unruffled. But in truth, my stomach churned. The butler must have informed him that Harriet had gone out with me the day before, and now Gillingham wanted to drag me over hot coals to pay for it.

Gillingham's top lip peeled back from his teeth. "Where is my wife?" he ground out.

"What do you mean?" I asked. "Isn't she at home?"

"You've taken her somewhere and I demand to know, *witch*."

Harriet, gone? *Oh God, no.*

"Don't play the innocent with me. Where is she?"

"I, I don't know. I brought her home last night after our drive. She was there when we left. Ask your butler. He saw us."

"She left again. Snuck out of the house somehow, despite being confined to her rooms. Not a word to anyone, not even her maid. *You've* encouraged her with your immoral talk, your *wickedness*." He spat out the word along with a spray of spittle, and shook the walking stick at me.

Lincoln grabbed the brass head and wrenched it through the window. Gillingham shrank back inside. I suspected he'd remained in there because he was afraid of Lincoln.

"Your wife's disappearance has nothing to do with Charlie," Lincoln said.

"It does! It must! She's never done anything like this before, never even entertained the thought of defying me, until *she* visited. You should learn to control your woman, Fitzroy, or—"

Lincoln reached into the cabin and grabbed Gillingham by the coat lapels. He dragged him along the seat and half pulled him through the window. Gillingham's face had been mottled red with anger, but now all the color drained away, leaving his freckles to stand out against the stark whiteness.

"You have only yourself to blame," Lincoln growled. "If you didn't forbid your wife to leave, she would have told you where she was going." He let go with a shove that sent Gillingham rocking back.

Gillingham smiled, a slippery tilt of his lips. "I'll ask you if you still think that in a year. I'll wager you'll understand then, when Charlotte's being willfully disobedient."

I placed a hand over Lincoln's arm. His tense muscles relaxed a little but not completely. "I have an inkling she might have gone to the East End," I said. "To see a man named Gawler who is like her. We spoke with him yesterday and your wife had more questions of him but didn't get to ask them."

"You took her to meet another! My God, you're more stupid than I—"

Lincoln grasped Gillingham's coat again. Gillingham flung his arms over his head to protect himself, dislodging his hat. When no punches were thrown he peeped out, blinked, and lowered his arms. Lincoln let him go.

"If you ask around the East End for a man named Gawler, you ought to find him," I said.

Gillingham stopped straightening his tie and coat. "You expect me to look for her? In the East End? Think again."

"You won't go there even to find her? Are you that afraid?"

"Of course I'm not afraid." His nostrils flared. "It's just that I can't be seen in that sort of place. What will people think?"

"That you're deeply worried about your wife, whom you love and wish to protect."

He sniffed and picked his hat up off the floor. "That is certainly not what they'd think. You really are a—" He glanced at Lincoln and sniffed again. "*You* must fetch her, Fitzroy. Be discreet. Nobody important must know. Understand?"

"I'll find her," Lincoln said. "But only because I want to learn more about her kind too, not because I think she's in danger. I'm busy this morning. I'll go later."

"Later! No, you must go *now*!"

"Go yourself if you're that worried."

Lincoln and I walked away, leaving Gillingham spluttering protests and threats.

"You don't think she's in any danger?" I asked him.

"She has her animal senses to protect her."

I wasn't so confident. I didn't think Gawler would pose a threat, but the East End was full of unscrupulous, dangerous types who could easily take advantage of an innocent like Harriet.

"I can't stay here and do nothing, Lincoln," I said as we re-entered the house. "I have to find her."

"I suspected as much."

"We'll go now? Before you pay King a visit?"

He nodded and explained the situation to Seth and Gus. I couldn't help but feel it was my fault that Harriet had disappeared without telling anyone, but then I remembered what

Lincoln had said to Gillingham. If he hadn't confined her to the house and turned the servants against her, she would have taken footmen.

A pounding knock on the front door had me jumping out of my skin. I'd heard Gillingham's carriage leave, so I knew it couldn't be him.

"Charlie!" came a shout from the other side. "Charlie, open up!"

"Finley?" I opened the door and Finley rushed inside, his face red.

He bent over at the waist and sucked in air. We crowded around him, waiting for him to catch his breath enough to speak. If I'd had a dreadful feeling in the pit of my stomach before, I now felt positively sick.

"Mink," he finally gasped out, still doubled over. "He's gone."

I groaned.

"Gone where?" Lincoln asked.

"Don't know." Finley straightened but his fingers pinched his side. He must have run most of the way from Clerkenwell. "He went out for a walk last night and never came back. Then today we heard about a lad being kidnapped in Whitechapel."

"Kidnapped!" I pressed a hand to my throat where bile burned. My blood ran cold. "No, no, no. This is all my fault. First Harriet and now Mink. If it wasn't for me, they'd both still be tucked into their beds. Lincoln...what have I done?"

CHAPTER 13

incoln's hand rested on the back of my neck, gentle yet reassuringly solid. "It's not your fault," he said. "And we don't know if anything bad has happened to either of them. Street children get kidnapped in Whitechapel more frequently than you'd think. The child may not have been Mink. He may have simply gone out for a longer walk than usual."

"He ain't never been gone this long," Finley countered.

Lincoln narrowed his gaze at the lad, but Finley wasn't intimidated.

"Well, he ain't," he repeated.

"I know," I said heavily. Finley wouldn't look so worried or have run all the way to fetch us if this was a normal occurrence.

"Harriet also went out voluntarily," Lincoln said.

"I don't like this at all," I said. "We have to find them both."

He nodded. "We'll leave immediately. Wear your trousers."

I hurried off, relieved that I didn't have to ask to go with them—because I would go, whether he wanted me to or not.

* * *

LINCOLN, Seth, Gus and I did not take our own coach but caught a hackney cab that deposited us out the front of the Smithfield meat market. The market was at its busiest—and loudest. Butchers' apprentices shouted over the top of one another in the long avenue, vying for attention. Carcasses hung from the hooks today like macabre garlands, and one stall even had over a dozen whole pigs arranged on the floor with their heads resting on front trotters. They looked as if they'd leap up at any moment to frolic among the straw.

We asked the butcher Gawler had spoken to the day before if he'd seen him. He hadn't and didn't know where Gawler lived, but he knew he drank at the Jolly Joker in Shoreditch.

We walked there. The tavern keeper was just opening the doors to let in the early drinkers who waited outside like flies around meat. After money changed hands, he told us we would find Gawler in Myring Place.

I expected Lincoln to try to put me in a cab and send me home, but he didn't. We headed to Myring Place in the Old Nichol district, a small court set amid one of the areas I'd learned to avoid when surviving on the streets. The half dozen or so dwellings surrounding the open yard were in varying stages of decay, the outbuildings little more than lean-tos that must leak terribly. Windows were shut, but even if they were open, no air or light would have entered the buildings, as not a breath of wind or beam of sunshine entered the yard. Children huddled around a brazier near a broken costermonger's cart that looked in danger of being sacrificed to the fire next. They watched us through wary eyes, their faces bearing the pallor and scars of illness and misery.

Lincoln handed out coins and the children's eyes lit up.

"We're looking for a man named Gawler," he said. "We were told he lives around here."

Some of the children hesitated and exchanged glances, but one pointed at the second house. "In there."

"Is he home?"

The lad nodded.

Lincoln handed them all another coin each then approached the house. He didn't knock, but pushed open the door. I covered my nose and mouth to block out the smell of meat. A narrow flight of stairs led up to the next level. Cobwebs clustered in the ceiling's corners and something scuttled in the shadows.

Lincoln put his finger to his lips and climbed the stairs quietly, slowly. He signaled for Gus to remain by the door and for me and Seth to follow. The staircase was only wide enough for one, so I went up last.

The door to the court closed, plunging us into semi-darkness. We headed up the stairs as silently as we could, but it wasn't silent enough.

There was no warning. One moment there was nothing at the top of the stairs, and the next, a dark shape hurtled toward us and slammed into Lincoln. If Seth hadn't been right behind him, Lincoln would have tumbled down the stairs under the force of the impact.

He grunted, but the only other sound came from the punch he landed on the other man. It was definitely a man, not a beast, albeit one with superior speed and a strength that allowed him to land a sickening blow into Lincoln's stomach. Lincoln doubled over, coughing, just as Gus pushed me into the wall and stormed past.

He and Seth tackled the man and Lincoln pinned him to the staircase. A low, fierce snarl curdled my blood. I'd heard stray dogs snarl like that right before attacking.

"Stop!" I cried. "Stop at once, Mr. Gawler!"

My voice seemed to startle him, and he stilled. "You?" He squinted past the men at me. "Bloody hell."

"These are my friends. We're not here to harm you. Lincoln, let him up."

Gawler threw up his arms, dislodging Seth and Gus, but not Lincoln. He slowly stepped back of his own accord and held out his hand. Gawler hesitated then took it and stood.

"Do you always greet guests by assaulting them?" I asked.

"Guests don't usually enter without knocking," he said, rolling his shoulders forward. "I don't get many guests anyway. Not until last night."

"Was that my friend Harriet the shape shifter? Was she here?"

"Aye. Bloody toffs. I knew this would happen. Ain't get no peace with you lot, demanding this and that. Clear off! Go on. I don't want nothing to do with any of you."

"Mr. Gawler," I said, "please. If you know where she is, you have to say something. She's not used to places like this. She could find herself in a great deal of trouble."

"Aye, she could, if she didn't make it to King's in one piece. Pretty thing like that would fetch a good price around here. If I were a different sort—"

"You sent her to King's?" Lincoln cut in.

Gawler shrugged. "Why wouldn't I? She wanted to speak to him and the other pack members, so I sent her. It weren't me she wanted, it was them. They're welcome to her, I say. She's got too many questions for my liking."

"But she wanted to speak to women," I said. "So why not introduce her to one of the females?"

"They *all* went to King's last night," Gawler said. "When I told her they were meeting there, she decided to go. Said she wanted to meet the leader too, and ask to be in his pack." He wiped his nose on his sleeve. "They always want to meet King, see. They can't help themselves. It's in their nature to want to run with the leader, and it's in his nature to take 'em."

I put up my finger. "Let's be clear. By take them, you mean...couple with them?"

"Aye, but she's a toff so he won't. King's got principles, I give him that." He snorted. "Principles and manners. Guess that's why they all like him. Even me," he added, quieter.

"What about a lad?" I asked, indicating Mink's height with my hand. "He was with me last night, too. Did he come here?"

"No."

If Mink hadn't come here, where was he? What had happened to him? Why had he and Harriet both gone missing at the same time?

I headed down the stairs, but when Lincoln didn't follow I stopped.

"How does King change into the form of others, but not you?" he asked Gawler.

"I don't know. No one does." Gawler backed up a step. "You got to go. I ain't going to talk about King with you. You want answers, you speak to him yourself."

"He impersonated the prince consort," Lincoln told him.

Gawler huffed out a humorless laugh. "So he finally managed it."

"Managed what?"

"To shift into the prince's form." Gawler looked at Lincoln like he was a fool. "Ain't that what you just said he did?"

"Why did he do it? What's he up to?"

"How'd I know? He don't tell me nothing no more. Doubt he tells any of the pack, neither. He don't confide in no one, these days."

"Why not?" I asked.

"He got secrets, and he keeps 'em close to his chest."

"What *kind* of secrets?" If he couldn't tell me what the secrets were, perhaps he could tell me that much.

"The kind that sees him move out of here and into a nice place in Bloomsbury."

"You don't know where he got his money from?"

"No, it ain't my business no more."

"But you must hear the gossip from the others."

"They're just guessing, like me. Now go away before one of the pack sees you here and tells King. I don't want no trouble."

We headed back into the yard. The children were still there, warming themselves by their meager fire, their intent gazes watching us until we exited their domain altogether.

No one bothered us as we walked briskly along the greasy streets. Even ruffians knew to leave three tall, well built men alone. Once outside the slums, we caught a cab to Bloomsbury, getting out around the corner from King's place. The air wasn't all that much cleaner than in the Old Nichol, with soot clogging the sky and settling onto skin and hair like black snowflakes. But the buildings were in better condition and larger, the streets wider and cleaner. People huddled into warm coats as they hurried past, not threadbare jackets, and no one eyed us with desperation and wariness here.

"If the pack is there, we can't just burst in," Lincoln said as we turned into Rugby Street. "We'll wait and watch. After they leave, we'll go in and retrieve Harriet."

"But what if she's in danger?" I asked.

"I doubt she is. Gawler seemed to think King would treat her with respect, in deference to her station, and I believe him. He had no reason to like King and paint him in a good light to us."

"True," I hedged. "I hope Mink's in there, too. Perhaps he followed the trail here, as Harriet did, out of curiosity." But I doubted it. Mink wouldn't do that. He was much too careful to wander about alone in search of a mysterious shifter.

We stood on the corner of Rugby Street, and Lincoln

pointed out King's place. "He rents rooms on the third floor. According to the landlady, Widow Griggson, King is a nice gentleman who keeps to himself. He often goes out at night, but he's quiet when he returns. When his friends come over, they're respectful and cause no problems."

"You had quite a conversation with her," Seth said.

"She thinks he's a writer using a pen name, and that's where he got his money."

"Quite the conversation," I said. "I'm impressed."

"She was lonely and I was nice."

Seth and Gus exchanged smirks behind Lincoln's back.

"There." Lincoln nodded at the window where a man appeared in profile, smiling. "That's King."

A slender man with an unremarkable face and a receding hairline laughed at something someone said then disappeared from view. We waited several minutes. A light rain began to fall, enough to make the roads slick but not run with water. A moment later, Harriet stood in front of the window. My heart leapt in relief.

"There she is!" I said. "She looks well."

Harriet glanced up at the sky and wrinkled her nose. She spoke to someone behind her then King and another woman appeared too. They also looked to the sky. The woman shrugged and crossed her arms. Harriet looked uncertain. King laughed again and placed a hand on the woman's shoulder. He seemed to be appealing to her, and her arms lowered. She glanced at the sky, nodded and moved out of sight.

"They're discussing the weather," Lincoln said. "But I don't know why."

"Why does any Londoner discuss the weather?" Gus said with a shrug. "Because it's rotten."

"We're too visible here all together," Lincoln said. "We need to split up." He eyed me and I suspected he was considering whether I ought to be there at all.

"Why not go in and simply talk to them?" I asked. "We can ask Harriet if she wishes to stay."

"Aye," Gus said.

Seth shook his head. "And ask King if he goes out pretending to be the prince consort? We won't get a straight answer. I think we need to bide our time and watch him, catch him in the act, perhaps. Harriet seems fine, and there's no rush to return her to Gillingham."

"True." I glanced at the window where Harriet now stood with her back to us. She seemed perfectly at ease. "Very well, let's watch for a while."

We separated and moved along the street. I huddled into a doorway several houses away, but the owner came out and asked me to move. I found another doorway, deeper and more protected, but the cold still managed to penetrate all my layers of clothing and seep into my bones some two hours later. I was thoroughly wet and my teeth chattered so loudly that I didn't hear Lincoln approach.

"All right?" he asked, giving me a warm pie.

I cradled it in my hands. "Where did you get this?"

"A pie shop around the corner. Hungry?"

"Starving." I bit into the pie and sighed. How had I ever coped without the comforts of pies and warmth in my years on the street? I'd been hungrier and colder than I was now, yet I had trouble remembering how I felt in those days of famine and misery. Perhaps I'd blocked it out. I certainly didn't have the nightmares anymore.

"Go home," Lincoln said gently. "There's no reason for you to stay."

"I want to."

"I suspect we'll be here until the rain eases. Harriet doesn't want to come out while it's wet and King is indulging her."

"What do they want to come out for?"

He leaned one shoulder against the wall. "You won't go, will you?"

I shook my head.

He watched me a moment then pushed off from the wall. "It's going to be a long day."

He returned to his position at the far end of the street, where he settled beneath a tree sprouting through the pavement. Seth and Gus stood at the other end of the street, barely visible in recessed doorways.

The day did indeed drag. The rain didn't ease but continued to fall in relentless monotony. Not too heavy; just enough to be maddening. And it was cold. So very cold. I blew on my gloved hands, tucked them under my armpits, and between my thighs. Nothing warmed them. I'd lost all feeling in my toes and ears around midday, and my nose constantly dripped.

There was no respite from the weather, but the occasional movement in King's room alleviated my boredom. The occupants merely talked and drank tea. Sometimes I saw Harriet, or one of the others, but rarely King himself. The faces of those I did see looked frustrated and bored. I knew how they felt. At least they were warm and dry.

As dusk finally settled over the street, and the lamplighter made his way past me, the curtains of King's rooms closed. Damn. Now what should we do?

I went to find Lincoln and was met by Seth and Gus as I headed up Rugby Street.

"Are my lips blue?" Seth asked. "I think they're frozen."

"I can't tell in this light," I said.

"I'm going to have a nice hot bath when I get home," Gus said dreamily. "Hot enough to sting."

"Get in line." Seth squinted up at the sky. "When did it stop raining?"

"Just now," I said.

We met up with Lincoln and I was about to ask him what to do next when the door to King's house opened. He came out, followed by Harriet, another two women and two men.

We fell back into the shadows. I held my breath, not daring to move or make a sound. Thank goodness we were downwind from them, or they might have smelled our presence. We all remained perfectly still as the party approached.

"It's too early," said one of the women, stepping quickly to keep up with King's long strides.

He patted Harriet's hand, tucked into the crook of his arm. "Lady Gillingham cannot wait any longer. She must get home."

Oh, thank God. She was unharmed and in no danger if he intended for her to return home. Indeed, they looked like a couple strolling to the theater. They passed beneath a lamp and I was relieved to see a look of happy excitement on her face, not fear.

But what did King mean that Harriet "cannot wait?" What couldn't she wait for?

They disappeared around the corner. We followed some distance behind, but when we turned the corner, they were gone.

"Where—?"

Lincoln cut Gus off with a raise of his hand. He signaled for us to follow behind him as he continued on. I had a bad feeling about this. There was a small lane up ahead to our left, but it was a dead end. We'd passed it on our way to Rugby Street earlier and had dismissed it as a potential exit point due to tall buildings on three sides. The only thing it was good for was storing things and hiding. It wouldn't have surprised me to find stray animals and the homeless hiding out in there.

But now I realized it could be used for another purpose— to change one's shape in private.

We approached the lane, but were still some distance away when six large creatures dashed out. Three looked like wolves, two were more bear-like, while the sixth was like no animal I'd ever seen. It was covered in fur, like the others, but had a wide, flat nose rather than a canine one. It, and one of the wolves, skidded to a halt upon seeing us while the others continued on. The wolf sniffed the air and made to approach us, but the other yelped and the wolf turned away. Both ran off on all fours after their mates.

Lincoln sprinted after them but only got as far as the corner. He came back, shaking his head. "They're too fast."

Seth and Gus stared at the corner. Then they turned as one to Lincoln.

"That was them, weren't it?" Gus asked. "Lady G, King and his friends."

Lincoln nodded. "I suspect so."

"Bloody hell," Seth murmured. "I don't know what I was expecting, but not...that. They weren't all the same."

"No," Lincoln said. "They weren't. I recognized Harriet, and I suspect the odd one out was King. As pack leader, he ordered her to follow."

I tried to reconcile the pretty, delicate Harriet with the beast I'd just seen running off through the dark streets of London, but I couldn't. I wondered how she'd react next time I saw her. Embarrassed? Liberated? Perhaps she'd refuse to see me.

"They were waiting for the rain to stop and darkness to fall, so they could go for a run," Seth said.

"I agree with the woman who reckoned it's too early," Gus said. "They should've waited until everyone was asleep."

Seth glanced at the inky sky. "It's dark enough and cold enough that no one will be out." But he sounded worried and glanced at the corner again. "Now what?"

"We wait," Lincoln said.

Gus groaned. "That bath ain't getting any closer."

"You can go home," Lincoln said. "Take Charlie with you."

"No." I folded my arms over my chest. "I'm staying."

"There ain't no point staying," Gus said before Lincoln could answer. "Lady G ain't in danger. King even said she was going home soon, that's why they're gone for their run now. Come on, Charlie."

"But once the group breaks up, King will be alone and we can confront him. If he doesn't want to answer, he could cause trouble. Lincoln and Seth will need your help to subdue him."

Gus groaned. "I ain't going nowhere, am I?"

Lincoln remained quiet, which I knew was agreement. He merely regarded me, as did Seth and Gus.

I sighed. "Yes, I know I said that Gus is needed, not me. Fine, I'm going home. I don't want to get in the way."

Seth huffed out a frosty breath. "You're going home because you want a warm bath and hot soup."

"Next time you mention baths and soup, I'll thump you," Gus groaned.

"We'll look around King's rooms for any sign of Mink," Lincoln said. "Then wait for them to return down here."

"Perhaps Mink's inside waiting, too," I said. "Or perhaps he has returned home already."

Lincoln squeezed my hand, depositing some money in my palm. "For the cab. Stay warm."

He walked off. Seth and Gus trotted to catch up then fell into step beside him until they turned the corner into Rugby Street. I headed in the opposite direction to the pack and made my way to a busier thoroughfare where I paid for a hackney to take me home.

The driver stopped at Lichfield's gates, unable to venture up the drive due to another coach blocking the entrance. It had begun to rain again, and my driver shouted at the other coachman to move on.

"Oi!" my driver shouted. "What're you doing?"

I hardly had time to register his words when the cabin door wrenched open. A man clad all in black, a hood covering most of his face, leaned inside. I swallowed my scream and scrambled out of his reach.

"You have to come with me," he said, much too politely for a kidnapper.

Still, I hesitated. I'd been abducted more times than I liked, and I wasn't prepared to add another to the tally. "What do you want?"

"Just come with me and all will be explained."

"No."

"Come on, miss, it's cold and wet out here. It's warm and dry where we're going."

"Are we going to my home, Lichfield Towers?"

He peered at me from beneath the hood, his eyes two shiny centers among blackness. I couldn't make out his features and I didn't recognize his voice. "Somewhere nicer." He offered me his hand.

I kicked it.

He cried out and cradled it against his chest. He wasn't a very good kidnapper. I kicked him again while he was distracted, hitting him square in the chest. He fell back, landing on his rear in a puddle.

"Bloody hell! What'd you do that for?"

I pulled out the knife strapped to my forearm and the other from my boot and jumped out of the carriage. Ice-cold needles of rain pricked my face. I was already wet, and didn't care, but I'd begun to warm up in the carriage, and now I had to endure freezing rain again.

"I am in no mood for this," I snapped. "It's damned cold

and I want to go inside for a bath. Unless you have a good explanation for accosting me, I'm going in right now."

"You seem to have this under control, lad," the hackney driver said, urging his horses onward.

"Lad? She's not a lad." My abductor pushed himself to his feet and shook water off his cloak. "Put those knives away, Miss Holloway. I'm not here to hurt you."

"Then why are you here? What do you want? Who sent you to fetch me? How do you know who I am?"

"You just confirmed it. As to the rest, I'm not at liberty to say."

"Then I'm not going with you." I skirted around him, careful to remain out of reach. I did not lower my weapons or take my eyes off him.

"Bloody hell," he muttered, brushing himself off and flicking water over me in the process. "I ought to have asked for extra to do this."

"From whom?"

"The question you should have asked is, for what?"

"I assume you meant for kidnapping me." Why was I having this very normal conversation with an abductor? It was absurd.

"I told you, I'm not kidnapping you. I'm asking you to come with me."

"Why would I go anywhere with a strange man who stops me from entering my home? I'm not a fool."

"No, but you do ask a lot of questions." He regarded me, taking particular note of my knives. "You look like you know how to use those."

"I've had weapons training and am skilled in the art of hand to hand combat."

He paused. "Really? Are you sure you're a woman? It's hard to tell in this light with you dressed in those clothes. Perhaps you're not Miss Holloway."

"I never said I was."

He sighed. "I don't have time for this. My master is waiting for you."

"I don't have time for this either—or the inclination. Either you tell me who you work for or I go inside and you can tell your master that you failed."

"I feel sorry for your man." He sighed again. "Very well, I'll whisper it to you."

"So you can get closer and capture me?" I snorted.

"Blimey, you're suspicious. Very well, I'll show you." He parted his cloak to reveal a red coat with a lot of gold braiding and highly decorated lapels. The royal livery. "Now will you come with me?"

I relaxed my stance but didn't put my weapons away. "Why the subterfuge?" I asked the footman.

"My master is concerned about spies and newspaper men. The fewer people who know he has employed you, the better." He directed me to his coach. "Will you come now?"

"If I must, but wouldn't he rather wait for Mr. Fitzroy?"

"I was told to collect both of you or one of you if the other was unavailable. I asked at your house, but was told neither of you were at home. They think I left but I decided to wait here for the first conveyance to arrive. I recognized you from your visit to the palace." He looked me up and down. "Although you do look different in that garb. Now get inside before I freeze to death. Please."

He opened the door for me and I got in. He folded up the step and climbed up to the driver's seat. There was no one else either inside or outside the coach. The interior was appointed in the same colors as his livery, the luxurious velvet soft to touch. I removed my gloves and buried them in the blanket provided. Perhaps I could ask for soup at the palace, and hot tea too. I would certainly demand to sit by a fire. Surely the prince wouldn't mind once he saw my state. The bath would have to wait.

I should have asked if I could speak to Doyle first and leave a message, but considering the lengths the footman had gone to, I doubted he would have allowed me to go to the house. I hoped I returned before Lincoln. Perhaps the prince would allow me to send a message once I arrived at the palace. It was unlikely the meeting would go for very long anyway, if he only wanted a report on our progress.

A cluster of lamps burning brightly in the street caught my attention. I peered at them as we sped past, and frowned. The lights lit up the dour stone arch of the Kensal Green Cemetery. Kensal Green! But that wasn't on the way to Buckingham Palace.

My stomach dropped. I'd been tricked. We weren't going to meet the prince. The footman wasn't a royal footman, but someone wearing a disguise. And the longer I remained in the speeding coach, the further away from Lichfield Towers I'd be.

CHAPTER 14

J placed my hands flat against the carriage window and looked down. Endless pavement and road slipped past, no grass or earth. Jumping out would break bones at the least and perhaps kill me. Escape was impossible.

I gripped the edge of the seat and bided my time. The coach eventually slowed to turn a corner and I prepared to leap out, but I changed my mind as we passed through a large iron gate guarded by two men dressed in great coats. It would be difficult to get past them.

We drove along a short drive to a mansion built in the formal Georgian style, but modest in size compared to Lichfield. Dark shapes loomed, some as high as the coach, but closer inspection revealed them to be topiaries. The estate was secluded behind high walls, and the house guarded by another two men who stood stiffly by the lamp posts either side of the steps. I should have risked jumping out earlier. My chances of escaping now would be minimal at best.

I gripped my knives in each hand and willed my heart to cease its pounding. I needed to remain calm so I could think.

The coach door was opened by a different man than my driver. I hardly even glanced at him before leaping out and racing back up the drive.

"Wait!" he shouted. "Miss Holloway!"

Other voices joined his, but one boomed over the rest. "Stop, Miss Holloway! It's only I, the Prince of Wales!"

I skidded to a halt on the gravel and glanced back. The prince did indeed stand near the coach, sheltering beneath an umbrella held by a footman. The footman who'd opened the coach door caught up to me, panting.

"This way...please...Miss Holloway." He indicated the house, the waiting prince, and the collection of servants watching me.

"Why didn't someone tell me earlier?" I growled, walking back.

I performed a small curtsy for the prince but it must have looked ridiculous, dressed as I was in boys' clothes. "Your highness." I did not repeat my question in his hearing, but he must have understood why I'd run off.

"I apologize for the subterfuge," he said as we headed into the house. His footman did not produce another umbrella for me, nor did the prince offer me his. Since I was thoroughly wet, it hardly mattered. "There are spies everywhere."

"There are? Have you caught one? What did he say?"

"Nothing like that. But I am certain there must be spies, and since this is a delicate matter..."

"Is that why we're meeting here and not at the palace?"

"It is."

Warmth hit me as soon as we entered the house. The footman with the umbrella melted away and two others replaced him, one taking my wet coat, cap and gloves and the other standing around doing nothing but staring ahead as if he couldn't see us. With so many servants about, the prince couldn't possibly expect this meeting to be kept a secret, surely. Or perhaps, to him, the servants were irrelevant.

He led me to a parlor off the entrance where a fire crackled. Despite the less than impressive proportions, the room was decorated in grand style with gilt leaves on the high ceiling, the walls and on much of the furniture. Crimson carpet offset the sage green color scheme of the furnishings and white marble fireplace.

"Is this your home?" I asked, and immediately regretted my question. Of course the prince didn't live here. It wasn't large enough, for one thing, and he must live at the palace, surely, since it would one day be his.

"Only when I crave privacy," he said, indicating I should sit by the fire. "When I feel as if I'm being watched."

I lifted my gaze to the footman standing by the door and the second one who entered carrying a tray with more things on it than two people needed. "Do you feel as if you're being watched now?"

"Now more than ever," he said.

"By whom?"

He dismissed the footman with a lift of his finger. "I wish I knew."

Both footmen left and shut the door, leaving us alone. If I had a reputation worth protecting, I would protest. But my reputation was ruined already, and Lincoln wanted to marry me anyway. He wouldn't be concerned if I met the prince in private, and nor was I.

"Please forgive this arrangement," the prince said, perhaps realizing how it must seem. "You are in no danger from me, and your reputation will remain safe. My men won't say a word."

"Thank you for your concern."

"Chocolate or tea?" He indicated the cups on the tray. "Cake or biscuits?"

"Tea, please, and cake would be most welcome."

He poured and handed me a cup and slice of butter cake then sat back with a cup of chocolate. He didn't look at all regal in his green and gold smoking jacket, open at the front to reveal a matching waistcoat, but his aloof bearing made up for the casual attire. There was little chance I could forget who I spoke to.

"Where is Mr. Fitzroy?" he asked idly.

"Watching the man we suspect is responsible for impersonating the late Prince Consort."

He lowered his cup to the saucer, and the angle of his chin dropped. "You have found him?"

"We believe so." I hesitated, unsure how much I ought to tell him. But he was our employer, the heir to the throne and, perhaps most importantly, a worried son. He should know what we'd discovered, if only to be reassured. "Mr. Fitzroy found the stolen picture of your father in the man's belongings. He plans on confronting the man tonight and questioning him about it."

"Who is he?"

"A fellow by the name of King. It doesn't seem to be his real name, but the one he now goes by."

"That tells me nothing. *Who* is he?"

"I, I don't know what you mean."

"Who are his relations, his friends? Do I know him, Miss Holloway?"

"I doubt it," I said. "He's originally from the East End, but now resides in Bloomsbury."

"I know a few authors and artists from Bloomsbury but none named King."

"His friends still live in the East End. They visit him occasionally."

He wrinkled his nose as if he could smell the foul stench of the rookeries. "Then how did he rise to Bloomsbury?"

"We don't know. Perhaps Mr. Fitzroy will discover the answer to that mystery tonight too."

"Yes. Good." He thumped the chair arm and gave an emphatic nod. "Hopefully that'll put an end to their rendezvous."

"Whose rendezvous?"

He looked as if he hadn't heard me, and I felt as invisible as one of his servants. But then the tension left his shoulders and he rubbed his forehead. "The queen informed me late today that she'd had a visit from my father's ghost, looking very much alive, as she put it."

"When?"

"Yesterday. She only told me about it a few hours ago, hence this meeting. I was going to put the wind up Fitzroy but that's not necessary now."

"Is the queen all right?"

"Quite. Indeed, she was in good spirits. She is utterly convinced it's him, you see, and no matter how often I tell her it's an imposter, she refuses to believe me. Once she makes up her mind, it takes a miracle to change it, and she's made up her mind that my father's ghost visits her for a chat."

"Did you question the servants? Did anyone see him enter?" They must have. A man looking like the late prince consort couldn't wander into the palace without being detected.

"No. Not a single one. It's very odd. They're all on the lookout for someone claiming to be him after the last incident, but nobody saw him this time. Hopeless, the lot of them."

Or perhaps King had taken on the shape of someone else, someone the servants expected to see in the palace. He could have changed into the form of one of the servants, another family member, or official. If he was capable of changing into any shape, the possibilities were endless. And frightening.

"Did your mother—did the queen—tell you what they discussed?" I asked.

"He made her promise not to tell anyone, and she won't break that promise. I tried to get her to tell me, as did one of my brothers, but she refused. She's a bloody—" He cut himself off and drank his chocolate instead.

I sipped, too, considering the possibilities. What did King want? Money? He hadn't asked for any yet, but he might. On the other hand, he could have simply taken whatever he wanted from the palace and sold it. An expensive vase, a gold frame or candlestick. "He must want something," I said, thinking aloud.

"Perhaps to influence her, in some way, but I don't yet know to what purpose."

"Does she have much political influence?" I asked.

"In certain quarters. There are other types of influence, however. If she endorses a business, say a jeweler or horse trainer, customers would flock."

I nodded slowly. "It's a sound theory." I wondered if Lincoln would think to ask King that sort of question.

"She is utterly convinced that it's him," he said quietly. "Nothing I say can sway her opinion."

"It must be frustrating for you and your family."

"My family?" He looked taken aback. "I meant frustrating because she's the queen and she knows she can do, say and think as she pleases. The opinions of others, even those of her children, are irrelevant to her." He studied his teacup then finally lifted it to his lips. "I'm sorry, Miss Holloway, I didn't mean to say such a thing to you. My family is a sensitive topic."

"It's quite all right. I'm not used to families, you see. I don't have one. Not really."

He smiled. "That is not entirely a bad thing. Family are sometimes a thorn in one's side."

"I'm sure they're a great comfort, too. One can depend on family to keep one's secrets. You can trust family."

"Trust them to tell you exactly what they think of you, you mean." His smile became a smirk. "To lecture you, point out your sins, and compare you to your upstanding father who *never* put a foot wrong." He went to sip his chocolate again but set the cup down, a sour look on his face. He got up and poured himself a drink at the sideboard.

I didn't know what to say, or if my opinion was even sought. Perhaps he simply needed to talk to someone who wanted nothing from him in return. Perhaps being here, he felt safe. Did he bring his mistresses here? Or his friends, to get away from the public? What secrets did these walls and servants keep?

"At least we have the fellow in hand now," the prince muttered into his glass, his back to me. "It'll shut her up when she finds out he's an imposter."

"Almost have him in hand," I corrected.

He turned, a scowl on his face, as if annoyed that I was still listening to his private musings. I put down my cup and began to rise, but he put up his hand to stay me. He did not, however, say anything.

"Is there something else, your highness?" I asked.

He returned to his chair, sighing as he settled down. He suddenly looked every bit middle-aged and weary, like a man with many burdens. Up until now, I'd thought him rather sprightly and reasonably handsome for a man nearing fifty. I wondered how he kept up with a wife, mistresses, children, a demanding mother and his duties as heir to the throne.

"Sir?" I prompted. "Is there something else you wanted to ask me? Or something you wish me to pass on to Mr. Fitzroy?"

"Fitzroy." He squeezed the bridge of his nose. "That's an interesting name."

Ohhhh. So *that's* the direction his thoughts took. I sipped my tea, keen to see where this conversation led. Very keen.

"Leisl's son," he mused. "And twenty-nine years of age."

I pretended to study my cup but I kept my gaze on him through my lashes. He suddenly looked up, however, and my attempt at being subtle failed. My face flamed.

"What's he like?" he asked.

"Er, well, he's nice." I winced. "He's interesting. He's been kind to me." Most of the time, I might have added, if I were being honest. "He's extraordinarily clever, highly capable at everything, and not someone who should be crossed without good reason."

What else should I tell him? That he'd been brought up by a cold man, who turned out to be a killer, and servants who didn't care for him? Should I tell Lincoln's father that his son had difficulty trusting and loving because of that upbringing? That he never cared for his own wellbeing until recently? That he would have turned out vastly different if only his mother had been allowed to keep him and love him? That he was chosen to lead the ministry because he was the son of the prince himself?

"Is he a good leader?" he asked. "Do his men respect him?"

"Very much so." Except for the occasional jibe out of his hearing, but I didn't think the prince cared about that. "Perhaps you ought to visit him and get to know him better."

"Why would I want to do that?"

I blinked. "I—I don't know."

"He's better off not knowing me beyond our current interactions. I can do nothing for him, be nothing to him." He spoke as if he knew I was aware he was Lincoln's father. He probably assumed Leisl had mentioned it. "Does he see his mother much?"

The question surprised me. "No. He never met her until that night at the Hothfields' ball."

"He was brought up by English parents? Thought so. Explains his accent, his bearing, manners, what have you. Best thing Leisl could have done for him, giving him up. But he knew who she was at the ball?"

"He did," I managed to say.

"And has he seen her since?"

"No."

He nodded approval. "Very wise. It could damage his reputation if his relationship to her gets out."

"It hasn't damaged your reputation," I spat before I could check myself. "Your highness," I added in a vain hope to appease him.

He bristled. His nostrils flared. I wished the chair would swallow me up.

"I mean…that is…"

His face softened. "She did announce it to the entire bloody world that night," he muttered. "Thank God it hasn't got into the papers. My mother would box my ears."

"May I be so bold as to ask you something a little personal?"

"My disapproval hasn't stopped you speaking up so far."

My face heated again, but I forged on. "You must have cared for Leisl then. If I could tell Lincoln that his parents were in love, it might…" I shrugged, no longer sure what I wanted to achieve. Did Lincoln even care if his parents had feelings for one another?

The prince shifted in his chair and studied his glass again. After a moment, he drank the contents to the last drop. He set the glass down on the table beside him with very deliberate, slow movements. "You are bold."

"So Lincoln tells me."

"You're close."

"He's asked me to marry him."

His eyes flared wide. "I see."

I didn't think he was interested because he cared about Lincoln's life, or mine, but because he wanted to know how much he could trust me. A mere employee or casual friend shouldn't hear certain things, but a lover was a different matter.

"I'm afraid I'm going to disappoint you, Miss Holloway. Love played no part in what occurred between Leisl and me. Not on my part, and I'd hazard a guess not on hers either. We came together for reasons I can't entirely put into words. She was very beautiful, certainly, but I see beautiful women every day." He studied his hands, clasped lightly in his lap. "I don't know why I stooped so low. A *gypsy*." He shook his head. "She worked at the fair, for God's sake. She told fortunes. I must have been mad." He looked at me, parted his hands, turning up the palms. "There you have it. It was madness that brought us together. How else to explain it? We were two people from very different worlds, with nothing in common, who probably couldn't think of two words to say to one another under normal circumstances. But something came over us that day. Something I cannot fully explain. I simply *had* to be with her. It was like a compulsion."

Did he mean lust? Had Leisl used her beauty to lure him to her bed because she knew about the prophecy? Or had fate stepped in and thrown them together?

"Thank you for your honesty, your highness."

"Will you pass on what I said to Mr. Fitzroy?"

"If he asks, yes. But if he does not...I'm not sure. It's hardly a comforting story. I'd like him to see his mother again, though. I'd like him to get to know a member of his family and she is the most...accessible to him."

He inclined his head in a nod, but his lips flattened in disapproval. I held my breath, hoping he'd invite Lincoln to a private dinner, but he simply said, "There may be occasions when we have to meet. I'd like to see the ministry take on a more official role."

"Official? Do you mean for the supernatural to be brought into the open?"

He smiled. "I admire your curiosity, Miss Holloway, but I'm afraid I cannot answer that. Not until I've taken some advice on board."

"Of course. If you need to discuss anything, I'm sure Lincoln would be happy to tell you more about what we do."

He gave no indication if he would consult with Lincoln, and I grew concerned that he would speak with one of the lords on the committee instead. I was about to tell him not to approach anyone else, but he rose and peered down his nose at me.

"My man will return you to Lichfield Towers when you're ready."

It would seem he expected me to be ready now. I rose and performed another curtsy. "Good evening, your highness. I do apologize for my attire, and my attempted escape earlier."

"It's quite all right. I understand why you were apprehensive."

I doubted he truly did but refrained from saying so. He tugged on the bell pull and a moment later a footman collected me. The prince remained behind in the parlor and I returned to the carriage.

"Take me to Rugby Street, Bloomsbury," I said to the coachman before climbing in.

We rolled away through the puddles and picked up speed once we left the gates behind, so that we reached Bloomsbury quickly. The coachman left me at the top of the street and asked if I was sure I wanted to remain.

Gus stepped out of the shadows nearby to see who'd arrived. He saw me and approached.

"Yes, thank you," I told the driver. "My friends are here."

"What're you doing?" Gus asked as the coach drove off.

"I wanted to tell you something before you spoke with King. Has he not come back?"

He shook his head.

"You must all be freezing."

"It ain't no picnic."

"Where's Lincoln?"

He nodded at the tree at the opposite end of Rugby Street. I couldn't see Lincoln. "He won't like that you've come back," Gus said.

"I know."

He melted back into the shadows and I ventured toward the tree. I couldn't make out anyone in the shadows, so when Lincoln called my name softly, I jumped.

"Up here," he said.

I tilted my head back. He sat in the fork of two branches, high up. I climbed and settled on the branch beside him.

"You're still wet," he said, touching my hair.

"I haven't been home yet. The Prince of Wales's coach met me and took me to see him. He wanted an update on our progress and to tell us the imposter paid the queen another visit yesterday. She believed him to be the spirit of her dead husband."

"How did he get into the palace?"

"He slipped past the guards and servants somehow and spent time with her alone. They merely conversed. He didn't harm her. I wanted you to know before you spoke with King. Also, the prince thinks King wants the queen to influence something, perhaps a business or a political matter."

"I'll ask him." He leaned against the tree trunk. "You sent the coach away."

"I can get another hack."

"Hmmm."

"You disapprove of me returning?"

"Does it matter if I do?"

"I'm not sure." I considered my options and decided I ought to leave again and opened my mouth to tell him.

He suddenly went very still and gripped my hand. It was difficult to see his expression in the poor light, but his body tensed, alert and ready to spring. Then I heard it too. Yelping. Not barking, but certainly animal noises.

They stopped and I craned my neck to see where. I didn't dare ask Lincoln if he could see them. Their hearing was far too good.

A few moments later, a group of six wandered past the tree, all of them in human form. They must have changed back into their clothes in the lane again after their run.

"I ought to go," I heard Harriet say. "Could you find me a hackney, Mr. King?"

"Already?" drawled a man. "But it's early. My dear Lady Gillingham, we would very much enjoy your company a little longer."

"Mr. King, I must insist. My husband will be worried."

"From what you've told us, your husband won't be worried for your wellbeing, more for his reputation. He doesn't deserve your consideration. Stay," he purred. "We appreciate you and wish to get to know you better." King's rich, honeyed voice resonated through the dense air. There was no hint of the East End in his accent, but it wasn't as plummy as Harriet's.

"I don't know." Harriet stopped and glanced behind her. "I do want to get to know you better too, but I've been gone quite a while."

The group spread out and surrounded her, as if King had given them an order. But I'd heard none. He took her hands. "I insist. We'll drink wine and eat cake into the evening. Doesn't that sound like fun?"

"Ye-es but—"

"No buts! It's arranged. You'll come back to my place."

"I really shouldn't."

King didn't answer. Perhaps it was simply my imagination but I felt the air close in. Harriet glanced at the people surrounding her and tried to pull her hands free from King's, but he didn't let go.

"You misunderstood." King's voice turned harsh, tight. "I *insist* you join us this evening. You're one of us now and your initiation is not yet over."

"I—I don't understand."

"It's simple. You've run with us. You're part of my pack now and that means there are rules to follow."

"Can you not write them down and send them to my home?"

His brittle chuckle held none of his earlier charm. "And risk them being intercepted? You are a sweet girl, but very naive. Let me be blunt. One rule is that I, as pack leader, am entitled to call upon you."

"By all means, do so. My husband will want to meet you, of course. I warn you, he won't like you, out of principle. He dislikes my—"

"You misunderstand. I mean, I expect certain…privileges from you."

"W—what kind of privileges?"

He lifted a hand and stroked her cheek. "Can you not guess, my sweet?"

She recoiled and stepped back, only to be caught by the two men. "What are you doing?" she screeched. "Unhand me!" She struggled against them but they held firm.

King hooked his arm around her waist, pulling her into his side. The other men let go and he forced her to walk on. She resisted every step but he was too strong.

"Stop!" she cried. "Stop at—"

He placed a hand over her mouth, but I heard her muffled scream. The neighbors in their houses would not.

Beside me, Lincoln whistled and Gus and Seth emerged from their hiding spots. "Stay here," he ordered me, then jumped down from the tree.

The shifters halted and swung around. They sniffed the air. Some bared teeth in snarls.

"Go away," King snapped at Lincoln then walked off again, forcing Harriet along.

He must have loosened his grip enough for her to break free, however, because she tore away and screamed. In a flash, King caught her and lifted a hand to punch her.

Lincoln rushed at him and grabbed his fist. He wrenched it back, unbalancing King, tackling him to the ground. Lincoln delivered a punch to King's jaw before the other two men leapt onto Lincoln's back.

"Harriet, *move!*" Seth ordered as he ran up. He drew his pistol but Lincoln's attackers didn't stay still and he couldn't fire safely.

Lincoln threw one of them off him but the other landed a punch to his stomach. He grunted and coughed but swung his fist and hit his target's cheek.

Gus, too, had pulled out his pistol but couldn't fire. The fight was much too close, the risks too high. With a growl of frustration, he kicked one of Lincoln's attackers. But he too was soon overset by one of the females. In that instant, he could have shot her, but he did not—out of chivalry, knowing Gus. Then it was too late. She knocked the weapon out of his hand. It skidded away, out of reach.

I remained in the tree, waiting for the right moment. But what moment? What could I do? Even the women were too strong and fast for me. Gus could only shield his body from the blows of the one attacking him, and he only occasionally got in a punch or kick. Seth fared no better with the other woman, and with two men attacking him, Lincoln had fallen to the road. They kicked him in the ribs, stomach and legs. He curled in on himself, but they showed no mercy.

Tears filled my eyes, blurring my vision. My stomach knotted with revulsion and fear and hopelessness. I prayed to a God I hardly even believed in as tears rolled down my cheeks.

"You brought them here, didn't you?" King growled at Harriet. "You led them to me!"

Harriet had descended into hysteria, crying and whimpering on her knees. King hauled her to her feet and half-dragged her toward his house. She didn't resist. She couldn't.

The blows kept coming. Lincoln, Seth and Gus could hardly even defend themselves anymore. Seth tried to retrieve his gun, but his hand was kicked away. He cried out and cradled it to his chest.

"Kill them," King said over his shoulder to his pack. "Then dispose of their bodies. Do it quickly before the neighbors see."

CHAPTER 15

$\mathscr{I}$ had one weapon in my arsenal; the same weapon I'd had my entire life, only I'd not treated it as such until last summer—my necromancy. And with time against me, there was only one way in which to use it.

My gut protested at the what I must do, but I ignored its churning, ignored my conscience. I had to save my friends, no matter the cost.

I climbed down from the tree as silently as possible. It wasn't silent enough. One of the men attacking Lincoln looked up. His lips peeled back in a snarl and he prepared to spring at me.

I dove for Gus's gun at the same moment the man leapt at me. I rolled out of the way, as Lincoln had taught me in training, and the man landed on the road with a sickening thud and a yelp of surprise. In that blink of a moment, I rose on one bruised knee, steadied my aim, and fired.

The bullet hit him in the shoulder. He jerked back and cried out. His friends paused, looked up. They stood as one, and spread out to circle me. They would risk their lives to capture me, or perhaps they didn't think I would kill.

"Don't come any closer," I said, aiming at the injured man.

They did not stop. They stepped in, tightening the circle around me. The injured man joined them, his shoulder damp with blood. They snarled deep in their throats. I'd heard stray, hungry dogs snarl like that, right before attacking their prey.

I clutched the gun in both hands. It shook. "Get back!"

But instead of stopping or retreating, I heard a noise behind me. I swiveled in time to see one of the women leaping at me. I fired.

The bullet hit her square in the chest and she fell to the ground. She did not get up.

Oh God.

I lowered the weapon and stared at the body. Blood seeped out from under it and pooled on the road. A white mist rose and hovered in the air. It formed the shape of the dead woman, in human form, and wailed.

"You killed her," the other woman said, her eyes huge. "You killed Maggie."

"You attacked me," I said. "You attacked my friends."

She continued to stare, but her face hardened, her nostrils flared. "You bloody killed her!" She ran at me.

"Get into your body!" I managed to shout at the spirit. "Lie on your body *now* and—"

The woman tackled me and we hit the ground together. My head smacked the road and the air left my lungs. Everything went black. I couldn't see if the spirit had done as I ordered. I couldn't even move. The woman sat on me, pinning me. I braced myself, expecting her fist to smash into my face.

But it did not. My vision returned. I blinked up at her, but she wasn't looking at me. She stared at the corpse, now lurching to its feet. The other pack members didn't move. All gaped at the dead woman standing on unsteady feet, inspecting herself with eyes that couldn't really see. It was her spirit eyes that saw, not her human ones, and what she saw amazed her.

"I...I am alive." Her voice came out thin, brittle, struggling as it did through muscle, flesh and sinew that had to learn how to work again in dead form.

The two men approached her, touched her, checked her wound. The one who looked into her eyes suddenly recoiled with a yelp.

"Not alive," I told her and the others. "You're dead. I've brought you back to occupy your body."

They all stared at me. The woman who'd attacked me scampered back, falling over in her haste to get away from me. "What are you?" she whispered.

I got to my feet slowly, careful to keep them all in my line of sight. Behind them, Seth, Gus and Lincoln moved, groaning. They were alive, thank God, but in a bad way. "I am the person who will kill you all and bring you back from the dead to do my bidding unless you do as I say. Stand over there together where I can see you." I pointed the gun at the middle of the street.

One man moved, but the other caught his sleeve. "She won't do it," he said. "She's lying. Ain't no one can bring back the dead."

I aimed the gun at him. "Until recently I didn't know that people can become wolves and bears. Yet here you are." I nodded at the corpse. "And here she is. Dead yet walking. Force them to stand together," I ordered the corpse.

She moved toward the men, her arms herding them like cattle. "I can't stop," she muttered. "Why? What're you doing to me?"

The men edged away from her. The other woman raised her hands in surrender. I aimed my pistol at them. Seth got to his knees and aimed his, too. He cocked it with his forearm, not his injured hand. Despite the blood streaming from a cut above his eye, he looked furious and very much prepared to pull the trigger.

Behind him, Lincoln and Gus stumbled to their feet. I did not go to them but immense relief flooded me. I concentrated on our attackers. The danger was not yet over, not for Harriet.

"Go inside and insure King doesn't harm Lady Gillingham," I ordered the dead woman. "Do whatever it takes to free her."

"No! I won't do it." But her feet moved even as she protested. The others watched her go, a mixture of wonder and fear on their faces. The dead woman clomped toward King's house, her gait awkward, as if her feet were rooted to the ground and she had to rip them up with each step. By the time she reached his door, however, she'd become used to her dead body and moved more freely.

Curtains fluttered up and down the street. Neighbors peered out but remained indoors, too afraid. How long did we have before constables arrived? The gunshot would have been heard from one end of Bloomsbury to the other.

"We all go," Lincoln said. Somehow his face only bore a single cut to his cheek. The rest of him, however, must be black and blue.

I did not help him as he limped after the deceased, his body bent slightly, his arms folded over his stomach. He didn't utter a sound, however, but I knew every piece of him must burn with pain. I ached to inspect his wounds and apply salves, but it would have to wait.

Seth and I forced the others to follow at gunpoint. They went meekly and headed up the stairs to King's place without uttering a sound. There was no sign of the landlady. I didn't blame her for hiding.

The dead woman already had King pinned to a wall by his

shoulders in the parlor. He could use his hands to push at her, but get no strength behind it. She was too strong even for him.

Harriet huddled in a corner on the floor, whimpering, her feet tucked under her skirts, her face buried in her hands. No one took any notice of her.

"Let me go!" King ordered.

"Can't," the dead woman said. "Sorry, King, she controls me."

His gaze slid to me. "How?"

"Harriet is walking out of here," I told him. "You will not come near her or anyone associated with her. Is that understood?"

"I didn't plan on harming her."

"We heard you say you would have your way with her."

"She wanted me to. Didn't you, Harriet?"

"No!" she cried.

"But I'm your pack leader. You belong to me now."

"I belong to my husband. I wanted to *run* with you. Nothing more," she added in a mumble, all the fight gone out of her.

She picked herself up and came to stand beside me. I hooked my arm through hers and she seemed to take comfort in the close connection.

"If you come near Harriet again, I will send London's dead to your door," I told King.

He swallowed. "All of them?"

"As many as I can muster." Sometimes, a little white lie felt good. Wickedly good. "Now, answer our questions and we'll let you go."

Lincoln had remained by the door. He'd straightened but his face was racked with pain. I let Harriet go and went to him. I touched the tips of his fingers, an offer of encouragement. He gave me a flat smile and walked steadily toward King.

"You changed into the Prince Consort's form," Lincoln said quietly yet firmly.

"Did I?"

"How did you do it?"

King's lips pressed together. He looked away.

"Punch him in the stomach," I told the dead woman.

She protested, but did as I ordered. "Sorry," she said to King as he coughed over her.

"I will have her kill you," I told King. "After what your friends did to mine tonight, I have no qualms about that. We know you went to the palace and used the prince consort's form to speak to the queen. How can you change into his form, and others?"

"I don't know," he said. "It's just something I can do, like you can do..." He indicated the dead woman. "This. I learned years ago that I could shift into other shapes, but not easily. Anything other than my natural shapes took practice, and if I wanted to copy someone specific, it took years of practice."

"Your natural shapes?"

"This one and the one I run in."

"You've been trying to look like the prince consort for some time," Lincoln said. "You wanted to *be* him, didn't you? Hence the name you adopted."

"I've been told I resemble him a little." King tried to shrug, but with his shoulders pinned to the wall, it looked more like a twitch. "It was just a game. No harm done."

"No harm!" I marched up to him and poked him in the chest. "The queen thinks she's been speaking to her beloved dead husband!"

"And how is that a bad thing? She adores him still. Why not give her some happiness and allow her to think he pines for her as much as she pines for him?"

"You sicken me," I said.

"I know what I'm doing."

"And what is that?" Lincoln asked. "What do you want from her?"

King sniffed. "Nothing."

Lincoln smashed his fist into King's face. It was so sudden that even I was caught by surprise. King's head smacked against the wall and for a moment, he looked dazed. Blood trickled from his mouth, and he spluttered then spat out a tooth. "Bloody hell, aren't you in a fine mood."

"Is it any wonder?" I snapped. "You ordered your people to kill them!" I had a mind to punch him myself.

"I can wipe out every last one of your pack," Lincoln said with a growl that was more animal than human. "I can see that your kind become extinct after tonight. Don't presume I will show mercy, because I will not. Not after you showed us none."

Harriet gasped. King's pack exchanged worried glances. "Tell him," one of the men urged King. "The secret don't matter no more. You tried and got caught, and that's the end of it. Tell him what he needs to know!"

"It's not as simple as that." King sounded as if he were weighing up his options. "There will be repercussions."

"Seth," Lincoln barked.

Seth limped forward. "Yes?"

"Shoot one of them. I don't care which."

Seth blinked at Lincoln then took aim at one of the men. The man stumbled back and fell onto a chair, his hands in the air. "I didn't want to harm no one."

Seth cocked the gun. Harriet turned away and covered her ears. The living woman screamed.

"Don't!" King bit off. "All right! I'll tell you what you need to know. I, I simply wanted to convince Her Majesty that shape shifters are harmless, and that no one should fear them."

I frowned. That was all?

"She's weak," he went on. "She's impressionable and was easily guided by her late husband when he was alive. I hoped he could influence her in death, too."

"Influence her to do what?" Lincoln asked.

King's tongue darted out and licked his lips. "I, I mentioned that shifters are just as much her subjects as everyone else, and deserve to walk freely in England and not hide."

"But *you're* not harmless," I said. "You proved that tonight."

"Exceptional circumstances," he said with another attempt at a shrug. "You clearly knew too much about us and wanted to threaten us. When my people are threatened, I act according to my instincts."

It was madness and yet it made sense, in a way. He was acting on animal instinct; the instinct to protect one's pack and fight for territory.

"Who put you up to this?" Lincoln asked.

King's head snapped back. "No one. I acted alone."

"Who did he work for?" I asked the dead woman.

King's gaze turned icy. I shivered.

"I don't know," the woman said in a steady voice.

King shot me a triumphant smile. "I told you," he said, silkily. "I work alone. There is no one else like me, you see. No one else who can change into anyone, anything. It was easy to get into the palace, rifle through the letters and steal a picture of the prince."

"You needed a picture to perfect your impersonation," I said. "And the second time, yesterday, how did you get in?"

"I took on the form of a young maid. No one specific. Nobody notices a plain girl in a maid's uniform. There are so

C.J. ARCHER

many in the palace. When I reached the queen's private apartments, I changed into the prince consort's form and put on the clothes I'd brought with me. Simple." Smugness touched his smile. He was proud of his deception.

"Charlie, any more questions?" Lincoln asked.

"Just one," I said. "Where's Mink?"

"Who?" King asked.

"A young friend of mine, slim, about fourteen or fifteen."

He shook his head. "Ain't seen no young brats about."

Gus opened the door for us, and I exited with Harriet.

"Oi!" the dead woman called. "What about me?"

"I will release your spirit when we're safely away."

"Oh, and thank you," Harriet said to the woman. "Your advice earlier was invaluable."

The bloodless lips of the corpse stretched thin. She went to spit on the floor, but the dead can't produce spittle. "Traitor."

Harriet's grip tightened on my arm. Tears spilled silently down her cheeks. I led her away and down the stairs. Gus, Seth and Lincoln followed.

"Shouldn't you question him further?" Seth asked, falling into step alongside Lincoln. "About the person who paid him, I mean."

"He won't give us an answer," Lincoln said. "I'll need to follow him or go through his correspondence. But not tonight."

"No," Seth said quietly, cradling his hand to his chest. "Not tonight."

"What if he tries to leave London altogether?" I asked. "Perhaps this will frighten him off."

"He won't leave without his pack, but I'll make arrangements to have him watched."

We walked as quickly as the injured men could go,

passing two constables heading in the direction of Rugby Street. They didn't seem in any particular hurry and didn't stop us.

I worried that we wouldn't find a cab on such a miserable evening and indeed, there were no hansoms to be seen, but larger hacks waited outside St. Pancras station. We managed to all squeeze in one. Seth and Gus groaned as they sat, with me between them, and Lincoln winced when Seth accidentally trod on his foot.

We drove toward Mayfair first to take Harriet home. I didn't say the words to release the shifter's spirit until we were almost there.

"How did you know to come looking for me?" Harriet asked.

"Your husband informed us of your disappearance," Lincoln said.

She winced. "Was he very cross?"

"Very," I said. "Will he punish you?"

Her fingers wrung together in her lap then suddenly stilled. She smiled at her reflection in the darkened window. "We shall see."

"Did you tell King about us?" Lincoln asked.

"No! Not a word. I did not mention names, the ministry or Lichfield Towers. After the attack and before you joined us, I told him you were strangers, local troublemakers."

"He won't believe that now," I said.

"I won't tell him about you, I promise. I never want to see that man again."

"It's likely you will. You're part of his pack now. He thinks you belong to him."

She bit the inside of her lip and her hands resumed their wringing. "I only wanted to go for a run and meet others like me."

"I understand," I said gently.

Seth grunted and shifted his weight, only to groan again. "Next time you want to go for a run, come to Lichfield. I'll ride alongside you."

"Thank you, Seth, you're very sweet."

He didn't look at all sweet. He looked in pain, in between his scowls.

Gus checked his bruised and bloody knuckles. "Everything hurts. They were bloody strong."

"I feel awful," Harriet said, dabbing at her eyes with her little finger. "Everyone is injured because of me. And Charlie, you look like a bedraggled urchin. Were you up that tree? You poor thing. And Seth, your eye is closing up. Here, take my handkerchief and let me take care of you."

Gus rolled his eyes. "Heaven help us if that pretty face gets messed up. Don't want the golden boy to lose his looks."

"If I could be sure it wouldn't hurt me more, I would thump you," Seth said idly. "And my face is not pretty. It's ruggedly handsome."

"Who says? Your mother?"

"Yes, as it happens." Seth grinned but it quickly vanished. He dabbed the handkerchief to his wound. "She's going to have a fit when she sees me like this."

"You could hide out in the cellar until it heals," Gus said helpfully. "Or the kitchen. She don't go in there."

"Don't worry," I said cheerfully. "Alice's concern will make up for any lectures your mother doles out."

Seth brightened. "Good point. I wonder if she's still up at this hour. What time is it, anyway?"

"Eleven," Lincoln said without looking at a watch. "And Charlie gets the first bath."

Seth held up his hands. "Fine by me. I'm going to be busy reassuring Alice that I'll recover."

"Not your mother?" I asked.

"She'll be in bed at this hour, thank God."

We arrived at Harriet's house. Lincoln opened the door for her and stepped down to assist her from the carriage.

"Thank you," she said to us. She squeezed my hand. "You were all marvelous." She allowed Lincoln to escort her up the steps. "I am sorry for all the trouble I caused," I heard her say.

The front door opened and Gillingham appeared in the brightly lit entrance, not the butler. The three of them conversed briefly then Lincoln returned.

"She'll be fine," he said, thumping the cabin ceiling once he'd settled.

"How can you know?" I asked.

"Because she knows her strength now, and he's a coward."

"You think she'll use her strength to curtail his wrath?"

"I hope so," Seth muttered.

The drive from Mayfair to Highgate took some time. The rocking of the coach lulled us, including Lincoln. He closed his eyes but did not rest his head against the walls like the other two. I gently laid my hand on his knee and he settled his bruised hand over mine. He kept the other close to his chest. I suspected it sported broken bones, as did Seth's.

"I'm worried about Mink," I said quietly.

"I know."

"Where do you think he is? What's happened to him?"

He said nothing, and I knew he was avoiding mentioning the worst.

"And what about keeping an eye on King?" I asked. "Do you want me to do it tonight? Or Cook?"

"Gillingham will send men around, so he informed me."

"Is it wise to leave it to him? It's a great responsibility to watch a shifter as wily as King, and Gillingham's not the most competent."

"He has competent men working for him."

"But—"

"No more questions, Charlie. Please." He closed his eyes again and didn't reopen them until we reached Lichfield's gates.

The warm glow of the lamps at the front of the house welcomed us, and the door opened before we reached it. Doyle stepped aside to let us past, his features as schooled as ever, although I thought I detected a flicker of alarm in his eyes when he saw how gingerly the men walked.

"'Bout bloody time," Cook growled, hands on hips. "We thought you all be dead."

"Almost," Seth muttered. Then he suddenly beamed. "Ah, Alice, good evening."

Alice rushed down the stairs, a fringed shawl slipping off her shoulders. "Thank goodness you're back. We've been worried."

Seth held out his hand to Alice. She seemed confused by the gesture then took it. "I'm sorry I can't use my right hand," Seth said indicating his badly bruised right, cradled against his chest.

Alice gasped. "What happened?"

"I punched someone very hard." He jerked his head, flicking his damp hair off his forehead. "It's nothing."

Alice looked at Lincoln, Gus and me. "Are you all hurt?"

"Just the men," I told her.

Cook slapped Gus's shoulder in a friendly gesture and Gus yelped. "Where does it hurt?" Cook asked him.

"There." Gus shrugged off his coat, hissing in pain. "Everywhere."

"Doyle, fetch Dr. MacDonnell," I said. "Tell him there will be broken bones, bruises and cuts. A lot of them."

"I'll leave right away," the butler said. "Before I go, I must warn you that we have some visitors staying the night."

I lifted my brows at Alice. "Not your parents already, surely?"

She shook her head. "The children. Mrs. Cotchin put them all in the last bedroom. They managed to fit in the bed, but it's tight."

"Mink?" I blurted out. "Is he here?"

"I'm here," came a small voice from the shadows. He stepped forward and I ran to him and hugged him. I was happier to see him than I had been to see Harriet.

He wriggled in my embrace and I pulled away. He looked unharmed, but tired. "What happened to you?"

"Nothing." He dipped his head, sheepish.

"Tell them," Alice ordered gently.

"I went for a walk." He shrugged. "I had to think."

"You went for a walk!" I cried. "Without telling anyone? Mink, you ought to know better."

"Didn't think anyone cared," he muttered.

I hugged him again and ignored his protest. "Finley cared enough to race here when he realized you didn't get home," I said in his ear. "And I've been worried sick all day. Next time, tell someone where you're going."

He nodded and wriggled free again. He lifted his gaze to mine. "I had to think about the things you said, about staying here with you."

"And you've decided to stay. I am *so* relieved."

Mink glanced past me to Lincoln. He cleared his throat. "Sir?"

"You may stay," Lincoln said. "Until a better arrangement can be made."

"What can be better than here?" I asked.

But he didn't answer. He limped past us to the kitchen. "Is there anything to eat?"

All except Mink headed to the kitchen. The other boys had already gone to bed, and Mink looked tired. He'd only stayed up to speak with us and make sure my offer still stood. Lady V, Mrs. Cotchin and Bella had also retired, much to Seth's relief. He'd forestalled his mother's lecture until the next day.

He accepted a bowl of soup from Cook and sat at the kitchen table. "Both my hands hurt," he said to no one in particular. "I'm not sure I can feed myself." He blinked innocently at Alice.

She pretended not to notice and handed a bowl of soup to me.

Cook picked up Seth's spoon. "Open up for the choo choo train."

Seth snatched the spoon off him and fed himself.

"Charlie," Lincoln said, accepting a soup bowl off Alice. "You wanted to have a bath first."

"Actually *you* wanted me to have a bath first," I said. "I think you three ought to go before me. You were out longer than me and it'll do wonders for your injuries. I'm nice and warm by the fire."

"Speaking of fires," Alice said, "one has been lit in each of your rooms."

"You're such a kind, thoughtful woman," Seth smiled at her. "That's very sweet of you."

"It was Mrs. Cotchin's idea. I'll tell her in the morning that you called her sweet. She'll be delighted."

His smiled tightened. "Still, you *are* kind and thoughtful."

Alice somewhat reluctantly retired to bed and it wasn't until she'd gone that I remembered her dreams. I only hoped tonight they didn't come to life. I was too tired to tackle rabbits or battle armies, and the men too sore.

In the end, Gus went in the bath first, followed by Seth. Cook had to help him out of his shirt since he couldn't lift his arms above his head. He was still in the bath when Dr.

MacConnell arrived. The doctor saw to Lincoln first since he sported more injuries.

"Fractured bones in his left hand," Dr. MacDonnell reported when he allowed me back in to Lincoln's rooms after his examination. Lincoln sat on an armchair, his shirt open, revealing a triangle of black and blue skin. His face looked paler than when I'd left him. "Some broken ribs and various bruises on the torso and limbs. It's unlikely there are internal injuries or Mr. Fitzroy would have succumbed to them by now. It's fortunate that his musculature is strong. It's my belief it protected him."

"Thank you, doctor," I said without taking my gaze off Lincoln. He looked like a damaged warrior, badly in need of rest. "You haven't bandaged his hand."

"The bones are fractured, not broken. It should be bandaged after the bath. He assures me you're capable of doing it, Miss Holloway."

"I am."

"Be sure the bones do not move in that hand in the meantime," the doctor said with a stern glare at Lincoln. "Don't forget the salve. Apply it liberally to the bruises. There's nothing to be done about the ribs, I'm afraid. Now." He snapped his bag closed. "Where's the next patient?"

"I'll take you to him."

By the time I'd delivered Dr. MacDonnell to Seth's rooms and returned to Lincoln's, he'd gone. I poured myself a brandy and waited for him by the fire. My clothes and hair had dried but I welcomed the delicious warmth. It seemed to take an age for the chill to leave my bones, but when it did, I closed my eyes and sank into the armchair.

A light caress on my cheek woke me. "Lincoln?" I murmured. "Did I fall asleep?"

"Go to bed," he said, his voice as soothing and warm as the fire. "It's been a long day."

I sat up and yawned. He perched on the footstool in front of me, looking every bit a devilish rake with his damp hair falling around his face and his shirt open, revealing the bruises. He watched me with an intensity that made my insides weak. I cupped his jaw gently, just below the cut on his cheek, in the hope of capturing the look.

"I'll go to bed after I've bandaged your hand and seen to your wounds," I told him.

A mischievous gleam flickered in his eyes. "Dr. MacDonnell only mentioned my hand. I can see to the rest of my wounds myself."

"And deny me the pleasure of touching your bare chest?"

"You have no rights to see my bare chest, young lady. Not until you put my ring on your finger." He nodded at the ring in its box, sitting near the front of the desk. It had moved further forward. Was he moving it so I couldn't fail to notice it?

"Perhaps I wish to sample the goods before I buy."

The corners of his mouth kicked up. "You drive a hard bargain."

"Take off your shirt."

He hesitated then put out his injured hand. "This first."

I sighed. And he thought *I* drove a hard bargain. I ached to touch him, even clinically, but *he* seemed able to resist. He always was a man of iron self-control.

The doctor had left bandages and splints to keep Lincoln's fingers from moving. I gently positioned each splint beneath the fingers then firmly wrapped up the hand, fingers and wrist. It must have hurt but he made no sound.

"Remove your shirt," I ordered when I finished. At his hesitation, I added, "I won't ravish you."

"It's not you I'm worried about," he muttered.

I arched my brows but he didn't notice as he struggled to remove his shirt over his head.

"Allow me." I pulled the shirt up, revealing the dark bruises on his chest and stomach. "Oh, Lincoln. It must be painful."

He watched me carefully, as if he were unsure how to react.

I unscrewed the lid of the jar of salve and sniffed the thick, gluey contents. "It smells pleasant enough." I avoided looking at his face and focused on his shoulders and arms, gently dabbing the salve onto the bruises. When I got to his chest, however, I stopped. "It would be easier if you were lying down rather than sitting."

"You want me to lie on the bed?"

"The sofa isn't long enough."

"No."

"Why not?"

"You have to ask?"

My face flamed. "I suppose it is a little intimate."

"A little?" He grunted softly.

"You forget that I've seen you in your bed without a shirt on before."

"Don't remind me. I live with the guilt every day. In my defense, I didn't know you were a woman then." He stood. "This will do. Proceed."

I rubbed the salve into the wounds. They covered much of his torso, mostly the chest and stomach, but also covered his back. There was hardly an inch of him not covered in salve by the time I finished.

I concentrated so hard on the task, focusing only on the patch of skin where I worked, that I failed to notice his deep breathing until I stood back and admired my work.

"If you think this is any less amatory than lying on the bed, you're sorely mistaken," I said.

"That is your opinion." His raspy voice had me looking

269

up. His eyes were shuttered behind their lids, his jaw set hard.

I wanted to stroke away the firmness. Wanted to kiss his bruises, and whisper his name in his ear. I wanted to run my fingers through his hair and feel his fingers in mine. And I knew, without a doubt, that he wanted that too.

I rested my hand on an unmarked area of skin at his waist. "Lincoln..." I murmured. "Kiss me."

CHAPTER 16

*L*incoln placed his hand over mine then drew it away. "No," he said firmly. "No kissing, no touching, no more of…this. It's too…" He heaved a sigh. "I can't."

I dropped my hand and lowered my head. It may have been a demure gesture, but my heart was anything but. It rampaged in my chest, giving me no peace. "If that's what you want."

"It's not what I *want*, Charlie. What I want is for you to put my ring on your finger. This will be done the proper way or no way."

He was fishing for an answer, but I couldn't give it to him. Not tonight. I searched for something to say to break the tension and finally found a safer topic. "Lincoln, we should talk."

He had been putting on his shirt, but stopped. "Yes."

"I've had a thought about the boys."

"What?"

"The boys. Mink, Finley and the rest of their gang."

He resumed dressing, pulling his shirt over his head,

allowing me a moment to watch and admire. "What about them?"

"Their presence here makes Lichfield very crowded, and I'm not sure Lady V will cope with them all running about. Since the cottage you gave me for my birthday sits empty, I thought I'd give it to them. They can live there, get jobs or go to school. A dry, warm place to stay will do them wonders."

He hiked up his trousers at the knees and sat. "I've been thinking about them, too, and have a better idea."

"You've been thinking about Mink and Finley? I knew it."

His eyes narrowed. "What does that mean?"

"It means I knew you cared about them more than you admitted. You left them a coat while I was away, and perhaps more that you won't own up to. They certainly wore better clothes than when I lived there. It's not a weakness to care about them, Lincoln. It merely makes you more human."

His lips twitched. "Less like a machine?"

"I never thought you were a machine. I only called you that to rile you."

"You did not succeed. Not with that."

"Can we get back on topic, please? What's your idea and how could it possibly be better than mine? I think giving them the cottage solves many of their problems."

"But not all. It is a good idea," he added quickly. "And the boys may prefer it when they hear the particulars of mine." He stretched out his legs until his bare feet were alongside my booted ones. "I inherited more than the general's position on the committee. I inherited his house and fortune, neither of which are inconsiderable."

"You want to give them the general's house! But it's enormous and there are only five of them."

"Not them, Gus's aunt, Mrs. Sullivan."

Gus's great aunt had been a charwoman for more than forty years, but in her retirement had opened up her home to poor girls in need of shelter. She was a kind soul, full of vigor, wisdom and a generous spirit that outstripped her means. I knew Lincoln gave her money to provide for the girls, something he'd only begun to do after I noted how Mrs. Sullivan could have changed my life if I'd met her years ago.

"You win," I said, smiling. "Your idea is better than mine."

"You haven't heard it all yet."

"I don't need to. I suspect you'll hand over the running of the house to her, and let her take in as many girls as she can manage. Boys too. She'll need help with all of that."

"The house is staffed, their wages paid for out of the income earned from Eastbrooke's investments. There's enough to cover more staff, provisions, and wages for a permanent teacher."

"You have thought it through," I said.

"Do you think Mink's gang will agree to it? They don't strike me as the sort who'll take kindly to being told what to do."

"If they want to live in the free world and not behind bars, they'll have to get used to a little discipline in their lives. But not too much. Mrs. Sullivan is very fair. She'll have the right touch. And I know Mink will secretly want an education. He's so bright, he could be anything when he grows up." Tears pricked my eyes and tingled my nose. "Oh, Lincoln, don't ever let anyone tell you you're unkind. You're going to change their lives for the better. Few people can go to their graves saying that."

"I'm not dead yet, despite King's best efforts." But he smiled to soften the shock of his statement.

It still wiped the smile off my face. The beatings had been brutal, and the thought of King wandering freely around the city sickened me. He ought to pay for what he'd done. But how? Tell the police? That would involve a trial and we'd all be witnesses. It wasn't an ideal situation but I would do whatever was necessary.

Lincoln crouched in front of me and took my hand. "Thank you for staying in Rugby Street and not going home. If not for you, we would not be alive."

I looked down at our hands because I didn't want him to see me cry. Somehow I'd blocked out my role in tonight's events, but now it all came crashing back. "I killed her. I ended her life."

"It was kill someone or die ourselves. All of us."

"I know." I looked up and wanted to fall into the warm depths of his eyes and never come out. "I would do it again given the same circumstances. If it's in my power to save you, I will."

He kissed my forehead. I closed my eyes and listened to my thundering heart, my ragged breaths. I knew he meant it as a platonic kiss, but it still affected me deeply. Everything about him did.

* * *

GAWLER ARRIVED mid-morning as Lincoln and I prepared to go to the palace. With so many people now living at Lichfield, it was difficult to find somewhere private to talk. We had to ask Mink to leave the library. He took a stack of books with him.

Gawler screwed his cap in his hands and stood with his back to the fire. He met Lincoln's gaze steadily, albeit warily. The mix of uncertainty yet determination were at odds. "Thank you for seeing me, sir. I thought you might not let me in."

"We're not enemies," Lincoln said. "You've done nothing wrong."

"Aye, but my friends...my pack...I heard what happened. It affects all of us, not just them."

"You mean that woman's death?" I asked cautiously. My stomach churned and I worried I would toss up my breakfast. "We're sorry for your loss."

"I appreciate that, but I know she done wrong. They told me what happened."

"Her family," I muttered, hardly daring to ask the question, but knowing I had to ask it. "Did she have a husband? Children?"

"A husband but no children."

I nodded, numb. Lincoln placed his hand on my lower back. "What else did your friends tell you about last night?" he asked Gawler.

"That King ordered them to kill you while he took your friend to his rooms to—" He shook his head. "I...I didn't expect that. You must understand, I thought he'd be different with her. I wouldn't have sent her to him if I thought he'd treat her like one of the females in his pack, like he had a right to her."

"Why are you here?" Lincoln asked.

"King's dead."

Lincoln's hand at my back tensed.

"My God," I said. "How?"

"Someone stabbed him in the night, right there in his lodgings. Police are crawling over it now, looking for clues, interviewing the landlady."

I felt a little weak and had to sit down. Lincoln rested his hand on my shoulder. I didn't look at him. Couldn't. Had he ordered King's death? Or had he told Gillingham to do it? Had that been what their brief conversation had been about last night?

"Who did it?" Lincoln asked. "Do your friends know?" It was impossible to tell from his voice whether he was surprised by the murder or was simply asking the question to deflect suspicion.

"They'd gone home. They saw nothing." Gawler cleared his throat. "I came to tell you that with King dead there's no need to trouble my pack no more."

"You're their leader now?" Lincoln asked.

Gawler nodded. "They'll follow my orders, and I ain't like King. I won't put them in danger like he did. I won't order them to hurt anyone. So you can leave them in peace."

"I intended to, but I need their names and current addresses for my records. The whereabouts of people like your friends must be known at all times."

Gawler hesitated then nodded. Lincoln retrieved paper from the desk by the window and dipped the pen in the ink. Gawler recited the names and addresses of his pack, including that of the deceased woman.

"I'll be off now," he said as Lincoln returned the pen to the stand. "Give my regards to your friend, miss. Tell her if she wants to go for a run again to come see me. There won't be no initiations with me. She won't have to do nothing she don't want to. Just run."

"Thank you, Mr. Gawler," I said, offering up a weak smile. "I'll pass on your message."

Lincoln saw him out just as Doyle drove the coach around. With Seth and Gus too injured, he'd volunteered to drive us to the palace. I secretly suspected he wanted to glimpse the elegance of the place, even if only from the outside.

Lincoln assisted me into the cabin then ordered Doyle to drive on once we settled. We sat in silence for a moment until Lincoln broke it. "You have something you wish to ask me," he said.

Sometimes, his ability to know what I was thinking unnerved me. "I'll just come out and say it. Lincoln, if you had a hand in King's death...if you ordered it, I want you to know that I understand why. You don't have to lie to me."

"I didn't do it, nor did I order it, but I don't blame you for jumping to that conclusion, considering my past."

I blew out a breath, more relieved than I expected to be. King had been thoroughly unlikable and was incredibly dangerous; not only because of his own power to change into multiple forms but because of the power he held over his pack. They would have done anything for him, including committing murder.

"I assume the man paying King to impersonate the prince consort did it," Lincoln went on. "Or possibly Gillingham. It wouldn't surprise me if he ordered King's murder out of revenge."

"It wouldn't surprise me either. Gillingham doesn't like to lose. He's a fool if he did order it, though. We needed to follow King to learn about the man paying him."

"Yes," Lincoln said with a measure of frustration unlike I'd heard in his voice before. No doubt he regretted not taking care of the situation himself. "I'll have a word with him later and see what I can learn."

"I do hope Harriet's all right and he hasn't locked her away again."

"We can visit her after we leave the palace, if you like."

I shook my head. "I don't wish to be turned away. I'll write to her."

We fell into silence, and my mind wandered to the task at hand, and to my recent conversation with the prince. I plucked at my skirts as I considered how best to broach the subject with Lincoln.

"Something's on your mind," he began. When I nodded but didn't go on, he moved to sit beside me. He gripped the edge of the seat. "Tell me, Charlie. Please, just get it over with."

"You seem very earnest. Very well." I blew out a breath. "The Prince of Wales talked about you last night."

"The prince?" he echoed, dully.

"Yes. You and Leisl. Perhaps he felt he could talk to me about your relationship more easily than he could talk to you, and knowing how close we are, he trusted me."

"I don't wish to hear it." His face shuttered, as it did when he was determined not to show any emotion.

"You have to. They're your parents, Lincoln, whether you like it or not. The prince told me that he was captivated by Leisl's beauty at a fair where she told fortunes." It wasn't quite how he'd put it, but I thought it a reasonable explanation for his actions.

"He regretted it later, I assume," Lincoln said.

"In a way." He had nothing to say to that so I added, "He was very interested in your welfare and upbringing."

"How much did you tell him?"

"Only that you had an excellent education but your childhood was somewhat lacking in affection. I mentioned that you had never met Leisl until the night of the Hothfield's ball."

"And I have no plans to see her again."

I sighed. "Lincoln, don't be so hasty with your decision. She's your mother. You may not feel any connection to her, but I doubt she can set aside thoughts of you so easily. She must have wondered how you fared over the years. I cannot begin to know how she felt when she saw you at the ball."

He had turned to look out the window as I spoke, presenting me with his hard profile. I turned the other way, not prepared to sympathize with him on this. I *did* feel for Leisl. I may never have been a mother, but I'd seen women forced to give up their children because they were too poor to keep them, and it had devastated them. Most never recovered.

Fog hung low over the skeletal trees of St. James Park, a canvas of ominous clouds behind them. It would rain later, perhaps even snow. I tried to think about that, and the book I'd curl up with by the fire, and not the man beside me.

"It's possible that she did not want me," he said quietly.

My concentration shattered. "Leisl?"

He nodded, although he still did not look at me. "I think she saw me in a vision, before my conception, and knew what her role had to be. I think she sought out the prince not because she desired him but because she knew he was the piece needed to bring the vision to life."

"You think her that calculated?"

"Only she can answer that."

"Let's say it's true," I said. "Let's say her vision made her aware of what needed to be done...that doesn't mean she never cared for you, and has no interest in how you turned out."

"It's best left the way it is. There's no point in pursuing a relationship with her if we've got this far without one."

I gave his point careful consideration, but in the end, I couldn't agree. I took his hand in mine, but when he still didn't look at me, I touched his jaw. He finally turned my way and gave me the full force of his frostiest glare. It used to chill me, but no more. "Lincoln, you never knew you wanted a relationship with me in the beginning, and look how that's changed, in time. Don't dismiss her yet."

He sighed. "Next you'll be telling me to call the prince Papa."

I smiled. "One step at a time."

We arrived at the palace and a footman led us to the queen's private apartments where we'd met her last time. The Prince of Wales was with her, standing by her side. They looked as if they were an ordinary mother and son sitting for a portrait, her in widow's weeds and he in a modest charcoal gray suit and tie.

"Miss Holloway," the queen said. "I'm so pleased to see you again. Are you here to speak with my husband's spirit? Bertie wouldn't tell me."

I glanced at the prince. He looked a little sheepish but unrepentant. So he was leaving it up to us to tell her.

"No," I said. "We were summoned here to report on our investigation into the imposter."

She blinked and looked away "It's cold in here. My shawl, Bertie."

The prince plucked a black shawl off the back of a chair and draped it around her shoulders. "You remember the conversation we had about that man," he said, impatience tightening his voice. "Miss Holloway and Mr. Fitzroy have been investigating. It turns out that the man had an unusual quality. He was able to change his appearance to look like anyone."

Was? Had? How did he know King was dead?

The queen held the shawl's edges at her throat with white knuckled fingers. "Did he admit to impersonating my husband?" Her voice sounded frail, old. It was easy to forget that she ruled the most powerful country in the world.

"Yes," Lincoln said. "The man known as King admitted his trickery, although it's possible he was paid to do it, ma'am."

"Can't you ask him?"

"I did. He denied it. Now he's dead."

I watched the prince carefully. He gave no reaction, not even a flicker of his lashes. "I cannot even ask his spirit," I said. "If I don't see it rise at the time of death, I must know his full name to summon him back. Everyone knew him only as King."

"So he is gone," she said, her voice quavering. "And I am alone again."

"Not alone," the prince said. "You have your children and grandchildren, your ladies."

"It's not the same."

The prince sighed. "We wish to thank you," he said to us. "It cannot have been easy." He nodded at Lincoln's bandaged hand and the bruises on his face. "Were there any casualties?" He spoke as if it had been war. I suppose, in a way, it had been a battle.

"Two of my men suffered broken bones and bruising. They'll recover."

"Please pass on my thanks for their service to the crown. It's pleasing to know that we have such loyal and capable subjects protecting us against the supernatural."

"Not all supernatural people are dangerous," I said. "I, for one, am not."

"Of course. But we must be vigilant. Your ministry is all that stands between order and chaos."

I glanced at Lincoln, but he remained unmoved.

"Is there anything the ministry requires?" the prince asked. "Funds? Resources?"

"From what source?" Lincoln asked, rather boldly, I thought.

The prince, however, seemed unperturbed. Perhaps he liked directness. "The public purse."

"That would require an act of parliament to be passed, and the ministry would become public knowledge. Is that wise, your highness?"

"Why not legitimize what you do? Perhaps the public has a right to know about the supernatural. Perhaps they *should* know."

I held my breath, hardly daring to consider the implications of what he suggested. What would happen if the public knew? Panic, I suspected.

"I'm not sure it's wise," Lincoln said.

The prince nodded slowly. "You may be right. I'll think on it some more. In the meantime, there are ways of supplying funds that would keep the ministry's existence a secret. Money can be funneled through various channels."

"That's done already."

"It seems you have it under control. I am glad, however, that I am now aware of the ministry. My mind is eased knowing you are looking after the realm in matters supernatural. And it is even more at ease knowing someone of such competence, efficiency and loyalty is at the helm."

It was positively glowing praise. Did he go to such lengths because Lincoln was his son, and this was his only way of showing his pride?

The queen held out her hand to Lincoln. She seemed to have recovered from her disappointment, or at least covered it with a regal façade. Lincoln took her hand and bowed over it.

"You're a remarkable young man," she said as he rose. "And you, Miss Holloway, are quite remarkable too. Would you mind remaining behind and summoning my husband again?"

"She can't," Lincoln said before I had a chance to think of an excuse. "I have need of her this afternoon."

"Another time. Soon."

I could not let her go on in hope forever. "Your majesty," I said, approaching her. "The dead don't like their afterlife being disturbed. Your husband wishes to be here with you, of course, but every time he returns, it pains him. He is best left where he is, in peace, waiting for you."

Her chin and jowls wobbled, and she dabbed at her eyes with her handkerchief. For a moment I thought she might order me. "If that is his wish, then I must abide by it." She lifted her hand to dismiss us. "Good day to you both."

A footman escorted us outside where Doyle waited with

the coach. Once settled, I mentioned the prince's response to King's death. "It was as if he already knew."

"Yes," Lincoln said drily. "It was."

"Do you think…" I leaned toward him and whispered, even though we were quite alone in the carriage. "Do you think he had a hand in it?"

He considered his answer for a moment before replying. "It's possible Gillingham informed him last night, perhaps suspecting the prince would take care of King."

"So he didn't have to do the horrid task himself."

"Or they may have colluded to remove King."

We didn't speak further on that matter, or any other, for the rest of the journey back to Lichfield. My heart felt too full, for one thing, and I couldn't stop thinking about the pride in the prince's eyes as he praised Lincoln. Any doubts I'd had about whether he knew Lincoln was his son were dashed entirely. But I couldn't talk about that with him. He wouldn't want to hear it.

"So?" Gus asked upon our return. "You getting a knighthood now?" He winked at me. "Be worth getting a broken hand for a knighthood."

Lincoln closed the parlor door, piquing the curiosity of Lady Vickers, Alice, Seth and Gus. "What's happened?" Seth asked.

"The Prince of Wales is considering giving the ministry a more formal role," Lincoln announced.

"Blimey," Gus muttered.

"Madness," Seth said, tapping his temple above his cut eye. It was almost completely closed today, and the surrounding flesh sported a rainbow of colors. He looked terrible, and I'd even caught Alice giving him a sympathetic glance.

"What did you say to him?" Lady Vickers asked.

"We managed to convince him that keeping the ministry secret for now was in England's best interests," Lincoln said.

"But I suspect he wants us to be more official than we have been."

"To give us access to funds and resources," I clarified.

"He'll tell people," Seth said with certainty. "Let's just hope the people he tells are liberal-minded."

"You mean more like Lord Marchbank than Lord Gillingham."

"Precisely."

Gus sat forward, his eyes bright. "We need a symbol."

"What?" Seth scoffed.

"If the ministry becomes more official, it needs a symbol, an emblem. We can get paper printed with it, and get it etched in the silverware."

"Did your brain get squashed yesterday?"

Gus's enthusiasm would not be curtailed. "We could get it painted on the coach door."

I rolled my eyes and caught Lincoln smirking. "I don't think the ministry is at the point where it needs an emblem," I said.

"We need someone to draw it," Gus went on. "Alice, you said you're good at watercolors."

"I can sketch well enough," she said, "but only if I copy something. Creating a design from scratch is not a skill I possess."

"Seth's creative," Lady Vickers piped up.

Alice looked impressed. "Is he? I never suspected."

Seth gave a nonchalant wave of his good hand. "I've dabbled."

"Aye, but dabbled at what?" Gus said wryly.

"Fetch a sketch pad and pencil," Seth ordered him. "I've got some ideas already."

"You can't," I reminded him. "Your hand."

"Oh. Right."

Gus rose anyway. "I can work a pencil as well as him."

I left them to it and went to sit beside Lady Vickers. Lincoln joined us. "Maids and a footman have been employed and will begin tomorrow," she announced. "Mrs. Cotchin is proving to be a marvel. Lichfield is in safe hands with her."

"My thanks, madam," Lincoln said.

"I could never have done it on my own, and nor could Lincoln," I said. I hoped he would offer to give Lady Vickers something as compensation, but he walked off. It was left to me. "As a token of his appreciation, Lincoln would like to take you shopping. Well, I will be the one to take you."

She patted her hair and her cheeks blushed. "That's very kind of you."

"I thought a new gown, something to wear to dinner parties. Something to wear to *our* dinner party."

She clapped her hands. "Charlie, what a wonderful idea. I already have a list of guests. There are invitations we must reciprocate, of course, and some dear friends who've been kind to me since my return. And eligible young ladies, too," she added, eyeing Seth and Alice, their heads bent together in discussion.

I almost mentioned inviting Lady Harcourt but bit my tongue. Did I want her at my first dinner party? She may be in an unhappy situation, but how was that my fault? It was her stepson's doing. *He* ought to be the one making it up to her. I would think about it some more.

"It's not so bad," Lady Vickers said quietly.

"Pardon?"

"I know what you're thinking, and I want you to know that it can be as wonderful as it can be awful. It all depends on whether you love one another enough to endure the lows."

"Hosting dinner parties?"

She laughed. "No, marriage."

"Oh!"

"I have had one awful marriage and one good one," she went on. "Take it from me, Charlie, how you feel about one another makes all the difference. If there is no respect between you, no genuine friendship, and no love, then you'll end up despising one another." She looked to the door through which Lincoln had just left. "Mr. Fitzroy is not like any man I've ever met. You can't compare him, and your relationship, to any other. You are both unique individuals, and what you have now and what you'll have in the future has no precedent."

"Thank you for your advice."

"Will you put him out of his misery?"

"I...I think I need to talk to him."

I rose in something of a daze but did not leave to follow him. I wanted to be among my friends and their lively chatter, so remained in the parlor. We ate an informal luncheon in the cozy room, although Lincoln was absent. Doyle informed me he'd gone out, but he didn't say where. I found myself alone in the parlor with Seth after lunch, the others having gone in search of more paper for their sketches.

"You look contemplative," he said, stretching out his legs. "Anything you want to talk about?"

I shook my head. "Oh, wait, yes." I lowered my voice. "I've been meaning to talk to you about Alice."

He straightened. "Has she mentioned me?"

"Yes, but not in a good way."

It took a moment for my words to sink in, then he sat back with a deep sigh. "What do I have to do, Charlie? Why doesn't she like me when everybody else does?"

"Alice is very perceptive," I said. "And she's a lot like you, in that she has been admired for her beauty all her life. But unlike you, her beauty has led to complications."

"You're referring to the engagement she never wanted with that older fellow."

I nodded. "So she's careful now, wary, and you...well, you aren't subtle, Seth. You've praised her beauty often."

"I thought women liked to be told they're pretty. Would you have me call her ugly?"

"Don't twist my words."

"Sorry," he muttered, rubbing his temple. "Go on."

"Point out her other good traits."

"Like her needlepoint?"

"Like her cleverness, for example. Her creativity," I said, indicating the scraps of paper with half drawn designs on them.

"She's not overly."

"Don't tell her that."

"I'm not an imbecile. I know how to praise women, Charlie."

"And another thing. Be yourself."

"I am."

"No, you're playing a role around her. The role of charming, affable gentleman."

"That's not a role."

I never knew he could be so recalcitrant. Perhaps I'd offended him by pointing out a fault. He probably wasn't used to it. "Be sincere with her. Don't worry if she sees a bad side to you. It'll make you a more interesting person. I fell in love with Lincoln despite his faults. Owning up to yours won't push her away, if she does really like you enough."

He looked to the ceiling and shook his head. "I can't believe I'm listening to the advice of a nineteen year-old. I can't believe I need advice at all. What is the world coming to?"

"You're maturing, Seth. That's the problem."

He pulled a face. "Maturity is for the aged, like my mother."

"Don't let her hear you say that."

He huffed out a humorless laugh. "And what about you? How does your love life fare?"

"I've been too busy to contemplate it."

"You're not busy now."

I glanced at the clock on the mantel. Lincoln had been gone for nearly three hours. "Indeed I'm not." I kissed the top of his head and left as Alice and Gus returned, chatting excitedly about designs for the ministry emblem. I hoped they wouldn't be disappointed if it was never used.

I headed up the stairs and walked quickly to Lincoln's rooms. The fire in his study was unlit, the room cold. I picked up the box and plucked the ring off the velvet bed. It slipped easily onto my finger.

I stared at it. The diamond looked so large and bright, even in the gloom. Was it really mine?

I tucked my hand into my skirts and headed back downstairs. I didn't join the others in the parlor but sat in the library. Mink and Finley had returned to Clerkenwell that morning with the rest of the gang to prepare for the move to the general's house. Perhaps Lincoln had gone there too.

It was another two hours before he finally returned. I met him in the entrance hall and beckoned him into the library, just as the rain started. It pummeled the windows, drowning out the laughter from the parlor. "You've been gone a long time." I indicated he should sit in the chair by the fire. "Are you cold? It looks fierce out there. Take off your boots and warm your feet."

His eyes narrowed. "You're fussing. Should I be worried?"

I knelt on the rug and knotted my fingers behind my back. "Tell me where you've been."

"To Mrs. Sullivan's first."

"What did she say?"

"That she can't wait to move into the big house with her girls, as she calls them."

"You mentioned the boys?"

"I did, and she has no qualms about taking care of them, too. I think she's looking forward to the challenge. I then went to my lawyer's office to make the arrangements. He wanted to discuss what to do about your cottage too, but I told him you needed to be there for that conversation."

"Right. Thank you. Anything else?"

"I went to the general's house and informed the staff."

"What did they say?"

"The housekeeper protested. She thinks children should be neither seen nor heard. I told her she could find employment elsewhere, and so could anyone else unhappy with the arrangement. I expect to lose a few, but not many. I'll let Mrs. Sullivan choose her own housekeeper when she's ready."

"Finley and Mink were a little overwhelmed when we told them," I said. "I understand how they felt. They had nothing a mere twenty-four hours ago. They didn't even have hope. And now they have a future that can be anything they wish to make of it. Believe me, Lincoln, it takes some time for that to sink in."

He regarded me gently, his eyes shining. "Has it sunk in yet?"

I grinned. "Yes." I rested my hands on his knees. "Yes it has."

He stared down at the ring for a long time. He'd gone very still, and hardly seemed to be breathing.

"Lincoln." I sucked in a breath and plucked up the courage to say what I wanted to say. "Lincoln Fitzroy, will you marry me?"

He looked up, laughing, and drew me to him. He made way for me to sit beside him in the chair and I was careful not to put too much weight on his injured thighs. I cupped his face and smiled.

"Is that a yes?" I asked.

"With all my heart, it's a yes. It belongs to you, Charlie. *I* belong to you, and I want the world to know it."

My heart thudded in response, a signal that I'd made the right decision. Whatever storms lay ahead, we would weather them as a couple. Without each other, we were two separate halves, but together, we were a whole.

I stroked the side of his face and tumbled into the pools of his eyes. "And I belong to you," I whispered.

I kissed him and he kissed me back thoroughly, holding me against his chest. When he hissed, I drew back.

"Sorry," I said. "Did I hurt you?"

"It's not that. I had another vision."

My gaze connected with his. "Good, I hope."

"Very."

"Tell me about it."

He shook his head. "I don't want to make you blush. Not when we're about to have company."

I opened my mouth to protest but the library door suddenly opened and Gus and Seth burst in.

"There you are," Gus said, not even blinking an eye at me sitting so close to Lincoln. "Doyle said you were in here. Which one do you prefer?" He held out two pieces of paper with designs on them.

"I tried telling him that the one with the dragon is better," Seth said.

"We don't slay dragons," Gus shot back. "They ain't real."

"We don't know that for certain. They might be real. If they are, and we do find ourselves fighting fire-breathing dragons one day, you're going to be terribly disappointed if you didn't choose this one." Seth tapped the piece of paper with the dragon on it, flames spewing from its mouth. "It's clearly the better of the two."

"That's because Alice drew it under your guidance, and you're sweet on her. And you're a fool."

I took the pieces of paper, making sure to pass my left hand in front of their faces. Gus gasped and caught it. Seth drew me into a hug.

"About bloody time," he murmured in my ear.

He let me go and I was enveloped by Gus. Seth shook Lincoln's hand, somewhat gingerly, considering their injuries. "Congratulations, Fitzroy."

"Now, before we tell the others," Gus said, "you got to decide something."

"What is it?" I asked, grinning.

"Which one of us will walk you down the aisle?"

Seth looked at him like he was thick-headed. "Me, of course. Who would a lady rather have at her side? Lord Vickers or Mr. Ugly?"

"Lord Arse, more like."

"It's going to be a tough decision," I said, regarding them both. "I'll need a way of choosing between you. Perhaps I could flip a coin."

"This ain't a joke," Gus said. "Seth's a big fool, and his hair is ridiculous."

"My hair is lovely!"

"Or," I said, "I'll think of a number between one and a hundred and whoever gets the closest is the winner."

They both scowled at me.

"Trial by combat?" Lincoln suggested.

"Excellent idea," I said, taking his hand. "We'll wait until you're both fully healed, of course." I led Lincoln out of the library to the parlor to inform the others.

Behind us, Seth and Gus followed meekly.

"You'll have them eating out of your hand until you make a decision," Lincoln said, a smile in his voice.

"That's my plan."

He put his arm around me and kissed my forehead. "You're a wicked woman. But you're *my* wicked woman."

I tipped my head back to look at him. His warm gaze searched my face and his arm tightened. "Very much so," I said. "Very much so."

THE END

LOOK OUT FOR

VEILED IN MOONLIGHT
The 8th Ministry of Curiosities Novel
by C.J. Archer

Charlie and Lincoln's wedding preparations are interrupted
when a young gentleman with links to the royal family is
found dead, and the main suspect is a wolf.

Sign up to C.J.'s newsletter via her website CJARCHER.COM
to be notified when she releases the next Ministry of
Curiosities novel plus get access to exclusive content.

A MESSAGE FROM THE AUTHOR

I hope you enjoyed reading OF FATE AND PHANTOMS as much as I enjoyed writing it. As an independent author, getting the word out about my book is vital to its success, so if you liked this book please consider telling your friends and writing a review at the store where you purchased it. If you would like to be contacted when I release a new book, subscribe to my newsletter at http://cjarcher.com/contact-cj/newsletter/. You will only be contacted when I have a new book out.

GET A FREE SHORT STORY

I wrote a short story featuring Lincoln Fitzroy that is set before THE LAST NECROMANCER. Titled STRANGE HORIZONS, it reveals how he learned where to look for Charlie during a visit to Paris. While the story can be read as a standalone, it contains spoilers from The 1st Freak House Trilogy, so I advise you to read that series first. The best part is, the short story is FREE, but only to my newsletter subscribers. So subscribe now via my website AT WWW.CJARCHER.COM if you haven't already.

ALSO BY C.J. ARCHER

SERIES WITH 2 OR MORE BOOKS

Glass and Steele

The Emily Chambers Spirit Medium Trilogy

The 1st Freak House Trilogy

The 2nd Freak House Trilogy

The 3rd Freak House Trilogy

The Ministry of Curiosities Series

The Assassins Guild Series

Lord Hawkesbury's Players Series

The Witchblade Chronicles

SINGLE TITLES NOT IN A SERIES

Courting His Countess

Surrender

Redemption

The Mercenary's Price